ESTHER

QUEEN OF ALL PERSIA

By
HEATHER NUTTALL WESTOVER

AUTHOR
CATALYST
PUBLISHING

ESTHER 4:14

For if you remain silent at this time, relief and deliverance for the Jews will arise from another place, but you and your father's family will perish. And who knows but that you have come to your royal position for such a time as this.

Esther 4:14 NIV

DEDICATION

To all of the strong, spirit-filled women who were made to feel wrong for walking in the gifts God created them to have. Relax sister, you are worthy because God *says* you are worthy. No other set of circumstances or person's opinion carries any weight on your worth. God created you with the gifts you will need to successfully walk out the situations He is bringing your way. Rest ... and ... Trust

To my five daughters blessed with spiritual gifts, unique and individual. Your strength encourages and inspires me daily.

CONTENTS

FOREWORD

When Mama told me she was going to write a series on women in the bible, my mind immediately went to Mary the mother of Jesus and Mary Magdalene. But neither were on the list, at least not yet. When she said the first woman up would be Esther, I thought, *'Solid lady. This will be gold.'*

Then she went on further to let me know she wanted each of us girls, her five daughters, to sit for the covers. The series then became even more intriguing. What an honor to even be able to sit for the cover as one of these bold and courageous women who stood up, spoke out, and changed their world for God.

My Mama has always been drawn to strong women of faith, she is one, and she raised five more. I am looking forward to seeing how she unfolds stories full of suspense, in a world full of sin, lived out by normal women like you and me who are led by faith, and sometimes saved by miracles when the enemy strikes hard.

Chances are, even though I might recognize myself or a character trait from one of my sisters in these leading ladies, knowing my Mama and how she lets God hide things in her stories ... you'll probably find yourself in these books somewhere along the way as well.

Happy Reading ~ Ethel

Introduction

A letter from me to you ...

Esther 4:14: If you keep quiet at a time like this, deliverance and relief for the Jews will arise from some other place, but you and your relatives will die. Who knows if perhaps you were made queen for just such a time as this? NLT

Over the history of the Word of God, countless generations of believers have either read or heard this verse and it has allowed them to ponder the many events that have filtered into their lives uninvited.

"Was I born for 'such a time as this?'" I have asked myself this many times. It gave me the courage to keep walking, fighting, and climbing toward the mountain peak of the current challenge before me. Sometimes those challenges were created by my own life decisions, sometimes God placed them there to grow my faith or courage. But sometimes the enemy threw down on me to keep me from being effective for the Lord the way I should be. The origin of the challenge isn't quite as important as developing the habit of pushing onward and reaching for my 'such a time as this' moment.

I love the Lord and follow him now, but I spent too much of my life as a James 2:19 believer.

James 2:19 *You believe that there is one God. Good! Even the demons believe that—and shudder.*

I believed he was God. But I had never given him my life. I was no different than the demons. I had to wrestle with my pride to be able to release control. Once I gave my life to Him, I began to know Him in a much more powerful way than I ever thought was real. I'm still terribly flawed. Less so than before, but I'm still a work in progress.

When setting out to write a Christian fiction novel, I struggled with wanting to write it as real as possible. Wanting to portray the world Esther had to live in as filled with sin, as the world we have to navigate in today. I understood the goal is to *never* glorify sin. But in our overachieving attempts not to glorify sin, sometimes we forget to portray the *reality* of it as well.

We have been told we have to live *in* the world, but we are not of the world when we are believers. So reading some of the Christian fiction genres out there left me feeling like the square peg trying to sink into the round hole. Some of the books showed everyone in town had a good moral compass deep down inside somewhere. That's not the world I know. Other books depicted an environment where all people believed in God and wanted to please him even if they got a little off track sometimes. That was also not the world I grew up in. I could go on and on with examples but I've brought it up to say this.

In this recounting of Esther, not all of the sin has been scrubbed from the book. Not all characters want to please God, or any god for that matter. There are worldly thoughts, actions, and religions represented in this book so it represents the world Esther had to walk through. She figures out how to navigate the same kind of world we live in where greed, lust, perversion, violence, idolatry, and selfishness are the norm for the non-believers, and many followers of God as well.

She has to seek Yahweh, and her Papi (Mordecai) for wise counsel. She has to pray and use discernment to act in ways which are the most beneficial. Remember, the Holy Spirit wasn't a spiritual tool that had been unleashed for believers in the Old Testament. Her plight took more. More wisdom, more strength, more faith, more ... everything ... and it took a woman with just a little ... more as well.

We know the story of Esther from the tidy summed-up version rolled up into ten chapters. What many of us may not know is, from the time of Vashti's death until Esther is crowned Queen takes approximately three years. Likewise, five years pass between her crowning and Haman's death.

There is a lot of life to be lived in those eight years. Remember, whether she chose it or not, this will be the only opportunity she will have to be a wife. Once she is crowned, she knows she has to make the best of it. Hating the only husband she will ever get to have will not honor herself, Mordecai, the law, or Yahweh. She has to make the best of it. She has to reach out in friendship, give herself to Xerxes, to love him, to minister to him, and be a queen he can be proud of.

You cannot call her a sell-out. She was a wife. Women didn't have options back then. For the most part they were bought and sold with bride prices. Some fathers loved their daughters and tried to secure the best situations for them. A large majority of fathers ended up deciding their daughters' marriages based on who offered the largest bride price regardless of age, character, or social standing.

In Esther's new life she is surrounded by lifestyles of sin. Harems threaten to take her man's affections. Haman seduces Xerxes' moral compass into the dregs as often as possible. Haman is vile, every wife would have his number within just a couple minutes of meeting him. You wouldn't even need the gift of discernment to recognize the spirit of this man immediately. She knows it is even possible Haman could harm Xerxes for personal gain. We women can rival the Federal Bureau of Investigation with our gut instinct for certain players sometimes. Am I right? Women's Intuition, we get it and we rely on it.

There are wars, ruling drama, skirmishes among the people, and the pressure to produce an heir. Esther was an exceptional woman to walk through almost a decade of all of the things the Book of Esther records. While I use my imagination, and hopefully the nudging of the Holy Spirit along the way to fill in some of those eight years of events, I still hope to honor the foundational truths of what God wanted this book, and this woman to show us.

I hope this telling of Esther blesses, and entertains you as fiction is meant to do. But I also hope it makes you think about Esther, Yahweh, and life a little as you make it to the last page. So here we go, using Esther chapter 1, verse 1 as our starting point.

Blessings,
Heather

P.S. A cubit equals about 18 inches (give or take). King Xerxes is reported to be around 8 feet tall. Some people exaggerate, some don't know how to measure exactly, so all of the descriptions vary. Eight feet seems to be a good average of all the info out there so I'm sticking with saying King Xerxes was eight feet tall. To try and stay in the vibe of the time period somewhat, we're going with cubit measuring.

5 cubits = 8 feet
4 cubits = a little over 6 feet

Last helpful tip: Papi is pronounced more like the flower poppy. Not like - pappy. Hope that helps!

PROLOGUE

<Esther>

"**M**y dear, sometimes rebellion is the best course of action, no matter the consequence," Queen Vashti lifts my chin with her fingers and then cups my cheek with her elegant, jeweled hand. "May you never know the sting of this truth."

The queen lingers for a small moment, looking into my face. I see tears pool in her mesmerizing green eyes and wonder what has caused all of this to come about. With dark hair piled fashionably atop her head, Vashti appears every bit the royalty she is.

Fighting the threatening tears makes the rims of her eyes turn red, and then her nose. Sniffing back her emotions, Vashti stands tall, and squares her shoulders. Before continuing down the hallway, she leaves me with one last word. "Blessings my sweet, beautiful girl."

Standing in awe of the interaction with the queen, I remain frozen. All the people of the land have been invited to the banquets hosted by the King and Queen, but never in all the world did I expect a one-on-one moment with Her Majesty. Rachael, my best friend, squeals and shakes me by the shoulders. She's so excited, even her lazy eye is wide open.

"The Queen was just touching and embracing you! What did you do? What happened? What did she say? What did *you* say?"

Coming out of my stupor, I shrug my shoulders from Rachael's grasp. "I don't know. I don't know what caused her to speak to me. I didn't ask any questions. The Queen had tears in her eyes Rachael. There must be something going on we're not privy to. She told me sometimes rebellion is the best course of action ... no matter the consequence."

Chapter 1

VASHTI'S REFUSAL, THE KING'S HUMILIATION

<Xerxes>

"All of my possessions are the finest you will ever find, including my wife. There is none whose beauty can compare." I smirk at the other guests and dignitaries in the banquet hall. Tonight is the feast for all the men of the lands, whether rich or poor.

"So says you," King Aramath shouts, raising an eyebrow in a good-natured challenge from across the way as the rest of the room erupts with raucous laughter, prodding me to prove myself.

Feeling smug, I make direct eye contact and chuckle. "And *any* other man who has ever laid eyes on her. Her body is flawless. Her eyes are mesmerizing. All of your wives combined don't even come close and you know it!"

Taking another long pull from my wine goblet, I hold it up for a refill. Aramath might as well be a street rat. They say his parents are of royal blood, but I smell street rat. I would lay money down his mother got lonely, and filled her empty nights with one of her bodyguards.

"Beauty is nice, but is she a shrew brother?" Now the crowd is relaxing into the teasing banter men do when in one another's company.

"Does it matter?" I grin at them knowingly, "Now men, drink up!"

Speaking of her body and her physical beauty, my mind wanders to numerous trysts and intimate encounters we have had in bed. The strong drink pulsing through my veins is probably adding to my desire to prove myself, but why shouldn't I? I am the most powerful King in the world. If I see something I want, I take it. If I already have it and want to show it off, all I have to do is say the word. Only the finest of wives would be acceptable for a King such as me.

The laughter and teasing of the men in the room doesn't sit well with me. My pride and the drink are pushing me to silence their laughter once and for all. Anger builds in my stomach. Standing to my imposing 5 cubit height, I push my shoulders back. Looking down at the crowd of men, letting my deep brown eyes challenge each of them, I stare for a minute commanding their attention. The only indication of my mood is the twitching muscle above my jaw.

"Eunuchs!" I bellow, "fetch me my wife... make sure she wears her crown ... *only.*"

The room falls silent, but only for a moment. King Darapth is the first to speak. Addressing me by my formal name, he speaks, "King Ahasuerus, surely you don't mean this?"

"You dare to call me a liar?" Glaring at him, my fists clench and unclench as though I'm inviting him to use his physical strength to back up his words. I really hope he will. I am itching for a fight.

Not getting the challenge out of him I wanted, I settle back into my chair, savoring the smooth sensation of the finest wine in the country sliding down my throat. From my throne, I gaze around the room and connected courtyards. The garden has hangings of white and blue linen fastened with cords of purple and white that connect the material around silver rings on marble pillars. There are couches of gold and silver on a mosaic pavement of porphyry, marble, mother-of-pearl, and other costly stones. Yes, my lands and possessions are the finest and most beautiful.

Wine is served in goblets of gold, each different from the other and the royal wine is abundant in keeping with my intended liberality. Each guest is allowed to drink what he wishes. I love being able to lavish my people and visiting dignitaries with our finest assets to show my generosity, wealth, and power. People talk about me year 'round for my generosity.

When the eunuchs return, my brows furrow at the sight of them coming through the door, alone. Hegai approaches, and leans in to be discrete.

"Your Majesty, Queen Vashti respectfully declines your invitation citing she is too busy hosting the banquet for the ladies," then Hegai clears his throat, "and she will not appear unclothed."

He backs away quickly, fearing my heavy hand for delivering such news. Unmoving for several moments, the rage builds inside me. She denied me in front of the men of my country. In front of the men from other countries. She would pay, and she would pay dearly. I am not only her King, and husband, I am a god! Coming up with a plan for how to present this little problem, I finally stand, gathering everyone's attention.

"Gentlemen, please continue to enjoy your drink and feast on the food generously provided tonight. I must confer with my Council regarding an urgent matter. Servers! Bring the next round of delicacies for my guests!"

"Trouble in paradise with *the finest wife in all the world,* Your Majesty?" Lord Jaren jests, receiving rounds of snickers and a few pats on the back from the other men in the room.

"There is *never* trouble in my kingdom, Lord Jaren." Fixing my darkening stare on him, showing a glimpse of the ruthlessness that has kept me in power thus far. "Not for long anyway."

Not only my look, but my words spread a sobering feeling over those at the banquet. The chattering grows quiet as people lower their voices, sensing how upset I am. I know there are those in attendance looking for ways to weaken my influence and cut my power. Some of them must be secretly gloating, and contemplating how to use this moment to their advantage. I will never allow it to happen. This blatant disrespect by Vashti must be dealt with harshly, and publicly.

"Councilmen, trusted advisor Haman, Queen Vashti has expressed she is too busy hosting her banquet to grace us with her presence, but if she did ... she would only come fully clothed. This is a direct assault on my authority and rule. Me, King of all Persia! If my wife refuses my commands, she rejects the teachings of the husband being the head of the household. What do we feel will be an appropriate punishment for her disobedience?"

Most of the Councilmen were horrified. If the women of the kingdom heard of Vashti's stubborn refusal of her husband's wishes, they might begin to have thoughts of their own. This is absurd. These thoughts would lead to disobeying their own husbands. No this would not do! We can't have women thinking they're equal with the men. What would they expect next? Should the men help out by washing the clothes for the family? No, this insolent woman had to be put in line *immediately*. They must send a message to all women. Persia could not be expected to have such unruly females. This is the way it has always been. Men are the leaders of the home and what they say goes.

If any of them were honest, they would have to admit Vashti's refusal struck pure fear and anger into their hearts and challenged the way of life they've known for generations. Men who fear their authority being challenged can be dangerous ... very dangerous.

"My King, the Queen has wronged not only the King but all the officials and peoples of Persia. I propose Queen Vashti suffer the consequences of her bold, and perverse way of thinking. I feel we have no other option but to banish Vashti and her family from our lands, never to return. Furthermore, they can only take what they can grab in one hour as they leave Susa tonight." Other Councilmen nod their heads and murmur their agreement with Councilman Tarshish.

"If it meets the King's approval, he should personally issue a royal decree. Let it be recorded in the laws of the Persians and the Medes so it cannot be revoked: Vashti is not to enter King Ahasuerus's presence, and her royal position is to be given to another woman who is more worthy than she," Councilman Meres ponders before continuing. "The decree the King issues will be heard throughout his vast kingdom, so all women will honor their husbands, from the greatest to the least."

"Just send the guards to retrieve her and remove her clothing, bringing her to perform the wifely task requested by her husband. Force the obedience, and respect," Councilman Carshena offers as though this is not really that big of a deal.

Haman, my Second in Command, is sitting back pondering the moment. He's a sneaky rogue who only looks out for himself. In every situation he is looking for ways to get himself more money, women or power. Manipulation is his showcased trade, but it has come in handy during times of war. Just turn him loose in negotiations with the enemy and watch him work. Each time he finds a way to make himself a little wealthier, hide another concubine, or torture some poor soul. But he always has my back, so I do turn my head to a lot of it, but I'm curious to know which direction his performance will take this time.

"King Xerxes, if I may, your generosity knows no bounds. Look at all you have provided to every citizen of our lands tonight. What other King invites even the lowly to the palace for free drink and food? I am dismayed at the level of disrespect and insult the Queen and her family have displayed tonight. They raised this woman with a heart of treason towards her King. I believe if you do not deal with this harshly, other members of the kingdom may start looking at you as someone to be taken advantage of rather than to be respected for your endless protection and generosity." I am aware he feels like the crowd's reaction will place more pressure on me to make a rash decision. I already have my mind made up though. Let him boast.

"Has she not had the finest of everything in life? Yet she still humiliates you in front of dignitaries. I believe the only proper punishment for this behavior is to have Vashti face beheading this very evening without her clothing as you instructed her to appear. And her family should be banished without returning home to collect the things you graciously bestowed upon them. You cannot show weakness, Your Highness."

Haman watches, seeing if the effect of his words have settled over me, the Councilmen, and the crowd as well as he wanted. The whispers between guests are almost deafening. I have my hands intertwined in my lap, staring down at them while twirling my fingers around each other as I often do when deep in thought. My dark hair falls forward over parts of my face giving me the illusion of privacy.

Clenching my teeth, I feel the muscles in my jaw jump as I contemplate the level of punishment I might wish to hand to my incredibly stubborn wife. Her beauty is beyond compare, but she has never connected with me on any other level. My heart honestly won't miss her. I have never had one ounce of soft feelings toward her or any other woman. She was just okay in bed, and hasn't even produced an heir. It is time to enjoy another. Maybe I will actually like the next wife a little more.

One at a time, members of the Council approach me offering their opinions privately, but Haman knows his words have had the proper impact. They are all on board with his plan. He prides himself on being a master manipulator. I'm sure he can't wait to oversee the clearing out of Queen Vashti's family compound, keeping as much of their wealth for himself as possible before putting the rest back into the palace coffers. I tire of his games at times, but having a sinister Second in Command does come in more handy than I'd like to admit. So fine. Put another feather in Haman's cap - for now.

"The King looks furious! He could punish all of us for witnessing such an embarrassing moment. Do not laugh, make eye contact, or smile. We will leave as soon as possible," the voices behind us sound urgent and full of fear.

Haman catches my eye and silently chuckles as he hears the lowly father-son duo move to position themselves closer to a quick exit. This is all working in our best interest. Maintaining obedience from one's subjects can sometimes be helped by making them carry a healthy dose of fear.

My Councilmen, Haman, and myself approve an edict made from all of the suggestions that evening. We send letters out to all of the provinces in my own handwriting and have them translated in each language for all of the ethnic groups in our lands. In summary, the edict ends, emphasizing that every man, from the least to the greatest, should be the master of his own house. It is a message to warn every woman and encourage every man.

"Furthermore My King, if I may," Haman saunters through the tables projecting his voice to garner as much attention as possible. "A King such

as yourself should not be without a wife. We should find your new wife
by contest! Make a decree stating all of the young beautiful virgins in
the land be brought to the palace where they will undergo months of
purification rituals to be worthy of the King's presence, etiquette lessons
to teach acceptable behaviors for a queen, and on a night when you desire
to have them brought to you, they will appear. You can share a meal or
conversation, and … if you choose, indulge in an evening of pleasure. If
they don't meet your standards, you can send them to the harem until you
find our next true queen."

Haman knows I would likely let him pull and keep a maiden for another
concubine. I see the truth as he hid his smile behind cold emotionless
eyes. I know he has been watching one particular girl in town, but having
two wives already, he can't pursue her through proper channels. He is
determined to have her though. He will find a way to gather her for himself,
and this could be the quickest way to accomplish that without making
anyone angry. Yes, tonight has turned out to advance his own selfish agenda
quite nicely. Again, he is a means to an end for me. I'll let him think he
has succeeded. The contest sounds horrid and exhausting but at least I
will mostly see them one at a time. It gives me a chance to observe their
personalities and avoid those hateful, manipulative women I have grown
so tired of. Ahh, sobeit.

"You mean the King is to take all virgins with the intent to sleep with each
one until he finds one he wants to make Queen?" Kavan asks as his throat
constricts. Obviously, his thoughts are turning to his five daughters and
fearing their enslavement at my hands.

"Kavan, are you suggesting our King go without a wife to help him rule?
Our country still needs an heir! One of your fine daughters could become
the next queen! Surely you wouldn't deny your King his queen or your
daughters the opportunity to birth the next heir to the throne would you?"

Haman knows he must spin this so everyone sees it as an honor, and one they would be remiss at missing out on.

Clearing my throat, I address the room, "Upon choosing my queen, any damsels who remain pure will still be allowed to return home, and search for a husband to give her an honorable life. You have my word," I say, rising from my chair. "But I am in agreement, a contest shall determine the next Queen of Persia. Let's finish our meal before the unpleasantry that is to come. Blood coming from men is a trophy. I don't love it as much, pouring from women."

Haman excuses himself to summon the guards and have them secretly place all of Vashti's kin in a holding cell until her death is completed. I can almost visibly see his excitement bubbling to the surface. He believes he is about to add to his wealth, see Vashti naked, and accelerate his plan to possess Janeth for his group of concubines. I know he is gloating inwardly, believing he will finally begin receiving all the blessings he thinks he deserves. I guess he will. I am allowing it, again. But he doesn't know that I do see through him. He truthfully is a wretched man.

The only redeeming quality he has is his love for children. He cannot resist them. When we are out in the city, he joins in any streetball game he can find. The dagger he carries in his waistband has carved more falcons, cats, and camels than it ever has seen time in battle. He genuinely lights up when visiting with a child. Maybe it is because he has ten sons and who knows how many daughters. I have heard non-stop stories about them all. I do not know how both men live inside one body but they surely do.

Chapter 2

VASHTI'S DEATH

\<Haman\>

"Unhand me this instant!" Vashti's father struggles against the guards. Looking around, he sees his sons and brothers being restrained as well. He knew his daughter's refusal was going to bring punishment upon all of them the minute Hegai returned to the banquet hall alone. He hurriedly tried to round up the family and make a quick exit from the festivities but I was too fast. I am always a few steps ahead of situations like this and had sent the guards to prevent them from leaving before the King and Council could come to a verdict. I think like a criminal so I am always ten steps ahead of them. *'I think like one because I am one.'* I chuckle to myself.

"Hegai, please fetch the Queen. Tell Vashti, her King requests a private meeting between them." I had instructed once all decisions were final. "And there is no option other than her immediate attendance. Guards, two of you accompany Hegai but only step in if she tries to flee."

Walking outside to the wagons full of children and family members we had retrieved so all of her kin could be banished at once, I truly only had one regret. The fear I see in the children' s eyes.

Nearing the back of the cart, I place one foot up on the end and rest my forearm on my leg. Pointing at the child who is visibly shaking, I ask if he feels brave enough to come to me. Hesitating but a moment, he finally decides he is. When he nears me, I place him on my knee.

"How old are you son?"

Puffing his chest out, he says in a shaky voice, "I am four summers old sir."

"I figured as much," I replied, nodding my head. "You see, at about four years old is when you learn being brave means you can do hard things even when you are scared. Being scared doesn't stop you from being brave and doing what you have to do. That's how I knew you were about four."

He raises his quivering little chin to me and finally meets me, little blue eyes looking into my brown ones. Nodding his head, he said, "Do we have to leave sir?"

"What is your name?"

"Amir, sir."

"Well Amir, sometimes the adults in our lives make decisions. Those decisions change our lives in big ways when we are little. We don't understand it and we don't like it, and sometimes we get real scared. Oh ya, it happened to me when I was a scrawny little guy about your age. I was smaller than you at four."

His eyes got round as dinner plates and I knew the other kids must be teasing him for being so small. I remember it well.

"The thing is, sometimes the adults make good decisions, sometimes bad ones. You can't change it. Your job is to eat all your food, sleep when your mom and dad tell you to, and work very hard. First, work hard in school. Then, when you know what you want to be when you grow up, work very hard at that. I knew I wanted to be in the King's army, so I worked at being strong."

Looking at all the children in the cart, I knew I had all of their attention.

"I do not know where you will go, but you do not have to fear. Where you will go, is where you are supposed to be. You will grow up, take a wife ... or a husband, and have little ones like yourselves. One way or another, it will all be okay. Do you believe me?"

"Yes," Amir says, hesitantly.

"Oh come on, you can do better! All of you, do you believe me?"

A chorus of 'Yes' rang out with a little bit more belief behind them.

"Now, I only have one ready, but Amir I am giving this to you to remind you of what I said tonight. Do your jobs, and eventually everything will all be okay." Pulling out a camel I had carved, Amir hastily wipes a tear with the back of his dirty little hand and grabs it.

Clutching the carving to his chest with both hands, he lifts his tear streaked face to me and says, "Thank you sir."

Putting him back in the cart, I return to the palace. Now I have about twelve more little reasons to hate Vashti more than I already do. I was looking forward to her punishment with a vengeance. I would get justice for upending little Amir's life, leaving him and the rest of the children afraid and without any means to affect even one detail about their future. Ready or not Vashti, here I come.

***

\<Vashti\>

"Hegai, I'm not sure it's a pleasure to see you twice in one night. What is your business?" I inquire, stopping his forward advancement.

"My Queen, King Ahasuerus requires your presence for a private meeting in the council chambers immediately," Hegai responds.

Noticing the guards I ask, "Am I to assume the guards at the back of the room are to ensure my attendance?"

"Yes, My Queen."

"I suspected this would come to pass. Let's remove ourselves without causing panic among the women in attendance, shall we?"

I raise my chin, smile at the nearest guests when we pass them by, and try to look for my family to give them a sign to leave. Not being able to find any of them, lets me know Haman is farther ahead of me than I suspected. Fear settles in the pit of my stomach. For refusing to be Xerxes vulgar naked trophy on display, I know what fate awaits me.

Masculinity in all of its toxic glory will be the end of me tonight. It was never meant to be this way. Men were to be the stronger, yet equal part of creation. To protect the physically weaker vessels, to fight the wars for protection, to provide for us, and to cherish the females as though we were the most precious and costly jewel in the world.

The females would bring the gift of life, companionship, passion, nurturing, and wise counsel to affirm the males and be a helpmate to them. Somehow, somewhere through the years of life, love, and sin, both sides had perverted their calling. The men possessed women as though they were an object. Buying them with large bride prices in marriage, treating them as

something to be owned and traded or even discarded if she couldn't produce an heir. Bride prices originally were supposed to be held in reserve for
the woman in case she ever became widowed. The fathers could hold onto
the money, and use any interest that might have been earned off of the bride
price, but the original amount was never supposed to be touched. Over
the years many fathers decided it was fine to keep the original investment
as well.

Women had become emotional, manipulative, and irrational, always trying
to gain trinkets and rewards for their time and gifts. Not giving freely to
their husbands the boost of strength, courage, and bravery that having a
compassionate, hard-working mate can give a man, but striving to control
him in return by withholding the very things they were created to give
away. The whole thing was upside down and only now, walking to my final
punishment did I really see the bigger picture and the portion of guilt I
carried, along with the rest of the female race.

"My King, to what may I owe the pleasure of our meeting during the
busiest night of the year?" I'm trying to buy myself some time to finish the
banquet before they deal with my earlier disobedience. Maybe I can find a
way to escape. All Xerxes can focus on is that it *is* the most important night
of his reputation and I've done my best to destroy it.

"Yes, and isn't it pleasant that on the busiest night of our year my Queen,
my *wife*, damaged my reputation making me appear weak in front of all
the men in attendance from both near and far?" His teeth are clenched,
but saliva is frothing at the corners of his mouth. His rage can almost be
touched by reaching out a finger. "You must be punished, Vashti. I will not
have a wife who does not obey."

"Xerxes, I was trying to do the best job as your queen I could do! I was also
trying to protect you from yourself. If I were to show up there unclothed,

who is to say your adversaries wouldn't plot to steal me away from you? They could think abducting me would weaken you enough to be overtaken and killed. I was trying to save you from yourself, Xerxes!" It was more manipulation, but I had lived this so long, I didn't know another way to communicate with him.

"I do not need saving from a *woman*! You and your family will all pay the ultimate price for your disobedience. I don't need you to think for me. I have the finest council in all the world and a Second in Command who works tirelessly to protect me. You don't get to *think* for me!" The table shakes as Xerxes slams his enormous, powerful fist into it from frustration. "Tonight you shall pay with your life and your kin will be banished with only the clothes on their backs."

My senses take over, and the blood begins pumping through my veins so loudly, it presses on the inside of my ears spreading into my head, and my breath begins coming in short bursts. It feels like someone has tied a heavy chain around my ribs and it is pulling tighter and tighter. "My love, No!"

"My *love*? How can you call me your love now Vashti? You denied me, you weakened me, and you dishonored me in front of dignitaries from across the lands as well as being disobedient in front of our people. I am through with your tireless manipulation." His voice is so loud even my skin is shaking as the table shook moments ago. Maybe it is fear making me shake, but nevertheless, Xerxes' anger is the cause.

"The baby, what about the baby?" I plead in one last attempt.

Xerxes advances on me, and my neck twists violently to the side as his giant hand sinks into my hair. "What. Baby. Vashti?" His hot breath on my face gives me goosebumps, and my adrenaline spikes even more.

"Xerxes, we lay together just last night. I could be with child this very moment. It could be the heir we've been waiting for," I plead, already knowing it won't work.

"If you are with child, it is best if it dies with you this very night. For I would kill her with my bare hands the moment of her first breath for carrying your betraying, manipulating, disobedient blood inside of her." He lets go of my hair and storms out of the room.

Moments before I collapse, I see stars, the room begins to spin and something pulls away all of the oxygen. I place one hand on the marble pillar next to me to steady myself. But it doesn't help. The darkness overtakes the rest of my vision with its heaviness.

"Wake up you traitorous wench." Haman kicks my side urging me to regain consciousness. "Tonight you will finally carry out the King's summons and when everyone sees you in all your naked glory, I shall make the guard swing the axe taking your head from your body."

Shaking my head, trying to clear the fuzziness left behind by losing consciousness I stand and say, "Haman, until I am dead I am still your Queen. Address me properly."

Without a second's hesitation, he grabs me by the throat, backing me up swiftly until the breath is knocked out of me by the impact of being thrust against the nearest pillar of marble. "You are nothing anymore. All your days of looking down your nose at me are over. Women are not above men. You don't make decisions, you don't think for us. You do as you're told or the consequences will be dire. Now take all of your clothes off. The guards and I will be enjoying the sight of the high and mighty Vashti being humiliated and exposed for all to see!"

He lifts his forearm and presses it into my neck. Oh, how I hate this man! He carries such perversion, it's always there simmering underneath. I feel dirty merely being in his presence.

"Obey quickly *My Queen*, otherwise I shall find time to partake of the spoils of your body at my pleasure before you are disposed of. Then we will find time for the guards to do the same. One or two at a time," he says as spittle leaks out of his mouth and drips down his chin. Two or three of the guards are chuckling at the thought of getting a go at me as well. Though it is nauseating, I know he's not bluffing.

With shaking limbs, I start by removing the satin blue slippers that match my dress. When the nude stockings join my shoes on the floor, Haman backs up to get a better view with his lustful beady eyes. I think about trying to scratch them out, but then I know what would follow and decide to control myself. The sneer on his face makes me want to vomit. His tapping foot lets me know I am not shedding my clothing nearly fast enough for him. He is handling me roughly and does not care. He is enjoying torturing me as though he has a personal vendetta against me, or those like me. He is a man driven with hate.

After removing my beautiful blue outer dress sewn with tiny crystals, I stand erect. "I cannot remove the binding undergarment myself Haman, you know there are handmaidens who must attend while dressing me."

His eyes are roaming lustfully across my body and it makes me shiver in disgust. My repulsion makes him angry, but I can't help it. Snapping his fingers, he points at a guard in the back of the room. The guard draws his knife and advances behind me. I know anything can happen in these moments because I have already been sentenced to death.

I will not enter eternity weeping and begging, but I will try to enter forever with as few violent wounds as possible. Maybe whatever god will be waiting on the other side, will be as taken with my beauty as the men in this life. Maybe my eternity can still be purchased with my flesh as it appears to be the most important asset I have been given. Standing still, I let the guard take one swipe with his blade and my binding garments fall to the floor. I feel the blood seeping from my skin where he used too much force and went through the thick material, but I refuse to act like I feel anything. Maintaining eye contact with Haman, I remove my lower undergarments.

"Keep your jewelry on. The guards will cast lots for them. They thank you in advance for the addition of wealth to their families," he sneers.

"It is my pleasure to make the lives of the women I lead better," I boldly respond.

"Didn't you have on an ankle bracelet and two other rings at the beginning of the evening? I don't see them now. Maybe a body search is in order." With me glaring at him, Haman pauses. "No? Just remember, I'm in total control here. Keep showing that stiff neck of yours and it can be broken. Guards, take her to the executioner's scaffold and tie her to a pillar while I check each piece of the equipment to ensure it's in working order. I'll take my time, so all those in attendance can look at the nakedness you so desperately tried to withhold."

My body is now fully on display ... wearing only my crown. The humiliation I feel is maddening. I hate Haman with all of my heart. I hear several men making comments about my body, and laughing at a woman being 'taught a lesson'. Many of the banquet's attendees have shuffled out to the courtyard to look at me, and watch Xerxes' strength on display. I'm sure it is supposed to send a strong message to the women of Persia. *'Never refuse a request from your husband.'*

Once Haman sends word everything is ready, King Ahasuerus, and the council arrive in the courtyard. Without so much as a glance in my direction Xerxes says, "You may begin Haman."

He takes his royal seat and views the stage as though he is overseeing the punishment of a common street beggar. His face betrays no emotion. No thought for all the time we were married. Well I will not beg him, it would not change my fate anyway.

Over-pronouncing his words, and projecting his voice so even the people in the back can hear, Haman addresses me, "For refusing a request from King Ahasuerus, committing treason in the eyes of Persia, dishonoring your husband, and encouraging rebellion and rioting of the women in all the lands of Persia, Queen Vashti you are sentenced to death. Have you any last words?"

"Sometimes rebellion is the best course of action, no matter the consequence." I repeat my phrase from earlier, remembering the beautiful chocolate-haired girl with stunning light-brown eyes. Ironically, I thought I was so very clever returning to the women's banquet after refusing the request to be paraded in front of these men. The sentence had rolled off my tongue instinctively and seemed so wise and so smart. Now that choice of words is the sum total of emotions, actions, and words which will end my life. It is obvious, rebellion should have been walked out in another way.

"We shall see about that, *Your Majesty*." Haman chuckles as he unties me from the wooden pillar on the platform. Stumbling as he jerks me forward and forces me to rest my head on the stool created to cradle the face of the offender, my breathing turns heavy. The stool was built to hold the face of a man and doesn't quite hold mine very well. This is a problem, I would prefer it if my head was severed with one blow. Fear is flowing through my veins, choking me strenuously at the thought it could take a couple swings of the axe to complete the execution. Expressing my thoughts to Haman will be the last thing I would ever do though. It would bring him too much joy to know of my fear and apprehension. No, I will keep my mouth shut and deny him any pleasure I can.

'May the gods shine upon me and allow me to enter the after-life with a clean cut so maybe it can be cleanly re-attached in the next life. That is all I have left now. My journey into the next life. The gods have all promised a bountiful after-life if we have been good worshippers. I have upheld all of the teachings since my youth. I am ready. Send me on. Nothing on this side would make my situation better here with men like Haman and my dear husband.'

Looking at the executioner, he is meant to strike fear into the hearts of those to be punished. He has to be taller than Xerxes, maybe closer to six cubits. His muscles ripple like the hills descending the mountains. His cleanly shaven body is sweating, and those droplets of sweat make their trek down his muscles like a river flowing downhill. His eyes are lifeless behind the required mask. Personally, I would prefer he take it off. I wish to die on the first blow. Take that silly thing off so nothing obstructs your vision you fool.

His axe stands almost as tall as his body. The blade is circular on one side, and a blacksmith has secured it to the shaft on the other side, requiring a smaller, more narrow build to merge with the shaft on the other. I wonder if there are any reasons for the holes cut into the blade other than design, but before I can examine it closely, Haman's grunting and pulling grabs my attention again.

He adjusts the stool a little more, making sure my neck will still be within the proper cutting area for the axe swing. If anything goes wrong with this beheading, Xerxes will be very unhappy with him. Haman may not show it, but he too is scared. Haman knows he will be punished if anything goes wrong with my execution. Finally, a thought that makes me smile.

Seeing me smile sends his anger rising like smoke from the communal fires. While securing my head, he pushes it firmly into the wooden stool making my nose bleed. Seeing the drops of blood appear below me, I can only imagine his smile. Haman's debauchery could never be satisfied in just one night no matter who he was being allowed to defile. Many in the crowd laugh, others do not. Before nodding at the guard, and giving the go-ahead to swing the final blow, he makes a great show of berating me for my disobedience. I am sure he thought it would bring more celebration to the moment of punishing a rebellious woman.

He receives outrageous laughter from most in attendance, except King Xerxes. His darkening glare reminds Haman, he too is capable of stepping over lines not acceptable in the eyes of the King.

Sobering quickly, Haman clears his throat and quickly continues. "As The Council, and King Ahasuerus have found you guilty and sentenced you to death. I send you to your gods on this day." Nodding to the executioner, he swings his axe with the giant blade. The crowd swallows back nausea, disgust, and fear at the final thud that signals my end.

Chapter 3

SIDE EFFECTS OF REBELLION

\<Esther\>

My Papi, Mordecai, works in the Palace Gates, this was the reason Rachael and I were able to attend the King and Queen's festival this year after coming of age. Normally, I wouldn't have been allowed to attend without a mother to escort me, but since Papi worked for the palace in a formal position, I was allowed to come with a guest. Rachael's parents had no desire to go, but they were okay with us going together.

Papi had seen the trouble brewing at the palace that evening. He sent word for Rachael and I to return home in haste. Shuddering when he heard of my encounter with Queen Vashti, he made us repeat it again. Finally, as his big shoulders slumped forward, he told us the Queen no longer lived, and the words she said to me were also the words she repeated out loud right before the axe swung to remove her head from her body. I don't know that I'll ever understand how something like this could have happened.

***

\<Mordecai\>

"Papi, you're home! Thank goodness. There were so many things happening tonight. I am so grateful Rachael and I were old enough to finally attend the yearly Celebration of Riches King Xerxes throws. It was very elegant and so exciting. But Papi, you are never going to believe this…"

"Queen Vashti talked to Esther! She lifted her chin with her fingers, stared into her eyes, spoke right to her, and then embraced her face before walking away! Can you believe it?" Flinching involuntarily, I reach up to place my hands over my ears. Rachael is so very excitable. Her voice can reach decibels no human ear was ever meant to endure, I am sure of it.

She is Esther's best friend and lives in the same part of the city as we do. With her home being just a few structures away, I see a lot of Rachael, and she helps me work on my tolerance for such a friendly, outgoing, screechy young lady. She is generous, compassionate, and always willing to work hard. Her hair is a shiny blue-black, and other girls in the village envy that about her. But not in a kind way. They feel it is a waste on someone who also has a lazy eye. It bothers me that they could say such things about her.

Her lazy eye is the only thing to mar her physical beauty. When out in public she becomes very shy and tries not to initiate eye contact or conversation to keep attention away from it. With its predominance in her physical features, she has trouble believing she is beautiful no matter what Esther and her parents say.

Growing very serious, I speak just above a whisper with a slight smirk. "Esther, please repeat … quietly … what Queen Vashti said to you this evening."

Settling into her cushion at the table, Esther begins with a smile, "It was when I was returning from relieving myself in the bathhouse. I turned the last corner at about the same time Queen Vashti appeared. Stopping, and backing against the wall, I lowered my head while she passed. When she had almost reached me, I curtsied as you taught me. She reached out, and lifted my chin with her fingers. Then she cupped my cheek and said 'Sometimes rebellion is the best course of action … no matter the consequence.' Then she sniffed back tears, straightened her shoulders, and returned to the women's banquet hall."

"*And* she gave you her blessing. That was eerily incredible," Rachael added, somewhat softer than her usual tone.

Reaching over to squeeze my daughter's hand, I said, "Thank you for following all of the protocols we've worked on over the years. Your respect for the queen in your actions tonight was commendable. Now, I must tell you some news. It will not be easy to understand." Breathing a sigh, I continue, "Queen Vashti was executed tonight. If I were to venture a guess, when she met you in the hallway, she was returning from denying a summons by the king to show up at the men's banquet, wearing only her crown."

Both girls sit unmoving for a bit. "Dead?" Rachael asks quietly.

"Papi, why would the king want other men to see his wife without clothing? It would be humiliating," Esther asks, trying to understand what she has heard.

"My girl, not all people follow Yahweh. Not everyone's preferences for modesty or loyalty will be the same as ours. Also, in almost every religion, the people at the top tend to become full of themselves and create their own rules to live by. Too often, the only rule followed is what feels right at the moment."

I wait for that part to sink in before continuing. "The drink was flowing liberally tonight. King Xerxes had told the men he had the best of everything, including his wife, who surpassed all of their women combined. After receiving much teasing, claiming he was simply exaggerating, King Xerxes summoned her to appear wearing only her crown so he could prove to the others his claims were true. She refused, and it grew like a raging fire from there," I explain. "Once The Council and Haman got involved, I think it had outgrown even King Xerxes reach. They wanted her head. They were all afraid if Queen Vashti got away with refusing the King's summons, every wife would begin to rebel and refuse to listen to their husbands. I am not sure His Majesty would have sentenced her to death himself. Punished her yes, but killed her? I think that was Haman and The Council myself."

"Will Persia continue without a queen?" Esther inquires.

"Ughh," I sigh with disgust, "there will be much you will not understand tonight. No, there will be a contest. All of the young beautiful virgins will be taken to the palace for a contest to see who will be the next queen."

"Thank Yahweh. I won't have to participate." Rachael breathes a sigh.

"What are you talking about Rachael, you're a virgin aren't you?" Esther says, confused.

Blushing profusely, Rachael says, "Esther, you know that I am. But your Papi said they would take all of the young, *beautiful* virgins, and we both know I won't meet those standards. It's probably the first time in my life I'm relieved to look the way I do."

Trying to encourage her friend, Esther states, "Stop it, Rachael. I think you're beautiful. So do others."

"Maybe what you say will be true, but if there is one thing that will save her from having to endure this contest, it will be her eye. It's just the truth. It is not an insult, Rachael. You are beautiful like Esther says, but it takes someone who knows what beauty truly is to see yours. Maybe Yahweh gave you that eye to save you." I spoke softly, hoping to reassure her, rather than to embarrass her. Rachael nods her head slowly, swallowing the lump of emotions in her throat.

"Rachael, look at me," I urge trying to console her. Reaching over, I cover her young slender hand with my much larger one. "Strong men of Yahweh see women with their hearts and the eyes of God. Yes, I won't sugar-coat it, you are not this world's standard of beauty. But you are a hard worker, full of joy and love for Yahweh, and you are intentional about trying to live your life according to the Book of Moses. Make no mistake, your heart and soul are even more beautiful than your outward appearance."

At my words, Rachael blushes and lowers her head. I meant what I said, and in a different set of circumstances, I myself might have considered offering a bride price for her. Maybe … if her voice could be lowered in volume.

"Well, if you won't be taken, then I don't have to worry either. My forehead is too big, and I have this mole on my lip." Esther decides.

"Esther, you are of the Tribe of Benjamin. The combination of thick chocolate brown hair, light brown eyes that seem to glow from within, and your personality make you even more beautiful than Vashti. Unfortunately for you, your physical body seems to rival hers as well. I will need to pray for how to guide you through this season when it comes." Standing to excuse myself for the evening, Esther isn't so quick to let me go. She has more questions to be settled.

"Papi, how did I get chocolate-colored hair anyway? Most people in this region have very dark hair," she questions.

Her question makes me smile. "Esther, it is a family secret. When you were a baby, I accidentally poured tea all over your head and it stained your hair the color of chocolate," I sighed, shrugging my shoulders as if admitting a dark family secret.

"Umm what?" She stutters.

"Yep, it was tea, the same color as chocolate. I'm sorry."

Esther and Rachael look back and forth at each other trying to decide whether this could be true. Finally, I threw a pillow at her laughing and say, "I'm kidding!"

"Esther, you know in the first book of Yahweh, He said Eve carried the seed of many nations within her. This blessing was passed down to all women. Over time, it seems different regions have adopted different looks by marrying within small groups, but the blessing still resides. Your birth papi, my uncle, had dusty blonde hair. I was so sad to hear he was taken into captivity and killed during the war. He knew you were on your way but he never even got to look upon you." Shaking my head I continue, "Your mother had light brown eyes close to the color of yours. They were so excited to know they had conceived you. At least your mom had the chance to hold you and see your face. I know she prayed over you before succumbing to the trials of childbirth. So even though most of the people in our area carry different traits, your parents, and the blessing of carrying many nations in a woman's womb worked with Yahweh to determine your looks. You were so loved ... and still are, Nesicha."

"Ugh, Papi, I'm almost grown. I have told you before I am not a princess anymore."

"Ahhshhh, you are *my* Nesicha," I tease.

Hugging Esther, I then insisted we walk Rachael home. We had a full day on the morrow and we need our rest. I probably would not get any though. I would most likely be worrying about how this contest for the title of queen would play out. I must do right by her, I had given my oath to my uncle. But I would not try to manipulate the events Yahweh had allowed to come upon Susa. This would definitely take many prayers, faith, and courage to walk out.

***

As the months go by, the things I learn by sitting at the Palace Gates begin to weigh on me. I know from gossip, the rules for the contest are about complete, and it will soon be time for the guards to begin collecting the virgins from each sector of the city of Susa and other surrounding areas that have been identified. The virgins from the Hills of Shechar were gathered months ago and are already halfway through their purification time. The King will begin seeing each of them as soon as the rules are signed into law.

The rumors are true, King Xerxes does, in fact, intend to entertain and sleep with whichever of the girls he chooses, taking their virginity as he goes. If he has slept with them but does not see value in them being queen, he will send them to the harem kept for his entertainment. My poor Esther, this cannot be her fate.

***

"Papi, Rachael and I are going to the town's square tonight during the fires. There are going to be some musicians there I am dying to hear," Esther shouts as she completes the final touches to her braid before applying her head scarf.

"Oh no, you must not! You are but two young sweet girls. Surely the jackals will sweep you up and devour you as tasty sweets after dinner!" I tease.

"Papi, those are just scary stories you adults tell children to make them stay in bed! I'm practically grown. I don't believe in such horror stories anymore," she rolls her eyes, very aware I am just playing.

Chuckling at the memories, I assure her. "The same stories you will tell your children when you are tucking them into bed for the four hundredth time of the night I assure you,"

"I would never," she laughs good naturedly.

Doing my best to hide my amusement, I reply, "Nevertheless, I shall accompany you. I'll do it from afar," I promise her as she pulls in a deep breath to argue. "You know the punishments for young women wandering the streets alone are harsh. There is no need to borrow trouble. Besides, I love good music. Maybe I want to dance in the village square and impress everyone with my skills!" I say, dancing for her as the youngsters do these days.

"Oh Papi, I shall bring an extra head scarf to wrap around my face," she mimics with her face completely covered, trying to find her way through the house without being able to see.

Bending over and placing her hands on her knees, Esther dissolves in laughter, and I throw an arm around her shoulders. At the sound of insistent, excited knocking, I groan and rub my forehead.

"Rachael has too much fire for life in her veins. Such a noisy one - that girl."

They chat happily all the way to the square while I trudge ahead. Hearing their laughter makes my heart both happy and heavy at the same time. I know from talk at the gates, the time of gathering the virgins will be soon. Oh, how I will miss her when she is gone. Esther is an exceptional beauty even though she cannot see it herself. I had tried over the years to be sure she knew her worth. That she saw herself through my eyes, but as is the way with girls, she never could see it.

I was sure the prideful, yet wise, gracious, strong-willed, and sex-driven King would choose to sleep with Esther. She inherited an exotic mix of her father's dusty blonde hair and her mom's deep brown. Much to my dismay in this situation, she also got her mother's perfect, curvy figure.

There is no way I can see her escaping that moment. But what then? If he chooses her as queen it will be one thing, but if she is sent to the harem afterward, what kind of life will my daughter have then? Sure, either way, she will never want during a famine or hard times in our country. However, if there were ever a war, the enemy always goes for what belongs to the King first! The things done to women during war are unspeakable, and they never recover - even if they live. Worrying never changes anything I tell myself. *'Trust Yahweh and stop fretting like a woman.'*

For now, I vow to myself and to Yahweh, I will focus on enjoying the life we have left together before the gathering. I will spend hours praying to and seeking the guidance of the I Am and trust He has a plan for everything that happens in this life.

When we get close enough to begin hearing the music play and the dull roar of the people attending, I start to dread the rest of this evening. Watching Esther take extra time with her hair and appearance was a painful reminder she is at the time of being able to be spoken for and betrothed to a righteous man for marriage. Jonathan has already shown interest in her and has asked permission to begin talking with her about a possible courtship. He did not believe in false gods and is an apprentice under his father as a blacksmith so he understands the value of hard work. Now it is time to wait for Esther, and see what she thinks of Jonathan.

I have always insisted I would allow Esther to have some say in who she marries, but whoever the man would be, had to be a devout follower of Yahweh. Our people have battled too long, and overcome by the strength and mercy of I Am to be lax on our devotion now.

Having a daughter proved to be a test of strength and self-control. To give her a say in who she married brought in the 'the unknown' factor. Females her age don't think with their head or their spirit, but rather with their emotions. Feelings change every day, sometimes every hour, and that could lead her to make a terrible decision.

As much as I don't want to be, I am also disappointed I will not be receiving a bride price for all my hard work raising her. I know it is wrong, she isn't an ox or a mule to be sold. But the human side of me sees other fathers using bride prices they've received, and I could have used the money to finally fix the roof on the house. I would maintain the proper amount as her widow's portion if something ever happened to her husband of course, but any interest that occurred was for the fathers to use. All of that would be gone now once the virgins are gathered.

I need to be sure I offer a sacrifice for my selfish thoughts regarding the forfeited bride price, but it just keeps creeping in on me at times. I am not sure why I continually give it a place in my heart.

"Esther, I'm pleased you came tonight. I've saved you a seat by the fire and close to the musicians so you can enjoy the evening. Mordecai? With your permission, may we go up there?" Jonathan rushes out all in one painfully practiced breath.

As I nod, Esther cuts in, "Is there room for Rachael? We would need seats for two before I can accept," she says, linking arms with her best friend.

"I'm sure we can squeeze in," Jonathan says, making me cringe a little on the inside. There really isn't a need to squeeze closer together until a wedding night if you ask me, but no one does. They just happily bounce off toward the saved spot near the musicians.

The evening didn't do anything to alleviate my worries over the events to come. Many were talking about forcing their daughters into spontaneously arranged marriages at the last minute to keep them from possibly ending up in the harem. This also goes against Hebrew tradition. There would be no time for a proper courtship, bride price arrangement, prayers needed to bless the marriage and so many other issues. This takes Yahweh out of the position to bless unions and move on behalf of his sovereign will for each child he has created. Nothing about this feels right to me. If we ignore Yahweh, and make a mockery of his intended course for marriage, would we be punished? It was a grave sin indeed to mock God. Rushing a marriage ceremony and not taking the proper days between the traditional wedding rites and sacrifices put a twisting ball of anxiety in my stomach. Would God remove his hand of protection from his people if we forsook the laws he set for marriage?

If I allowed her to be gathered like the other contestants, Yahweh could ... no, *would* watch over her. I know she is his child more than she is mine. I know he would provide, or make a way just like Shadrach, Meshach and Abednego or even Daniel. But do I have the ability to send my child into the fiery furnace? Because it feels exactly like I am the one walking her to the mouth of the lion's den and throwing her inside. '*Yahweh, forgive my fear. I am giving her to you even though she never was really mine. I will not stand in the way of your will for her life. Please deliver my Esther, my little Nesicha. ~ Amen'*

Chapter 4

Being a Single Parent

<Mordecai>

I was a younger man when Esther came into my life. Finding a wife should have been really high on my priority list, but with a newborn thrust into my lap, I didn't feel like I had extra time to pray and seek a wife the way Yahweh would have wanted. One month turned into another and here we are, sixteen years later. Now I am old, not too old to get married I guess. Men *twice my age* are taking girls the same age as Esther for wives and no one thinks it out of place, but I find it unsettling. The fortunate girls are allowed to have some say, and pick someone their own age. The unlucky ones have no voice, and their fathers pick the husband based on who has the biggest bride price.

More and more, Hebrew fathers take no thought for anything but the bride price. The world is changing, some of these trends lean away from the law, but technically still are close enough to it the people convince themselves it is okay to do what they want instead of following the law exactly as it is written. I fear these tendencies will bring the Hebrew people a time of punishment and resetting someday with Yahweh. When he gave us the commandments and the law, He was specific and intentional. I am not sure how we have decided maybe he was just suggesting possibilities we could … maybe try … as options to worship Him. It is silly, and gives Him very little respect. But life is hard, and I understand. I will not be the person who runs around shaming my brethren everyday, so here I am. Caught in the middle.

When Esther was little, Yahweh had provided a wet nurse named Elizabeth in the village to help me get her to the age of eating solid food. Then there had been a widow who needed an extra set of hands, and took Esther while I worked. Asnat taught Esther how to cook, the Words of Yahweh, and was more of a Grandmother figure to her than anything. She might as well have been family as Esther grew so close to her. Arriving to pick her up after work was always so fun. Little legs carried her to me as fast as she could toddle. Her little voice crying 'Papi!' was so endearing. I can't say what years were my favorite, but those chubby little toddler years were very fun.

Shortly after Asnat passed, Rachael's family moved into the neighborhood. The girls played and played together. Sarah, Rachael's mom, agreed to have Esther over every day. Esther brought our clothes with her on wash day. She would prepare our meals over there, and I would stop by to help her carry it all home when I got off.

Yes, Yahweh had miraculously provided for us over the years. I would not stop believing in His provision now. Sometimes I was forced to do things unconventional to the Hebrew way, but I believe Yahweh knew that would be the case when He gave Esther to me. I firmly believe He had given me the unusual calling of having to be both Mama and Papi at times.

I am not going to force a speedy marriage on Esther to keep her away from the possibility of a harem. It is impossible to pick the "right" thing from two "wrong" options. We will simply have to trust in God, that he already knows what lies before us and has a plan.

I just wished this traitorous mind of mine would stop reminding me about the children of Israel in hundreds of years of slavery, a fiery furnace, and a lion's den were also things Yahweh had allowed over the years. This dumb, traitorous heart. She is my baby after all. I might have almost been a child myself when I began raising her all by myself, but Esther's birth Papi, my Uncle Abihail, was my favorite relative. I honored him as deeply as I could. He was a giant of a man, strong and worthy of respect. If I hadn't known it was a sin, I would have almost worshiped him. He was so impressive. Instead, I focused every ounce of my energy into honoring the oath I made to her parents about this little woman child I had taken in to love and raise.

I was surely wishing I had a wife tonight. Things had to be explained ...delicate things. She had to know. The King would take one look at Esther and he would definitely choose to sleep with her. She couldn't go in there not knowing what it meant. Her friends had been telling her ridiculous things. One friend had told her if the King kissed her, and their knees touched, it meant they had sex and could produce an heir. Ridiculous.

Obviously the other parents were struggling, or simply not telling their daughters the truth about love making. If in the middle of her night with the King she didn't know what was to come, she would be so scared. I could not stand to be the reason she would be blindsided with fear, and unprepared for the truth of the act. I also do not want anyone to over exaggerate the act and scare her to the point of heart palpitations. No, this was my job, it is my own stupid fault for not providing her a mother to love her through moments like this. Breathing a short prayer, I prepare to go forward. *'Now Yahweh, please help me not completely mess it up before I'm done.'*

I went to the market and bought some vegetables. A gourd and a carrot. A. Gourd. and ... a ... Carrot ... *"uhhghh Yahweh forgive me! How am I, a man, supposed to do this?"*

"Papi. What are you grumbling on about? Are you okay?" Esther says, coming into the kitchen.

"Yes daughter, sit please," gesturing to a chair, I smile over at her. She sits and looks up at me. Those big brown, innocent eyes waiting for me to speak were too much pressure. Every time she blinked I swear I could hear her eyelashes. *whoosh *whoosh Or maybe it was my heart? I could not tell anymore.

"Papi, you are sweating, do you need water?" She sweetly fusses over me. Whether it is King Xerxes or not, she will make anyone a wonderful wife one of these days.

Lowering myself into a chair and wiping the nervous sweat from my brow I suddenly find my mouth as dry as all the sands of the Dasht-e Kavir desert. "Yes daughter, water would be good." '*What are you going to say you old fool? You barely have any more experience than the beautiful daughter you are going to teach about intercourse tonight.*' I chide myself. Even though it is less frowned upon for Hebrew men to have lost their virginity before marriage than for women, I had not indulged in many physical pleasures. I wasn't a saint before becoming a father, but for the last sixteen years I had abstained. Tonight, in some ways I couldn't remember what it was even like. In other ways, when I had practiced my speech, imagining trying to explain it to my innocent daughter I felt like certain words and images were screaming through my brain and maybe even my mouth without any control.

"Okay Papi, here you go," she hands me the water with a curious eye.

Taking a big drink with shaky hands, I stand and walk behind a table I have prepared for this very conversation. Everything is prepared. I have a knife, the gourd, carrot, and hand towel so I can wring my hands on something if I should get nervous. That was a genius thought, because I am already nervous and she isn't even aware of what I want to visit with her about yet. *'Alright, old man quit stalling and get this over with.'*

"Daughter," I say, holding up the curvy shaped gourd in my hands and raising my eyebrows.

"Yes?"

"No, ... daauuughterrr," I say, making my voice dip the opposite way while still pointing at the gourd.

"Yessss," she replies mimicking my tone difference as well as my eyebrow movement.

"Oh Mordecai you old ghabiun!" Smacking myself in the forehead I force myself to get on with it already.

"Esther, you are more beautiful than most. When your night with the King comes, I expect him to take advantage of all the rights he believes he has. So, I am going to do the best I can to prepare you for what might happen. This curvy, stupid gourd is your body."

Now it's beginning to dawn on her what I am trying to explain. Her eyes begin to grow big. "Papi," she gasps as her hands take up an immediate shield over her eyes, even though she peeks through her fingers and nods for me to continue.

"It's embarrassing for me too, daughter but you must know. Be quiet. I'll be fast. It'll be over, and we will eat. But if you have questions, even if you are as embarrassed as I am right now, ask your questions, Yahweh gave us to each other. I am the only parent you have. We will do our best. Together, just like we always have."

She closes her mouth, nods her head and stares at me with very wide eyes and then moves her hands back up over her face, waiting for me to begin.

"He is supposed to be gentle with you. To love you. He should embrace you, kiss you and put you at ease. All of your clothes will come off - at least they are supposed to... umm this part is your head..." I gesture with a knife to the top of the gourd.

She nods in pure fright.

"If he cares about your needs this is only supposed to be a little painful the first time for you and then it is supposed to be pleasurable for both of you." My breath is coming in embarrassed, short gasps, and I wipe my forehead with the towel one more time. Grabbing the carrot, I find it is shaking in my hand. "This is ..."

"I know what it is supposed to be; please keep going," Esther squeaks from behind her hands.

"How do you know what ..." Now I am heaving like a bull out in the fields, wondering what kind of discussions she and her friends had been engaging in trying to figure this out. My nerves are stretching and at the point of snapping, but I take the carrot and look at the gourd before pausing. "OH for crying out loud."

Realizing I forgot to cut an 'entrance' on the bottom of the gourd, I panic and grab the knife, whack off the bottom of the gourd, shove the carrot in the end and quickly say, "And if the whole country is blessed, you will be with child!"

Esther stands, slowly walks to the table, looking at me while picking up the piece of the gourd I chopped off before shoving the carrot into the gaping hole. As her eyes widen to the size of onions, her screams split the evening with the ferocity of the most horrific night terrors one could imagine. Racing to her bed, she completely disappears under the covers, not even taking a breath to interrupt the screams. Pretty soon, an arm pops out from under the blankets, finds a floor cushion near her bed, and pushes it on top of her head as the screaming begins to lose its power.

"A Girl! Yahweh, you had to give me a girl. I am too dumb for this! Did I do more harm than the King is ever going to do?" I say and slump to my knees, resting my head in my hands near her bed.

"Daughter, come out. I am sorry. I am embarrassed. I didn't prepare well and panicked. Please ask me all of the fearful questions I created in your mind so I can fix whatever I just damaged." I murmur.

From under the blankets I hear a terrified question, "Does he have to cut a hole in me?"

Wanting to cry for the first time in a very long time, I swallow the painful lump in my throat and answer, "No daughter, Yahweh has already prepared you perfectly to receive your husband. You know when your monthly issue comes? That is the spot where you will receive your husband's member. During the act of sex, he will release his seed. If it is the right time of the month and the will of Yahweh, your seed and his, will meet and an heir will grow in your womb. During birth, the baby will travel back down through that same opening. The journey of giving birth will be much more painful than the act of becoming one with your husband."

Waiting for her to respond, I offer prayers to Yahweh, asking him to please heal the wounds in Esther that all of my stupidity earlier may have caused. After a moment, Esther pushes the blankets from her body and forcefully swings the floor cushion at me, landing a solid blow on the side of my head. The combination of her tear-streaked face, crazy-disheveled hair, and the menacing, stare-down she levels on me is almost comical until I remember I am guilty of putting it all there.

"Papi, it is all very simple. It is science. Why did you have to frighten me so? A curvy gourd ... really?" She huffs as she pushes herself out of bed and stomps into the kitchen. With a look of defiance, she grabs the knife and chops off the end of the carrot, and takes a very aggressive bite, much to my discomfort.

Esther begins the final preparations to serve dinner for the evening, mumbling to herself as she goes, "Or maybe, 'hey Esther, remember asking me a thousand questions about the goats mating in the field when you were ten? In a more loving and spiritual way, that is how humans engage in love making and have sex, hoping to create a baby.' because it is *not super hard* to describe."

I am a little disturbed at the heavy-handed precision she is using to prepare the vegetables for this evening's meal as she mumbles her frustrations. However, given the way I botched the 'scientific' lesson on lovemaking ... I decided to give her a wide berth and accept her food preparation techniques as the most normal way to chop carrots I have ever seen.

When the meal was finally ready to eat, we were able to fall back into our normal routine discussing our day, matters at work, and anything else we could think of. The topic of the competition came up and we discussed how although it didn't align with God's Law, I felt it was better to endure the trial, than to intentionally break several of the laws God had laid forth as part of the Hebrew foundation of faith.

Even though our evening had been a little uncomfortable, we both knew the coming days would hold much worse, and we would have to cling to one another to make it through. Still, I vow to myself not to buy gourds or carrots for a very long time after tonight. They would be embarrassing reminders of my failure as a Papi.

Chapter 5

LIFE WILL NEVER BE THE SAME

\<Mordecai\>

It is the day before the gathering, and I am rushing to The Marketplace as soon as work is through. Choosing a new dress, scarf, and delicate pearl necklace with jade accents for Esther, I should have done this yesterday because today I am short on time. A few stands over, I notice the merchant with beautiful fresh cut bouquets. Seeing one with red poppies in it, I rush over to grab one. They are Esther's favorite and I hope to make her last evening at home as special as possible.

Before the merchant wraps it up, I spot a slightly smaller bouquet with wisteria and bluebonnets in it, and on a whim, grab it for Rachael. I know deep down Rachael will not be chosen, but something in my gut still twists at the thought there is a possibility it could happen ... no matter how slight. I know Esther is strong and can endure anything thrown at her. But Rachael will be teased and bullied by the other contestants every second Esther is not around and it makes all of the protectiveness inside me come alive.

Jacob, Rachael's father, had agreed to stop by and pick up the leg o' lamb I paid someone to cook over a smoke pit all day. Sarah had agreed to make bread and a few vegetables. Tonight we would all sup together as families, and honor the two girls who really should be referred to as women now, but old habits die hard.

There were many memories, laughter, and even a few tears shed during the evening in our courtyard as we reminisced over the mischief the girls had gotten into when we all first met, memories we would all enjoy forever, and how Yahweh had made us into one big extended family. Finally, I asked both girls to kneel and be surrounded by the adults. I recited a prayer of protection over both of them as they held hands.

Lie us down tonight, Adonai our God, in peace; and raise us up again, our Ruler, in life.
Spread over us Your Sukkah of peace, direct us with Your good counsel, and save us for Your own Name's sake.
Shield us; remove from us every enemy, pestilence, sword, famine, and sorrow.
Remove all adversaries from before us and from behind us, and shelter us in the shadow of Your wings.
For You are our guarding and saving God, yes, a gracious and compassionate God and King.
Guard our going out and our coming in for life and peace, now and always!

"Amen," everyone answered.

Awkwardly, Rachael stood and stepped back beside her family. They hadn't practiced anything, but Esther began:

"May the Lord be with me, that He may defend me;
may He be within me, that He may conserve me;
may He be before me, that He may lead me;
may He be after me, so that He may guard me;
may He be above me, that He may bless me,
God the Father lives and reigns forever and ever. Amen."

She had no more than finished when a royal proclamation sounded by a chorus of shofars being blown together, splitting the air. The Palace Guards had marched up in formation. Thirteen rows of soldiers, all wearing full armor, carrying spears, and each blowing shofars of various sizes.

Everyone in this quadrant of town had come out of their dwellings and were lined up outside their homes. All of the young virgins took a step forward waiting to be judged on whether they were 'beautiful' or not. Rachael and Esther held hands. Haman walked up and down the length of the street slowly, relishing the fact that all eyes must be on him. I took a step back so he would not see me.

"Citizens of Susa, tonight is the night your daughters have the rare privilege of possibly becoming the next Queen of Persia. Our next Queen will not be chosen by how much money her family has, nor by the title held by her father, NO! Your daughters, and even one of my daughters will have equal opportunity to become Queen and bless our country with its next heir!"

"Our King Ahasuerus is without a doubt the most generous of all royalty. When we come by to confirm whether your daughter will be coming with us tonight, you will then have ten minutes to say goodbye. Arguing with our decisions will most certainly end with you burying a family member come morning. The word of the King is final. Guards! Begin." With a sly grin, Haman spins on his left foot and approaches the nearest family.

Poor Kavan, he has five daughters and Haman seems desperately focused on Janeth. Tonight, Kavan will lose three of those five daughters. He rushed two of them off into forced and hurried marriages to avoid handing all of his children over on the same night.

"Esther, we both know I will not be going. I love you. Thank you for being a wonderful friend." Rachael squeezes Esther tight and I reach in to break the embrace.

"Well Nesicha, there really isn't anything to say. You know I'm incredibly proud of you. You are smart, logical, level-headed, discerning, ...and wise. But none of that compares to the value of being obedient to Yahweh. I'm proud of you, daughter. Walk with your head held high. I love you." When I pull her close to hug her I whisper, "Do not reveal your Hebrew heritage until the time is right. This is very important Esther."

"I love you too Papi," she rushes out the last few words in a half sob but adds a nod as well.

"Hello Mordecai, is this your daughter?" A guard circles Esther like a vulture.

"You know I am a single man, Arman." I shake my head as though she couldn't be my daughter, hating the implication that she is not. I just feel it is life or death to keep this secret.

"Young lady, gather your things, you are off to meet the King."

When his eyes land on Rachael, she is frozen in place terrified, with her head lowered. Instantly, I want to protect her. He reaches out and lifts her chin. There is a momentary flash of shock in his eyes when he sees her face. Seeing his black pupils zero in on her lazy eye, he bursts out into awful, mocking laughter. Seething on the inside, I desperately wish there were something I could do to erase this moment. How could a man crush the soul of a young lady so easily? My anger rising, I can feel my fingers swelling because I am clenching my fists so hard.

"Ooooh that lazy eye? You do have beautiful hair but," then he shouts, "Nahhh, you're good. You may stay with your parents."

Then he turns on his heel, laughing loudly and walks away.

"Mordecai, tell that girl she has ten minutes to be on this cart. If she's not, someone in her family dies," he shouts back in my direction.

"Understood Sir," I reply knowing how the army works, as well as how dangerous it is to speak against their final word. I wrap my arms around Esther bringing her into the house to calm down. Rachael follows us in.

"Rachael, let's go," Jacob insists, leaning his head inside the entrance. "I haven't said anything before, but now we know for sure you're not going .... well ... we have received no marriage offers for you save one. The bride price isn't good, but it's all we've received. We thought if you were chosen to go, maybe you would fall in love with a guard who wouldn't mind your eye or something but ... well, now ... Peter is waiting for us to bring you by and start the traditional rituals. I'm sorry daughter."

Stunned, Rachael stands frozen, looking at Jacob in the doorway. Her skin is already a pale version of herself, and I wonder if she is going to pass out.

"Peter is four hundred years old! How can you do this?" Esther shouts, surprising us with her outburst, making all of us jump. Normally she follows the standard etiquette for a lady and their expected behavior. But I had spoiled her over the years, giving her the same opportunities as many of the young men. I could tell that she was very intelligent, and deserved extra schooling beyond the primary school. Schooling was not the only exception I had called in favors for my little Nesicha over the years. Occasionally, when an injustice was too great, or something she was very passionate about was being debated, she might be unable to maintain her silence as women were expected to do. The subject of marriage and how husbands were chosen, was one of those things for Esther. And I knew immediately we would hear from her when Jacob started talking about marriage offers.

With the whole room staring at her in shock, she turns to me. I can feel my face turning bright red. My fists are clenched again, and a burning rage is building in my gut. I can feel my fingers swelling again.. Am I ... jealous?

"Jacob, I will not allow you to do this." I demand softly.

"How do you think you have a say, Mordecai? Are *you* going to pay to increase my flock?" Jacob scoffs, offended.

"How much?" I counter. At his confused look, I say again. "How much? How much is Peter's bride price?" My voice rises every time I have to repeat 'How much?' before he catches on.

"Twenty shekels and six sheep," Jacob says, lowering his eyes. It is not much of a bride price, but if there's no other offer, it's better than nothing."

"Everyone stand still, I'm running out of time. Papi, please come with me." Esther grabs my wrist and drags me into her bedding corner. Reaching under her mattress, she pulls out the trinket box which holds the inheritance her birth parents left for her. I had never used it and had vowed to let her keep it.

"Papi, I know it's a big ask, but please, take out what you need to fix the roof and use the rest for a bride price... take Rachael for a wife. She will love you. I think she kind of does already. I know she annoys you, but you could make a request of her to work on her screechy voice. Papi, please!"

"This is yours, daughter," I say with years of guilt on my shoulders, even holding the money.

"All I want out of there is my father's ring and my mother's necklace. The rest means nothing to me, but she means the world. Besides, you'll be lonely. And you owe me for the carrot and the gourd," she says with a smile, making me groan in embarrassment.

"TWO MINUTES!" A guard bellows from outside. "YOU GIRLS HAVE TWO MINUTES TO BE ON THIS CART OR THERE WILL BE CONSEQUENCES!"

"Papi, please I have to go," she pleads.

Taking several pieces of paper money out, I count the rest. There is more there than I thought. Saving a few more pieces of paper money back to buy Rachael some nice things, I hurriedly return to the outer room and present Jacob with a pile of money.

"Jacob, my bride price. Rachael, with your blessing, may I pursue permission from your parents for your hand in marriage?" I inquire, smiling at her.

"WHAT!?" she shrieks.

"Rachael, don't ruin it! You'll have to work on your loud, high-pitched voice for my Papi," Esther says laughing. "I really really love you all, but I have to go! Rachael, please say yes before I leave."

"Yes Mordecai, I won't let you down. You don't know how grateful I am for this," Rachael smiles at me softly.

Rushing outside, Esther climbs up into the cart. She didn't take anything with her, but she is going to be living in the palace. Which one of her things would be acceptable there anyway? Time to make the best of whatever is to come! As the cart jerks forward, Esther smiles, blows a kiss to all those she loves, and whispers a prayer of thanks to Yahweh for her Papi saving Rachael from that terribly old, disgusting man Peter, who smells like his livestock.

***

\<Haman\>

With carriage after carriage full of beautiful young virgins, I could care less about any of them, save two. My daughter Yasna, and the beautiful Janeth. Xerxes already told me he would not marry Yasna, and I challenged him that she had better not end up in his harem. Being Second in Command means the bride price my daughters bring are handsome ones. I would not be cheated out of it all because he wants to sleep with hundreds of virgins. He reminded me this was my idea in the first place, and Yasna would be treated like any other contestant in the ranks, but she would not be queen. Janeth is mine. I do not care how we have to make that happen, but it will happen. She will be in my harem before this competition is over or I will just take her.

There are days where Xerxes' arrogance truly makes me despise him. If he only realized how easily I could take his throne. I am but inches from his throat on a daily basis and it could all be over within seconds if I chose to act. I am a formidable opponent. Sure, I might not be able to take him in a fair one-on-one fight, but if I caught him unaware, I know I could overpower him. There are times he takes his frustrations and fears out on me almost like my past mortal enemies. Other times, he values me as a trusted brother. He needs to thank the gods daily because I choose to restrain myself. I am smarter than he is. Just because he towers over everyone in height, he believes himself invincible. His throat can still be slit like all others.

If he calls for either Yasna, or Janeth his drink will be poisoned enough to ensure he cannot see anyone for the evening. He will spend the night throwing up instead of deflowering my girl. Janeth shall be mine. I have had my eyes on her since she was a child. Even at a small tender age she stirred thoughts in me that probably should not happen. Only because I know how hard childhood can be, did I not take her at the time. If the King even thinks of calling her to his bed first I will find some way to prevent their meeting. She is mine. She has always been mine.

I love knowing I'll be closer to Janeth and her family will be nowhere around. I purposefully ride on her cart so I can be close to her. Looking down into her eyes makes excitement shoot through me like lightning from the sky. I am finally close to having her all to myself.

"Good evening, Contestant. May I have the pleasure of your name?" I inquire knowing full well what her name is.

"Janeth, sir," she replies, smiling up at me.

"Ahhh, Janeth, you may all call me Haman. I hope you will feel welcome and safe during your time at the palace. The eunuchs are trusted, and well-versed at caring for the needs of women should you need anything, but if you see me in the hallway you may approach me," I say, ending my speech smiling back down into the eyes that have captivated me for many years.

On either side of her sit her twin sisters Zahra, and Zeinab. They are pleasant to look at, but they are not anywhere near the same worth as Janeth. They look afraid and sickly. Janeth is taking everything in with wonder in her eyes and looking forward to her experience. I hope I can make it everything she has ever dreamed of...because she is never going home.

Chapter 6

THE CONTESTANTS

\<Esther\>

Being one of the last ones to climb onto the cart, I look around for a place to sit. Finding none, I stand near a pile of trunks and boxes. Raising my eyes, I see everyone on the cart has brought many personal items with them. Clothes, shoes, and trinkets of all kinds line the empty spaces. Young girls dot the landscape between the trunks. Some are nervous, their eyes are wide, and the cords in their necks are prominent as they take deep breaths trying to calm their anxiety as best they can. Their labored breathing helps me imagine their pulses beating in their necks. Anxiety attacks are taking victims down one at a time.

Others portray more of a haughty demeanor. Acting as though they've already been named Queen to cover up their insecurities, but it shows more on their faces than they think it does. As I look at each girl, to the ones who make eye contact, I offer a small smile. For the girl next to me, I whisper a quiet hello. I have to admit, as much as I am trying to be nice, I'm also trying to get a good feel for everyone's genuineness. Trying to see right off the top if they are a scheming personality, or a trusting soul. Does it make me judgmental? I don't know, I just know I've always been able to sense these things about people. As if knowing their motives comes as a second nature to me. I have found it to be very beneficial over the years when I am in a large group situation, especially when it is in a competition-type environment.

Nearing the palace, the murmuring and gossiping increases. Some of these girls have gone so far as to have already planned out how they assume to redecorate and make the palace their own when they become queen. Have none of these young ladies given thought to the fact they could end up in the harem easier than they could become queen? Silly foolish girls.

When we arrive, two of the eunuchs, Zethar and Carcas, stand on either side of the cart offering their hand to us as we depart, to steady us down the steps. Many of the girls are bossing the eunuchs, telling them where to take their belongings, demanding they be extra careful because 'there are family heirlooms in those boxes and lowly eunuchs shouldn't be careless with their handling.' Zethar and Carcas are not saying much, simply continuing to help the girls out of the cart. I receive the hand, smile, and say a modest 'thank you' as I descend, using the manners Papi drilled into me over the years.

"Maiden, what is your name?" Zethar asks.

"Esther sir," I say, with a curtsey and a smile.

"Thank you, be on your way. Line up to the right on the blue line," he says nodding in the direction I am to go.

As the night progresses, a few more girls end up on the blue line with me, but I'm not sure why. Did we do something wrong? I spoke without being spoken to but will I be punished for it? Am I not supposed to be polite and say thank you? Oh, Papi will be shamed if I messed up before I ever made it into the palace. What have I done?

"Ladies, you have been placed into groups. The blue line will enter first. You will be with Abagtha. He will be your go-between with Hegai. Hegai is the head of the eunuchs and has direct access to King Xerxes. If Abagtha determines your request is not worthy of bothering Hegai, your request will not be delivered and you are not to bother him yourself. Please nod if you understand." The guard looks up to see we are following along. "Great. Carcas is with white, Biztha is with purple group, and Zethar is with yellow."

"Blue, line up first, then white, purple, and last yellow. This is how you will go through your treatments and purification process. You will be taught proper etiquette, whom you may address and whom you may not. Even if chosen as queen, there are certain men you are not allowed to approach unless you are given permission, and yes ... that includes King Xerxes," he continues.

"Who does he think he is?" A girl from the yellow group says, "If I am queen, I will do as I wish."

"And that my dear, is exactly why you are in the yellow group. Shall I let you in on a little secret? Every year at the feast where the King is very generous with all of the land's luxuries, he gives even the lowest citizen endless food and drink. During the celebration week, he sets aside the most troublesome women from the harem for the guards to indulge in their carnal pleasures. My guess is I'll see you there someday. Any other questions ladies?"

The contestants are stunned into silence. No one had heard of this tradition before. What happens to the ladies of the harem? It was something we were completely unsure of. We knew there were too many women there to be pleasuring the king regularly. Did they live a life of luxury, without having to do anything for months or possibly years at a time? This news was indeed unsettling. The more delicate girls are crying, their hiccupping and sniffling can be heard as each group makes their way into the palace.

Heaving a big sigh, the guard says, "Ladies, the sniveling and crying only attract the guards with the most vile lustful desires who love to listen to their women cry and beg. I suggest for your safety, you learn to control your emotions. Now move along."

He acts as though their tears are no more moving than watching a turtle cross the road in front of him. Many of the girls have now begun to wonder what their lives truly will hold in the future. For several of them, it seems to be the things their childhood nightmares were made of.

Inside, we are brought into four separate rooms by group. Each eunuch over a group begins giving instructions to his charges.

"Ladies of the Blue Group, I am Abagtha. I will be your attendant during your purification time here at the palace. Your diets will be restricted and changed to healthy options *only* in the beginning. Each morning you will start with breakfast, you will be prompt and ready for the day before breakfast starts or you will have points taken off. Do I make myself clear?"

Looking around for everyone to nod their understanding, he continues, "Every day your schedule will be different, but you will go through purification sessions, and hygiene classes, have your hair and skin scrubbed and treated properly each week. You will also learn how to tend your nails so they look like royalty, and not like one who has been made to cook and clean."

At his remark, each maiden looks down at her hands, turning them over and over to examine her nails, and the calluses which had formed from the years of work. It was a way of life, and it was how everyone's hands looked. We had not noticed before the small details screaming out to royalty that we didn't belong.

"Your willingness to learn, your attitude, your ability to catch on, and your knowledge of manners will all be scored each week. When it is time to begin presenting you to the King for your intimate dinners, the ones with the highest points will be presented first regardless of group you are in. If you have questions, we are here to help. I will show you to your quarters. Tonight there will be a gathering at 9:00 pm sharp. Meet here in our hall and I will escort you to the gathering," Abagtha said pleasantly.

Upon entering the sleeping quarters, most of the girls stand still, taking it all in. I move quietly toward a bedding area that catches my eye. Setting my things down, I turn to find everyone else has done the same. Along the ceiling of each makeshift bedroom, were rows of golden rings that have been attached to golden runners. Each golden ring is attached to a curtain that can be pulled fully around the bedding area so we can all have privacy during any free time we might have, for dressing, or times of prayer, and any other privacy needs we may have.

"Did anyone else have their heart set on this spot? We could play Snap-Shoot to see who wins?" I offer.

Everyone smiles at the mention of the childhood game we played during breaks at the *bet sefer* many of us attended together to learn in our early years. But it appears, everyone is happy with their chosen spots. We begin to settle in and look around.

Each of us has a luxurious bed in a frame standing up off the ground. Many of the girls live in homes where the sleeping spaces still hold some kind of simple padding on the floor. Not all of them are made of the same outer material, nor are they stuffed with the same filler on the inside. It depended on what you can afford, what you find when other people discarded their excess, or any other material that might be comfortable to lay on.

Here in the palace, the outer material was the same on all of the bedding. It was a heavy canvas material seen in the marketplace being sold for outer garments and was meant for durability, comfort, and fashion. Mine was mostly yellows, browns, and greens. The yellow had tree branches with birds on them and it was what had caught my eye. That, and the fact it was placed near a window. I love animals, everything from birds to the largest camels. They all fascinate me. I hope being near a window, I will be able to hear some birds singing, or maybe even the call of a Red Sand Fox at night. Each girl has been given beautiful, soft woven sheets, one heavy blanket, and one lightweight blanket for the shifts in weather.

Beside each bed is a wardrobe carved from rich cedarwood, and on the other side is a nightstand made of white marble. Inside the wardrobes are several blue dresses of different styles, and shoes. In the nightstand are undergarments, makeup, lotions, and facial products. I have no idea what to do with any of the products in the night stand. Normally I use goat milk lotion on everything from my face to the soles of my feet. Everyone's wardrobes contain the exact same items. A little overwhelmed, I go back into the hall to seek out Abagtha.

"Sir, may I ask you whether we are supposed to stay in our own clothing or change into one of the provided dresses?"

"Today, young maiden, you are allowed to do whichever makes you the most comfortable. Thank you for asking," he replies.

"And there truly is no right or wrong?" I confirm.

Shaking his head no, I turn to start back toward my sleeping nook. I relay the information to the other girls so they can make an informed decision on what they might want to do for themselves as well. Deciding to stay in my dress from home for as long as I can, I rest on the bed until it's time to go. I cannot bear to take off the dress Papi sacrificed to buy new for me on this day. It is beautiful, but I am sure it will be the last day I will see it. Others opt for the palace dresses out of the excitement of being here.

Tonight will be a moment for all of the contestants to mingle and get to know one another if they should so choose. Since Papi already hosted a feast, I will not have a very big appetite, but I will do my best not to waste food. This kind of event is something I look forward to. I am not one who needs to be the center of attention, so I will not fall into the trap of competing with the loudest braggers of the evening. Sometimes, the quietest souls provide the longest friendships, as well as the most intellectual fun. One thing is for sure, we will find out a lot about our fellow contestants! Tonight will be interesting.

***

Entering the dining hall, we notice the purple and white groups have already been seated. They are sitting randomly around the room, not seated together. Upon closer inspection, it appears the chairs have color-coded cards on them. I look for several blue cards, trying to get a feeling for the people sitting at those tables, and finally choose a seat.

Introductions are made, and pleasant chatter ensues. When the yellow group enters, it is obvious most of the girls placed in this group are either spoiled rotten, extremely wealthy, believe they are better than everyone else, or just downright mean. Choosing a seat for each of them is extremely difficult because none of the other color groups are worthy of their presence in their opinions, and therefore choosing a seat next to one of us is a perceived insult to their station. After much drama, the yellow group ladies all finally choose a seat, and dinner is allowed to be served.

Some of the girls immediately complain about the meal being laid before them. "Umm, my three-month-old sister eats more than this in one sitting. Where is the rest of the food?"

"Right?" Another one leans over whispering, "I don't like fish. We live in farmland and not near the ocean for a reason."

As the murmuring continues, Hegai addresses the room "Contestants, if I may. Notice I didn't call you *ladies* because, from all of the complaining I've heard coming from certain groups here today, I'm certain very few actual ladies are in our presence during this round of The Gathering." This prompts a new round of murmuring from the yellow group.

"You may have been expecting the finest lavish meals the palace can afford. As you well know, you're not here to be entertained. These are your purification months. Starting today everything that goes in your mouth, in your body, or on your skin has a purpose. You will be given specific proportions, and you will eat them all. A few months later you might be served a dessert, it will probably be the size of your fingernail."

Hegai delivers this news as the rest of the plates and drinks are served around the room. He comes to a stop in front of my table and looks us over. Holding an outstretched hand toward me, he inquires, "Maiden, your name please?"

I lift my gaze and see his eyes focused on mine. Swallowing deeply to calm my nerves, I rise and perform a small curtsey "Sir, my name is Esther."

"What would be the reason we might feed you white fish as your main course this evening Esther? What health benefits would they bring?" He asks.

"White fish are known for good brain function, purification of the skin, enhanced mood, and when used with a healthy diet can help keep one from getting sick." I recite everything I can remember from my science class with the healers in my House of Study year.

I was lucky to attend for even one year. Females are often barred from attending the upper grades of study because they will only need to know how to cook and clean to be a wife and mother, but Papi had called in a few favors and paid extra so I could go. I studied hard and made excellent marks so I wouldn't embarrass him.

It was a hard year with much grief from the boys who never took a liking to having a girl learning with them. They were always threatened by me, especially if I scored better than they did, which of course, drove me to get as close to perfect marks as possible. Strong, smart women were not something to be beaten down. They were something to be treasured even more and I knew only the smartest of men would be able to see that. Unfortunately, there aren't a lot of men who were able to see my high scores as something to be proud of. *We* (as in society collectively) couldn't have the boys embarrassed by a girl, so I was asked not to return the following year.

"Correct, you may have a seat, young Esther," Hegai said, smiling at me.

When I sat, the girl from the white group next to me reached under the table and squeezed my leg to congratulate me. Smiling at her, I was grateful for her genuine kindness. Later during the meal, I learned her name was Sunita.

"Mister Hegai, Sir, I know why we are eating this green stuff." A girl from another table calls to get his attention. He doesn't acknowledge her so she waves her hand in the air and tries again, "Did you hear me?" *Whack* "Ahhhhh you hit me?" She cries out in pain.

"I don't know when so many of you decided that you could drop the customs of our day and culture. Do I need to remind you why you are here? Remind you why this country is in need of a queen to begin with?" A guard bellows across the room. His thick arms bend at the elbows, both hands holding daggers crossing at his abdomen. He is yelling so loud, spittle is flowing from the corner of his mouth and down his beard. There is a prominent vein reaching from his right temple, running down to the corner of his eye and it is bulging and pulsing as he yells. It looks like it could burst with his effort.

"In this country, the *men* lead. The *men* make the decisions, the *men* go to war, and the *men* are obeyed. The women warm our beds, the women birth our heirs, the women do the tasks we need them to do. The women make our food, and the women do as they are told. I can tell you a tale of even a queen who decided she could speak out of turn, make her own decisions, tell a man no, and think too highly of herself. It's not a bedtime story. I feel like many of you assume you are special because you are here. Take a look around. You are not special. You are one of hundreds if not thousands in our kingdom. Do not make the mistake of thinking you are above even Queen Vashti. I assure you, if anyone was going to break rules just because she was beautiful, it would have been her. But I myself, picked her body up in two pieces and buried them. Control your tongues lest your body be buried likewise," pausing as many gasps and quiet sobs twitter through the room he waits before he continues.

"Being the first day, we have been so much more than patient. From this very moment on, the first one of you who speaks to a man without permission will be put to death in the same manner our former Queen was silenced. Don't make the mistake of thinking the King will save you. The last thing he wants is another wife like the last one. The only man you have permission to approach is your appointed eunuch."

Chapter 7

WHY HE'S THE KING

<Tereh>

With his enormous fist wrapped around the hilt of his sword, Xerxes throws a jab at Haman and lands it solidly on his nose. By the time Haman grunts in pain, the King already has his dagger pulled from his waistband and is drawing a small amount of blood from Haman's throat. The training drills this week seem to be taking on a level of intensity that is unusual. It seems like he is making a point to someone, or several some-ones. I am going to stay on my toes to be sure I am meeting expectations. Someone is being tested here, I can feel it.

Crossing his arms, and shaking his head, Xerxes begins to taunt, "Haman, *tsk *tsk just last week my Aljada was faster than you when I stole a sweet from her table as I left, and she's old."

Growling in response, and still trying to stop the flow of blood from his nose, Haman grumbles, "Your creepy Aljada is the weirdest grandma I've ever met."

"Shhhhh, she has ears everywhere," King Xerxes ducks down as if trying to hide. "You'd better sleep with one eye open tonight, sadiq. She is coming for you for sure."

I like seeing the King playing around comically with Haman. I have seen him in battle and know how deadly he is. There are days here on the training grounds, he goes through every one of the warriors leaving us bleeding and gasping for air. It is nice sometimes to see him as a real person. But I'm not sure what is going on with Haman. He is not someone who can be trusted in my opinion. I don't share my thoughts with anyone I know for fear of him finding out, but I am sure he will not hesitate to betray any of us to make himself look better. Sometimes I wonder if he is even loyal to the King.

Haman rolls his eyes and checks his nose again. Seeing the bleeding has stopped, he washes his face in the water barrel on the edge of the training arena. The fun and games over, King Xerxes grows serious, and crosses his heavily muscled arms.

"Don't think we're done for the day brother. Your skills have been weighed and found wanting - something I will not tolerate in my Second. Friend or not, you are on thin ice." King Xerxes' tone has deepened, and his very dark eyes bore holes into the side of Haman's face. "I better be hearing reports of you training so much you are only getting three hours of sleep a day until you are sharp again."

"Your Majesty, the new group of contestants are due to arrive and watch training. Would you like to put us through any other paces before they get here?" I ask bowing, taking my right fist across my armored body to my left pec in a warrior's salute.

"We're good Tereh, when they arrive, we'll do the self-defense instruction. Each of us will call down a contestant for one-on-one instruction like last time. Then we'll do the two attacker situation, and call down another contestant. They'll be all excited. They will exit, and we can go back to training," the King explains.

"Don't act like this isn't exciting for you. You get to act like the *big man* in front of all these young women who can't wait to be taken to your bed hoping to become the next queen," Haman jests with a slight sneer.

That was it. I could tell it was the last straw King Xerxes was going to take before putting Haman in his place. Even the night of Vashti's execution a couple years ago, Haman pranced around taking liberties he had certainly never been given. Enough was enough, you could see the tolerance snap on King's Xerxes face. This had been building for years. Without warning, the King threw Haman to the ground with the dagger once again poised to take the lifeblood from his body. This time, it was no training exercise. "Haman, who am I?"

The predatory look in the King's eyes punches fear through Haman's veins. You could see it the way his eyes widen, and his veins raise a little under his skin in places. But pride and arrogance were always louder than fear and wisdom in Haman's soul. They cause him to reply with venom. "The. King."

I don't know what has gotten into him to continue to press King Xerxes in this manner. He doesn't show any respect in his tone, or in the look on his face.

King Xerxes' dominant spirit will never let Haman get away with anything but surrender. Countering with a higher level of lethality, he asks again. "Who. Am. I?"

The rest of the guards have filed in around me to watch our two top leaders go at it. Murmurings can be heard behind me, I am not sure if I should be making them do other duties or let them watch. I am next in command after Haman, so this falls on my shoulders. Pride, arrogance, and the drive to fight or challenge one another is simply born into men. Learning to place ourselves under someone else's authority is a trait we have to learn

– to practice. It is something that is addressed and battled within an army repeatedly. When a soldier begins to have success on the battlefield, it isn't very long before he needs reminded that he still has superiors. Looking around, I decide it is good for them to see respect is demanded at all levels of authority, and let them continue watching.

This time, I see Haman looking back and forth, searching the King's face. He was smart enough to know all of his men were seeing his disrespect. Forcing the King to a battle of skills one-on-one would never see Haman the victor, and he knows it. Reluctantly, he finally spits out between heaving breaths, "The King of all Persia. King Xerxes."

When the King only continued to stare him down, and further add physical domination to his hold over him, Haman adds his formal title, "King Ahasuerus."

"Haman, I *am* the King of all Persia. From Egypt to the Caspian Sea, and from the Balkan Peninsula to the Indus River. I don't get to <u>act</u> like the big man. I am *The Man*. My spirit tells me your next Queen is in this group of ladies. I don't think your attitude is worthy of meeting her yet. Take this time and go see to it all of the royal livestock are watered," then the King turns to me. "Tereh, assemble your guards to help assist our contestants."

Haman is silently dismissed, and the murderous look on his face as he leaves to perform the lowly task usually given to children wanting to become part of the King's army has not been lost on anyone. Giving me the order that should have been Haman's puts me at the top of Haman's list to be knocked down once his punishment is served and he is restored. I will be ready.

"Yes My King. Guards, you heard your King! Prepare! I see them coming now," I quickly instruct the other men. I don't know what is up with Haman but he has no fear when crossing King Xerxes. One of these days he will stick his neck out there only to get it chopped off, just like he did to Queen Vashti.

***

<Xerxes>

With the contestants filing in and taking a seat in the bleachers, I jump on top of the judges platform and begin to welcome them. Being used to commanding a crowd, I pace back and forth and turn on the charm. Knowing women find me irresistible, and knowing how to command the attention of any crowd, both male and female alike, I begin to set the tone.

It takes more primal, killer aggression to seep into my delivery with men, but with women ... primal, aggressive dominance does the trick for most of the shallow females. After losing Vashti, the manipulation game is kind of losing its appeal. I do not grieve for her as we did not have many true feelings for one another. But this game is getting old. This time, I am looking for someone who might let down the veil and be more than a power-seeking, status-hungry, aloof partner. I know they are very rare, but does a woman like that exist in my kingdom?

"Welcome Contestants, personally I want to thank you for taking part in this event to serve your country, ... and me, your King. The country and I are grateful to you whether you are chosen as my next queen or not, simply for following the rules of the contest and doing what's best for the people of Persia."

Most of the girls are swooning simply because of my looks. Many have said I am physically as close to perfection as one can get. Well if you prefer blondes ... you might find me lacking, but if you like tall, dark, muscled, and handsome, with a smile that paralyzes female and even some male brains alike - I am your man. But it is wearing thin. Show me a girl with more. Show me a girl with courage and brains and obedience and a body begging to be taken. *sigh ...Now I definitely am asking too much.

"Today, we are going to show you what our warriors learn when they first start out as youth. I hope this never comes in handy for you, but in today's world it might save your life someday. Now I'm going to show you what you or anyone can do if a bad guy or lady comes and tries to attack you. I'm going to let it happen real fast just like it might if you are walking home from The Market by yourself at night. So here I am with my basket coming home from The Market...."

Many were giggling behind their hands at the sight of their mighty king walking with a shopping basket in his hand. Even though I had told them what was going to happen, when the guard, who was pretending to be an attacker, appears and jumps onto my back, several of the women scream, and several jump. Very quickly, I have the 'attacker' thrown on the ground with my foot in his throat. Every contestant sat very still as if wondering what had just happened.

"That was really easy for me to do because I am so big. We will try to teach some of you how to do this move, but we will also show you another move that works much better for people with smaller bodies like yourselves. Let me demonstrate the second one you will be practicing today."

We pause to demonstrate both skills a few times both at regular speed and slowly so they could see the progression of the moves themselves.

"Now each guard is going to invite one contestant out to guide you through these moves. Please be serious learners," I continue.

As the guards approach the contestants in the stands, I see one young lady in yellow lean forward and scratch another contestant in blue across the left side of her face from behind. When the attacker sits back, she is holding not only a fist full of the contestant's hair, but her hair wrap and broken hair tie as well.

On instinct, the victim reaches a hand to her cheek and notices blood on her fingers as she lowers it again. To her credit though, she doesn't start crying. The companion beside her sputters, and picks up another fairly large clump of hair from between them on the bench as well. The victim turns around with a gasp and meets her attacker's smirk. Words are exchanged but I am yet too far away to hear what was said.

The contestant in blue grabs her hair tie, but the lady in yellow won't let it go. It snaps between them, flying back across the crowd out of reach. When she sits down in pure frustration, I wait a minute for her to gather herself. Soon, her friend from the blue group taps her leg and they look up at me.

With her hair a mess, her eyes dilated, and her neck corded from the heavy breaths as she tried to compose herself from the attack, she raises her chin. Her eyes are the same color as the pelt on the neck of a fallow deer. Such light brown, and with the sun shining in them they are alive with determination, frustration, and a touch of horror realizing I had seen it all. Mesmerizing.

"May I help you maiden?" I say, and reach down to my uniform, bringing out a scarf to wipe the blood from her face. Then tearing a loop from my waist belt, I bring it to my teeth. Ripping it in half, I hand both to her before saying, "One for today, and a spare for another emergency on another day."

Hoping to make her feel better, I shoot her a wink. Tying her hair back as quickly as she can with the makeshift hair tie and securing the other one deep inside her bun, she nods her thanks and rises to her feet.

Trying to calm her further, I continue, "A shame to tie up your beautiful hair, but it is a must. May I learn your name?"

"Esther, Your Majesty," she offers with a curtsy, but she is all business.

"Now, Esther, please join me on the battlefield to learn self-defense for the next time another contestant tries to sabotage you...."

"I did no such thing!" Rajia spouts in a panic.

Never breaking eye-contact with Esther, my arm shoots past her and retrieves Rajia by the neck pulling her from her seat. As Rajia squirms, making choking noises, I say, "Guard, mark her unworthy. Let her go from the palace. She's done here."

You could hear many of the other contestants breathe sighs of relief and murmur exclamations of thanks that this venomous woman would finally be gone. Physical beauty never wins favor in the long run. Outward beauty gets you a first look, but when the second look sees your black soul, you are immediately forgotten.

Offering Esther my hand, I escort her to the area where we will train. To settle her nerves, I tell her the name I responded to growing up was 'altasalul qalilan' meaning 'little sneak' because I was always sneaking extra treats from the table. Esther couldn't help herself and laughs out loud, because it is such an unexpected piece of information to ever learn about her King. She covers her mouth knowing it isn't considered proper or ladylike for a woman to laugh as loud as a drunken man living it up with his friends, but in that moment, I wish I could see it. To see her throw her head back laughing from something I said, all of a sudden seems to be a moment I want desperately.

Knowing she doesn't feel the freedom, I do it for her. I laugh right out loud at her reactions, this only made it worse for her as she continues to cover her mouth and giggle. Someday it will happen, and I will reach out to remove her hand so I can hear her laugh without restraint.

"Now that my dear Esther has had cause to laugh, we can begin. Do not be ashamed, for if anyone looks down their nose at you for genuinely laughing, I shall order the guards to be *off with their heads*!" I wave my arm dramatically, still grinning.

"You really must stop before I do it again," she replies softly, "Isn't there something we were supposed to be doing?"

"Yes, there is," I say and take her hand in mine.

Going through the paces with Esther, I am pleased she picks up on both maneuvers very quickly. When she leaves my side to return to her spot in the crowd, Rajia slips past her guard and pounces on Esther's back, clawing and screaming her vengeance. I hold my arm out blocking the guard beside me and hold a hand up to the guard who was ready to grab Rajia again.

Having just practiced this move on the field, Esther once again, shrugs off her attacker like she was shown. Rajia is momentarily disoriented at being tossed to the ground and Esther is able to deliver a blow to her collar bone, breaking it. The sound made her flinch, but she still continued through the maneuver like I made her practice on repeat seconds ago. Esther pulls her arm straight, and stomps on her throat before noticing it is Rajia, and not another drill.

Being so full of adrenaline, frustration, and nerves, all Esther can do is lean over, look down at Rajia and scream loudly in her face. Once she has screamed away her fear and rage, Esther straightens and steps aside as the guards secure Rajia once again.

Mary squeals, and grabs her by the biceps when she reaches the seating area again. Esther can barely contain her smile. As a giggle threatens to burst forth, she dares a glance at me. I had been waiting for her to do so. When we finally made eye contact, I was already smiling and began clapping for her. The rest of the guards follow my lead and she blushes. Straightening her back, she nods to me with a smile, then leans into Mary trying not to laugh out loud again. Beautiful.

***

<Esther>

"Esther! You were so amazing! She was nasty to everyone from the first day we got here. Did you know she caused another girl from the yellow group to get a scar all the way down her leg? She was a tyrant." Mary collapses onto my bed with me now that we have a couple hours of rest before skin care lessons.

"She did *not*! Ooh, she is such a viper. The King told the guards to mark her unworthy. Do you know what it means? How are you marked 'unworthy'?"

"It means she will be branded on her forehead for all to see she has been disgraced by the King and is never to be trusted," a deep voice answers.

Mary and I scramble to a standing position gasping as we realize the King himself is standing at my bunk with one of his guards.

"I apologize for disturbing your rest time, I wanted to be sure you are alright and do not need any healers to be called to your attention." The King says as he reaches forward gently grabbing my chin between his thumb and forefingers, inspecting my cheek. His eyes are doing his own examination, making sure I wouldn't lie to him.

"No your Majesty, I honestly found it quite exciting. Thank you for checking on me." He drops his hand when I once again follow royal protocols, and curtsey.

Offering both of us a wink, he smiles, "You're welcome, I'll let you get back to your duties."

"Oh, we are allowed some rest time right now before our next lessons start. You weren't keeping us from anything, but thank you, Your Majesty." Mary offers.

He gives her a polite smile, "Mary is it? If you two catch on as fast at your other lessons as you did today, you probably will get much more rest time than the eunuchs planned on giving you. You might be driving them crazy. Is your group this good at everything?"

"Mary puts me to shame at many of the tasks, but we are lucky as our group works together and helps each other catch up when something is hard. So far it's been a very enjoyable experience," I offer.

Seeing the King's amused grin, Mary pinches her chin as though deep in thought and says in a lower voice, "It's true I'm afraid. Esther really can't dance. She looks like a newborn baby camel, but we'll help her figure it out before the banquet," cutting a side-eye in my direction with obvious amusement.

Seeing King Xerxes raise a teasing eyebrow, I groan and throw an arm around Mary's shoulders. Acting as if I am embarrassed, I have plans of my own, "Yes Your Majesty, we work together on everything. We will find a solution to all of our problems no matter how hard we have to work," I say, making my face look very worried.

"You look troubled?" He asks me, "Is there something your eunuch isn't providing? Something you need?"

"It's just, Mary here has the *worst* case of bad breath, and your eunuchs have not been able to do anything for her. Look around, I'm her only friend, the poor thing..." Unable to contain myself, a smirk is starting to appear at the corner of my mouth and Mary is now blushing. "My neighbor suffered from the same thing and..."

Seeing the pillow being swung at my head from the corner of my eye, I swiftly duck the blow and straighten as I am already hearing the King laughing as loudly as he had done before on the training grounds.

"We really should have a scoreboard placed on the wall somewhere eh Mary? You might have scored a tiny point on me, but I had you all eating out of my hand for a second there. I do believe I should get *two* points for that one," I state triumphantly.

"Just you wait until I find some squid ink to stain your teeth with!" Throwing her arms around me she continues laughing. "With friends like you, who needs enemies?"

"Esther, Mary, you two have made this day stand out from so many of the other days that just run together. I honestly look forward to getting to know both of you. I have to go. I need to cure Haman of the madness infecting him lately, and the only way that is going to happen is with a strong beating. It has to end now." He places a kiss on the back of our hands, and wanders off down the corridor, chuckling as he heads back to the training grounds.

I'm glad I'm not Haman.

"Esther, he is really interested in you," Mary says softly. "He could not take his eyes off of you."

"Mary! Don't. I do not think any of us have a reason to believe we could trust the heart of a Royal just yet. Men in power, their feelings can be fickle. Feelings can change with their mood. If they feel like fighting, their feelings of love or admiration wane. If they are given to wine, their feelings of passion flow from one woman to another like the wine they drink. Men have different moods than women, but they have just as many of them. I think it is worse for those with power. I cannot let my heart hope yet, and you should not either. It is really too soon. This is the only chance any of us will have at an honorable marriage with a husband and children. It just makes the stakes too high."

Chapter 8

THE CREAM RISES TO THE TOP

<Esther>

As the months progressed, I had continued to build friendships with many of the contestants from each of the groups. Others saw me as a threat because no matter what we were supposed to be learning, I seemed to always rise close to the top. It annoys me the way they respond. Am I not supposed to give my best effort because they are too lazy to really apply themselves and learn new things? Well, I would not slow down. Many of the skills and knowledge we were being given were things that would benefit us in other ways if we weren't chosen to be queen.

Mastering these skills might be the only chance we would have to become valuable in other ways for this country. I don't plan on rolling over and accepting the fate of becoming a concubine. If I am not chosen as queen, I will not be living out all my days in a wing full of catty women like these. No, that would not be my fate. It couldn't be. For one reason, I would go crazy, and for another, I was capable of much more than just lazing around waiting for my name to be called for lustful pleasures. No, being a harem girl would not be my only purpose in this life. I would learn a skill which would make me irreplaceable to the palace, and I would be given a job. I do not care what it is, but I would not live my life as a mere harem girl. If I had to be named 'Head Bean Counter' because I had developed the best system for it, and worked the hardest? Then 'Head Bean Counter' I would be. Living with this group of ladies where the large majority were jealous and manipulating during all of their waking hours would not be my fate, besides, how would a life in the harem please Yahweh, and represent my people well?

This week was Blue Group's turn to decorate the banquet hall with a theme for the week's meals. As a queen we would have to be able to prepare for visiting dignitaries. It would be just as important as understanding the country's laws and providing an heir. We had voted on a color scheme and theme. The decorations had arrived, and we were given the day to transform the banquet hall into a whole new experience, save for our assigned hours of the oil purification appointments.

Each day, the menu highlights a different region of Persia, showcasing the many healthy foods and commodities that can only be found in each specific region. It had been my call to order pottery, vases, and flowers from the same regions as well. This allows each day to be transformed into a different feel and mood. We have decided to leave the draperies a neutral ivory color because changing the plants, flowers, dishes, linens and other decorations changed the room so much it was almost unrecognizable from the day before.

The first day of the week will be focused on the Anatolian regions. Breakfasts will feature some type of bread with cheese and a fruit. The first day would introduce Pide bread as it is boat shaped and easy to fill with fruits and cheeses for easy consumption. This will be served with a chilled fruit juice for a morning energizer. To chill the juice, we will have them stored in the yakhchāls the engineers of the Persian Empire had just invented. They were little rooms that kept things cold, sometimes for years at a time.

For lunch, there will be another bread, with cheese, a vegetable, and a light meat tray. Giant grapes will be served as a sweet dessert. The evening meal will feature a stronger protein serving to replenish the body as it sleeps. The first evening is scheduled to be Doner Kebab, a meat - usually lamb - cooked vertically on a spit - and served thinly sliced onto a warm pita with a variety of vegetables as the contestant so chooses. Of course, the dessert will be Baklava. It is a favorite across all of Persia.

Since the Anatolian region produces so much steel, copper and precious metals, an order of metal toothpicks and tongs had been ordered to represent their region as well.

The decorations were finished off with vines and flowers to highlight each location and their different sights, smells, and delicacies. Our group has put a lot of planning into this and really hopes everyone appreciates the tour of Persia we have tried to provide. Each day of the week, we will be changing to a different region.

"How did you come up with this idea? It is very creative," Hegai inquires of Nika, in the Blue Group.

"Oh it wasn't I sir, it was Esther. You might ask her. But it is a stunning idea isn't it?" She replies with pride shining in her eyes at the masterpiece her group has been able to pull off.

"It is indeed," he smiles before wandering in my direction.

"Miss Esther, the ladies tell me this was your idea? Very creative, how did you ever come up with it?" Hegai inquires again.

"Oh, good morning sir. Walk with me while I grab supplies?" I gesture, "my Papi works for the palace in an advisory role and once-in-a-while he would be required to go on trips for business. A few times I went on those trips with him as he couldn't find anyone he trusted to watch me. I would be forced to sit a proper distance away for business privacy, but within eyeshot so if I tried to run off, he could see me and then … discipline me later." I said, rubbing my backside with a grin.

"While I sat during those meetings, I had a lot of time to look around. I loved all of the differences in the places. Mostly though, I tried to catch as many animals as I could and sneak them home in my satchel," I said laughing at the memory. "One time I had a Red Sand Fox in my house for three weeks before my Papi caught me."

Hegai laughed at the thought of keeping it quiet for three weeks. "A Red Sand Fox, huh? They are not very trusting of humans."

"I'm very persuasive. My Papi calls it stubborn, but I remind him that he has his words mixed up and *meant* to say persuasive each time stubborn slips out." Smirking with a raised eyebrow, I continue, "We're making progress, he'll get it right one of these days."

"One poor single dad, raising a '*persuasive*' daughter all alone. You must have really been a handful," Hegai replies, chuckling. "I'll leave you to decorate Esther, have a nice day."

"Goodbye, Sir. You too," I say, with a little wave.

As the days and themed regions have to be set up and torn down, a few of the servants of the palace grew tired of the extra work. They grumbled - and some even began to purposefully go missing when they knew it was time to begin a new day's changeover. This began to make some of the girls in the Blue Group grow weary and frustrated.

"I know this week has been a lot of work, however, no one can deny we have had the most relaxing and serene dining experiences of all the hosts to this point. If we lay down now we will have wasted a significant amount of time, hope, and money putting all of this together," Mary challenges us, "We have two days left. Surely we can do this!"

"I'm tired of having to do things the servants were supposed to be doing but just stopped showing up for!" One contestant moans.

"Same," grumbles another. A few other murmurings can be heard rippling through our group.

"Does anyone want first dibs on taking care of the servant problem?" I offer, noticing most of them are now studying their feet and avoiding eye contact.

"No? Okay. If you begin the change I promise you the problem will be solved before the job is completed tonight," I reassure them. I didn't really have a plan, but something has to be done.

I heard a few snickers and saw some rolling eyes, but I had seen my Papi deal with challenges like this. I knew how to be fair, and I also knew how to be firm. It was time.

"Eunuch Hegai, may I beg a moment of your time?" I requested, approaching Hegai slowly.

"Esther, what troubles you?" He responds, taking a step in my direction with frown lines of concern directed my way.

Squaring my shoulders, I draw in a calming breath to keep me from rushing it all out in nervousness. "Is there anything in the procedure rules stating one of the contestants cannot address the servants and correct their behavior?"

Rubbing his chin, he is quiet for a few moments. "I'm assuming the servants have either been disrespectful, or have not done their job well? If it is the fact they have harmed a contestant in any way, I'm afraid I and the guards will have to handle it ourselves. Maybe tell me what the problem is."

"First of all, thank you for your concern, but no, no one has been hurt. The staff is not only not doing their job well, they are not doing it at all. This is an obvious sign of disrespect and must be handled. If we let it go, they will do it, and much more to the next group who comes along. It should end tonight."

"And you are the maiden to do this?" Hegai inquires.

"By volunteer, *and* default sir." I chuckle.

"Very well, I'll have them brought in." Hegai claps his hands at the guards and gives the instructions as I go to work on a nearby table.

When the servants are all accounted for and lined up against the wall, Hegai walks to me and whispers. "As you wish my lady."

"Let them watch for a minute please, Hegai. Thank You," I whisper back.

After a few minutes, the servants begin to get nervous and fidget from one foot to the other. Finally, one of them breaks formation and attempts to help work on the tables.

"Oh, so you do know what is expected of you?" I ask with a raised eyebrow.

"Ma'am?" The servant stops what he is doing and raises his eyes to meet mine.

"Why did you start working on that table?" I inquire.

"It is one of the jobs we were assigned Ma'am," he replies.

Raising my eyes to the two lines of servants along the back wall, I ask the lot of them, "And you, was it part of your assigned duties to be helping the Blue Group each night with the daily change-out for new decorations?"

Several murmurs of 'yes ma'am' could be heard around the room. Tapping my chin as if trying to recall something, I ask another question. "I do remember all of you staying on Monday evening and helping out. We got everything changed and we were all in bed pretty early. We appreciated it, and many of us thanked you repeatedly. But on Tuesday evening, several of you started helping, only to disappear after thirty minutes? Odd wouldn't you say?"

No one said a word this time, several heads were lowered. Several, but not all. I meet challenging male eyes in the front row, his arrogance battling my confidence. Hearing the chauvinistic 'harumph' I stand still, maintaining eye contact, waiting...

"Sir, you obviously have an opinion to disrespectfully interrupt me ... speak," calling him out, giving him the floor.

"Who are you to even be addressing us? You are but a contestant," he hisses, taking steps forward, getting in my face. "The King may never call your name. And if he does, most likely he'll use your body and toss you in the harem," he seethes, "You are nothing."

"Seth, oh - love that confused look on your face. Seth, I make it my job to know the things that might help me. Hegai, please confirm for me that Seth has had his weekly salary doubled for helping our group this week?" I ask, not breaking eye contact with Seth.

"Yes, all of their salaries were doubled for the extra help," Hegai responds. The rest of the servants are silent, many showing me in body language or looks they also thought we were beneath them and didn't have to help us out. Not even after being paid extra to do so.

"For Seth, Hegai, please continue to require him to go the extra mile and help us the rest of the week for his normal salary, only. For the rest of the crew who thought following the lead of a few bad apples could profit them, let's say if they continue to work hard the rest of the week, they may get paid as promised. If they are one minute late or leave one minute early, they forfeit the extra bonus plus any compensation for any of the extra work they have put in so far. I mean it's fair you would only be compensated if you completed your contract, correct?" I ask looking each one, looking them in the eye as they nod their consent.

Seth, breathing hard and clenching his fists, begins to rush towards me. "You will be nothing more than a filthy palace whore ..."

Seeing the guard approaching Seth's back, I turn around and hold up my hand. "Hegai, because of the extra outburst and vulgar language in front of ladies ... When recording this incident, please add that *If* I am named Queen, Seth will be reassigned as a shepherd in the mountains of Zagros." Seth let out a half roar and half growl before being subdued by the giant guard Tereh. "Now Seth, there's nothing to be upset about. I mean even you said 'I am nothing.' What are the odds ... right?"

***

<Xerxes>

I had just come down the hall as Esther had asked for permission to address the servants. My gut wanted to step in and say no, for so many reasons. But on the other hand, it would be one of the jobs a queen would handle. She had caught my attention on so many occasions, and she was very beautiful. Watching Seth disrespect her made my fist clench. I had to force myself to relax multiple times, because I was dreaming of having his neck between my fingers.

Standing almost five cubits tall, and having killed hundreds of men, I was intimidating and scary to anyone. I could have this servant sniveling and on his belly in submission within seconds. But watching this female. This … all woman, …intoxicatingly strong, capable, competitive, and confident woman standing toe-to-toe with a male bigger than her and never looking away from his venom, had me standing there fantasizing about her like a teenager peeking into the bath houses. I exhale, and laugh at myself because just like a teenager, I find the need for a woman immediately. It has been a while since a female has drawn out this kind of reaction in me. Yes, this Esther was someone to keep my eye on.

Her last little barb about making Seth a shepherd in the mountains of Zagros was genius and I almost gave myself away by laughing out loud. What are the odds indeed! Better than you think little one. Better than you think. I wander off down the hallway telling a eunuch to grab someone from the harem to take care of this little problem Esther has created. Soon, she would tame my desire - but not today.

***

<Esther>

As my eyelids were dropping, I heard it again. At first I told myself it was nothing and I was overly tired. Trying once more to drift off, it happened again. Hearing the unmistakable combination bark/squeal of a young Red Sand Fox, I couldn't ignore the call because it sounded in distress. Knowing I shouldn't, but unable to help myself at the sound of an animal in trouble, I grab my dagger, a handbag, and sneak by the kitchen for a couple cubes of cheese and lunchmeat.

Relieved I found the baby before anyone else did, I reach out and offer him some of the meat. He gobbles it up so fast I am afraid he might choke.

"Easy now boy. Take it easy. I see you hurt your back paw. Where's your Mama?" I whisper.

Looking around, I don't see the glowing eyes of a possible mama fox anywhere, so I decide to take him into the palace and try to help him heal. What would the punishment be if I were to get caught? Taking in a deep breath I decide to hope for the best. Maybe I can get him passed off to the palace animal doctor in the morning before anyone notices.

Keeping my head on a swivel, I am on alert for anyone who might turn me in and get me into trouble. I'm not sure how I will keep him quiet with this many people around me all the time, but I will give it a try. This little fox needs extra help while he mends, and I am not sure how long it will take me to find the animal doctor. Before stepping into the doorway, I look left, right, and behind to be sure no one is watching me sneak in.

Stepping up into the doorway, I run right smack into a chest. Gasping in surprise my eyes slowly look up until they meet the raised eyebrows and knowing look of Hegai. All of the wind in my lungs rushes out at once as I know I have already been caught.

"Oh, Hegai, Sir, I just, well I... you see ..."

"Stop blubbering and get in here before anyone hears you!" He sighs, frustrated. Putting his index finger on his lips in the shhh signal, he leads me to a single empty bedroom, and closes the door behind us.

"You! Why are you such a handful and such an outstanding woman all at the same time?" He pulls at both sides of his hair repeatedly. It makes him look like a tufted barn owl. I do not laugh because I know I am already in a lot of trouble. "I should make you take him right back outside is what I should do!"

"Sir, look. He has a very badly injured back leg. He will most certainly die, either from the elements, starvation, or at the hands of a predator if I put him back out there. Look at him..."

The little fox turns his face to Hegai, his big round eyes and the fuzzy ears standing at attention are so adorable. You would have to have no heart at all not to be moved by the sight. He had not grown into those giant ears yet, I do not know how the Red Sand Fox babies do not get carried away by the strong winds with ears so big, but nature is perfect and finds a way.

"Okay, I'm going to move you here to this wing. You can rehabilitate this little guy and you will stay here to do it. You will move your things in the morning. Whatever story I decide to give the other contestants in the morning when I tell you to move rooms, you will back it up and go with it, do you understand?"

"Yes Sir," I say, smiling from ear to ear. "Can I bring him to breakfast?"

"I don't see why not. Whatever lie I have to think up will have something to do with him anyway." Hegai heaves out a sigh, resigning to the chaos he's fully committed to with a smile.

Chapter 9

THE STAKES ARE RISING

<Xerxes>

"Hegai," I bellow down the hall, "I must see you *now!*" Raging like a beast of the field, I crash through another doorway looking for Hegai. He is in charge and was supposed to know where every contestant is. Most of them are alarmed and a few are even crying as quietly as they can so as not to draw any attention to themselves. My anger is truly frightening for their gentle demeanor. I do not have time to console them. They needed to get tougher or go home.

There are a few though, for whom the 'bad boy' excites places in their soul. The anger just makes them all the more excited. Not having many chances in their life to truly experience a man like myself, they simply stand in place running their eyes over my bulging physique. Indeed, everyone is experiencing something this morning, but none more than me, and it has nothing to do with any of these women or their reactions. I am used to women like them.

"Your Majesty? How can I be of help?" Hegai rapidly appears, answering me with a proper bow.

"In. Private." I growl, grabbing him by the bicep and all but lifting him off the ground by the one arm, carrying him into a nearby room. Slamming the door behind us, dust falls from the ceiling, onto the contestants and their beddings across the hall. Once again, the ladies all react according to their pre-disposed demeanors exposed during my rage-filled entrance, making me roll my eyes.

"King Xerxes, what has happened?" Hegai inquires with genuine concern.

"I have been here for over an hour, grabbed a bite in the kitchen and wandered the hallways. Are you aware you're missing a contestant?" I interrogate him with narrowed eyes.

"Your Majesty?" He asks, confused.

"Esther, Hegai. She's nowhere to be found. Her bed hasn't been slept in. With the altercation between her and the servant Seth yesterday, I am wondering if he might have done something to her. I am asking you first before searching the grounds," spitting my frustrations all over him.

"Oh, no Your Majesty, I apologize. She is not missing. You see, she rescued an injured Red Sand Fox last night and asked for permission to rehabilitate him for release. I moved her to a single bedroom so the young fox would not cause any other contestants to lose sleep," he hesitates. "I hope that's okay?"

"A Sand Fox ... why is this contestant always full of surprises?" I mutter with a smile.

"I'm afraid this might just be the beginning, even though she really is the most fragrant flower in the garden." Smiling at me, he raises an eyebrow.

"Ah, so she's also your favorite? What about her friend Mary? And just when do we get to begin the visits with this group anyway?" I sigh in frustration.

"*Also* my favorite, my King? So you've already singled out who you want, eh? What if I said she isn't the point leader?" Hegai teases.

Leveling an unimpressed gaze on my head eunuch, I say "I could care less about your points. I'm not going to waste mine or anyone else's time, she is first."

Using both hands as if he is pressing down a rising tide, Hegai says, "I'm just being difficult, Your Majesty. However, I think some of the other girls know you favor her slightly. Are you sure you might not want to have dinner with a few others and let them return to their families in a show of fairness?"

"I could, but we're only doing a couple. Then Esther comes to me. When?" I ask again.

"Two more weeks," Hegai confirms.

"Leave Mary, and any of Esther's close friends for after her night with me," I say leaving the room, and also leaving Hegai completely confused. I have plans. I don't have to share them.

***

Seeking out Esther's new room, I round the corner just as she exits and closes her door. Turning around with a gasp, she almost runs into me. Gripping her chest tightly and acting very nervous, I already know the fox Hegai told me about is hiding in her dress somewhere. *Alright Esther, let's see how long you can keep him hidden.*

"Good morning, young lady. Why are you looking so surprised?" I ask, enjoying tormenting her a little.

"Good Morning King Xerxes, I was just in a hurry to get to breakfast since my group is hosting this week to see if there is anything needing arranged last minute," she says, trying to scoot past me.

Leaning my large frame against one wall with my elbow and forearm braced at shoulder height, I cross my legs at the ankle against the other wall - effectively blocking her escape through the corridor.

"You have physical training outside today, correct?" I inquire with false innocence as I notice her chest is struggling with itself inside her dress.

Looking a little panicked, she clutches her dress tighter. Just as she says the word 'yes' the young fox escapes his cloth prison. First, his head pops out, and then his ears. They wiggle back and forth a little as they spring free from her bodice. Both the fox and Esther stare at me with the same horrified, anxiety-driven face to the point it makes them almost look like twins. I try to keep my cool, but looking at both of their big round eyes blink in unison, then turning to look at each other and back at me, it was just too much. I begin to laugh like I did when I was a little boy. Tears are escaping out of my eyes and I even snorted at one point.

Smirking a little, she realizes she'd been played. Scratching her new little friend with an index finger she tries to ignore my laughter. Pretty soon she is leaning against me, shoulder to shoulder in the hallway trying to regain control. And there it was. Since the day on the training field I had been wanting to hear her genuine laughter shared with me like we were old friends - and it was finally happening. Looking away from her mesmerizing eyes was agony.

Nervously, I reached over to grab him. Where could my fingers brush against her that wouldn't make a virgin embarrassed? I don't think I have ever been worried about how any woman has felt before. It's curious, the thought even passed through my mind at all this time. "Let me see this little scamp."

"I named him Shujae, as he was brave to call for help that night. Any predator could have gotten to him, but he just kept calling for his mama. She must have been killed because she was not hiding anywhere nearby when I rescued him. I looked everywhere for her," Esther said. "It will take a while for his leg to be usable though."

"If ever," I said, looking him over. "I had one I rescued when I was about nine. Kept it hidden for about four months before my father said I had to let it go. He didn't like animals at all."

"Well, he sounds hideous," she said, smirking.

"I suppose he was in some ways." I chuckle, landing a mock punch on her chin.

"I really must go. I'm glad you got to meet Shujae. Come for breakfast if you'd like. There is always plenty," Esther offers.

"I might be sort of a distraction, what with being a god and all," I say, flexing my muscles.

As if someone wiped the smile off her face with a cleaning cloth, all mirth and traces of laughter instantly disappear. I hated to see our moments of light-hearted banter leave. The morning had been perfect.

"Why did your face fall, Kitten?" Leaning in, capturing her delicate chin in the palm of my hand, I forced her to look at me again.

"While I certainly find you intelligent, really easy to talk to, and ... physically it's easy to see you are a man above all men... my God, ... my religion only believes there is one god. That just because a man is king, it does not make him a god. I will not leave my God. Could you tolerate a wife like this?" she inquires softly.

"You think I'm a man above all men physically?" I say with a broad smile.

"That's what you *got* from all the words I said?" Esther says with a smile of disbelief.

"Kitten, I will not make you turn your back on your religion. However, you must promise not to let it interfere with your duties as queen if chosen. Should a conflict arise, you must first act as queen, then address it in private with me to find a solution for the next time. Does that sound fair? That, and every time you speak formally, you must always introduce me as "The man above *ALL* men," I decide, smiling devilishly.

Blushing, Esther rolls her eyes and says, "Yes, Your Majesty, now I really must be going. Have a good day." Kneeling in a perfect curtsey, and a drop dead smile, she hurries off toward the dining room. Every time she drops a knee in front of me, my heart and my body stir. This one has not only gained my body's attention, but my head and my heart as well. A little foreign to me, she may have too much power over me.

'So she has given serious consideration to being queen. I like that. Yes, I like it a lot,' I think to myself as I head to the throne room.

***

\<Esther\>

Today's physical training would be on horseback. I chose a much more flowing dress than the others. I read over the rules again last night, and there had not been anything specified for which riding position any of the contestants would have to choose. Noticing most of the others had chosen a dress which would work best for the most common female approved riding style of sidesaddle, I went with the one that would allow me to ride astride like the men.

Sidesaddle was a technique where a lady would sit with both legs facing the same direction or hanging off the same side of the horse. The leg closest to the horse's head would reach up and wrap around a long stick protruding from the front of the saddle, thus giving the woman leverage to keep from falling off the animal. While it was much more secure than just dangling both legs from one side, it still somewhat hindered agility, speed, and balance.

Knowing all of our activities include some kind of competition, I wanted to be able to ride astride. I am too competitive to intentionally give up these decided advantages. I can ride like a man, and still act like a lady. And I challenge anyone to tell me I can't. While everyone was being paired with their horses, I took my place beside my sleek Caspian gelding. He was gray in color with black mane and tail. Flicking his tail, he kept moving his head. The whites of his eyes are a stark contrast to his pupils, which continue to move, trying to lock in eye contact with me.

I was familiar with this breed's intelligence and desire to read their rider for a connection. Papi had close friends who would let us come ride their horses occasionally and I loved every Caspian I had ever seen. I reached forward and murmured into his ear as my left hand rubbed up his face to grab the tuft of hair between his ears. Chuffing in approval, his warmth tucks in under my arm as he lays the flat part of his head against my body from my waist to under my arm. He wants more petting and nuzzling. It is a good sign of acceptance, and approval. He likes me and my touch. I can tell we will work well together.

Reaching down and grabbing the extra layers of my dress right in the middle, I feel the expensive royal material between my fingers. Twisting the layers until they begin to form a separation between my legs, I bring it up, twisting as I pull. Pushing the end of it through the belt at my waist, I tie a big knot at the end so it would have a difficult time slipping back through the belt once I was seated atop the horse. Then reaching up, I pull myself astride just as I planned all along. Hearing the gasps and murmurs when I trot my mount to the starting lines, I nod at the other contestants as if this were the same as preparing a table for breakfast.

When I make eye contact with Genet, from the purple group, we both smile at one another. Obviously she had learned some horseback skills somewhere along the way as well. She had picked the same type of dress I had and was riding astride also. I liked this a lot. It told me so much about her. Smart, capable, detailed, adventurous and skilled, no doubt. I imagine she had read through the rules last night to be sure she was within her rights like I had. Yes, today would be fun. It looked like someone else would really know how to race in this little competition.

"I see you know how to ride," Genet grins at me.

"I am pretty excited to see someone else knows how to as well. Let's do this!" I say excitedly, throwing my free hand in the air.

"That's my girl!" Sunita shouts from the White Group. A few 'whoot whoots' rise from other Blue Group contestants as everyone moves toward the starting line.

"Contestants, as you know, on occasion as queen, you may be required to travel with His Majesty for dignitary purposes. If your visit falls during festivals celebrating holidays of their kingdom, you may be asked to participate in their festivities. Something like today's events might be what you would face. Today, we will be doing a relay race. The first rider will start with this ball, you will go up and around the flag, return to the line and pass off to the second rider who may not cross the starting line until she has the ball. If you cross the starting line before you possess the ball your team will be disqualified. Each participant will only go once except for the Blue Team. You have one less person in your group so your first person will go twice. Any questions?" The guard on duty asks.

"No? Then, line up!" He shouts.

"Esther, you go first so you run twice. Everyone okay with that?" Mary shouts. All heads nod excitedly.

"Okay, but everyone, back up quite a ways. These horses will be stomping, excited to take off. You *have* to hold them back. If someone is right behind you with a stomping horse it is going to make yours want to bust out running no matter what you say so don't crowd each other, we don't want to be disqualified!" I encourage the Blue Group.

When the flag is lowered I shout "HAAAA" and my horse takes off in one powerful lunge. He is so excited to run, his nostrils are flaring wide enough I can see them from where I sit. When approaching the flag, he is a little hard to slow down, the turn is precarious and his left flank even drags the dirt a little. He is trying so hard to keep the momentum and keep his footing as well. He definitely understands competition.

With my left arm safely cradling the ball, I try to touch the saddle occasionally for stability. Completing the turn I feel his lead foot change when I see his right hoof throw farther than the others. Settling in I can feel the difference in the rhythm. The reins are swinging naturally from my right hand and he pretty much has a green light on the return. I remind myself to breathe, passing out under those hooves is a dangerous thing to do. When we get half way back, I begin making soft sounds to him and then start saying "whoa, whoooooa boy."

When I am about fifteen lengths from Mary, I start counting. 15 ... 14 ... 13 putting my weight further back in the saddle, I feel him shift his weight, 12 ... "Whoa boy," I say ... 11 ... 10 ...

Now I say it more firmly. 'WHOA!', and he obeys my command with firmly planted feet in the dirt and sliding a little to stop. The ball exchange happens without a hitch and Mary takes off.

"I didn't prepare well for turning the flag and stopping at the end. You'll have to lead them into the slow down and the stopping so you don't overshoot both of those skills. But don't let your horse go too fast. I was almost out of control the whole time." Breathing heavily, I cannot help but still be excited for when I get to go again. It almost feels like flying.

The Yellow Group got disqualified as one of their girls' horses charged ahead before she had the ball. The White Group had 5 seconds added to their time as a whole for knocking their flag down on a turn but they were still in it. Just the Blue and Purple Groups were still alive without disqualifications or penalties when the last participants were lining up to take the ball. It looked as though Genet would get the hand-off just a smidge before me but I thought given my first run, I might be able to let my horse take it a little harder and be able to hold on better. When the handoff happens, I turn my gelding loose.

"Okay Yahweh,

> *May you be with me, that you may defend me;*
> *may you be within me, that you may conserve me;*
> *may you be before me, that you may lead me;*

Turning the flag, I squeeze my inside knee so my gelding knows it's time. Moving the reins ever so slightly to give a little pressure on his neck as well, he has all the direction he needs. Once again, we threw dirt and left skid marks everywhere, but this time he stays on his feet, saving us precious time. He is confident in his skills. He just wants me to hold on.

may you be after me, so that you may guard me;
may you be above me, that you may bless me,
God the Father lives and reigns forever and ever. Amen."

I finish my prayer right as we are pushing across the finish line, a nose ahead of Genet, to the shouts of the Blue Group at the victory.

Everyone continued to congratulate one another and relive the exciting moments of the relay from atop their horses as the guards readied the next event. Sunita and her horse had moved to the outside of the crowd visiting with friends. When they backed into some rows of hay, it accidentally flushed out a flock of birds that had been nesting inside. The birds flew out in all different directions, her horse spooked, and bolted out of control.

Knowing Genet's horsemanship, I take off yelling, "Genet, you get Sunita, I've got the horse. Help me - flank it!"

Genet didn't say a word, with a 'HUPPP' she turned her horse and raced for the right side, where Sunita had lost her hand grip and was dangling dangerously with her arm flying everywhere, trying to reach for something to hold onto. The only thing keeping her on was one knee squeezing very tightly to the saddle. I was gaining speed on the left and we were closing in.

Sensing our approach, Sunita's horse panics and breaks hard left causing my mount to stumble. If my horse would have gone down I could have been killed. I swallow down a lump of fear because I cannot think about that now, Sunita is in serious trouble. Several guards are mounting their horses, and everyone is shouting.

"Hold On Sunita!" I yell.

"Esther, get out of there. You could be killed!" King Xerxes shouts, racing toward the danger. "Genet, pull out, I don't want you hurt!"

Reaching down for the reins of Sunita's horse, I am barely a breath away. My fingertips graze them twice but I am still just a bit shy. I know it is stupid to get too far out over the head of your horse, but I am so close. Leaning over his head just a little farther, and barely able to still hold the saddle, I feel him surge. The moment Genet is able to pull Sunita to safety, I am finally able to grasp the reins of this runaway horse, and I tug. He panics and jerks his head in my direction, making hard contact with my forehead and eye. The last thing I saw was blood. And *a lot* of it.

Chapter 10

THE KING'S GROWING INFATUATION

<Esther>

With an inhaled gasp, I regain consciousness yelling for my friend, "Sunita!"

Instantly, I was enveloped in strong, warm arms, rocking me back and forth. Recognizing his scent, I instinctively grab at him for comfort, for safety, for... everything. As tears start rolling down my face, he scoops me up into his lap and holds me. Brushing my hair back gently, he closes his eyes.

"What were you thinking?" His masculine voice at my ear sounds tortured by the what-ifs and it sends goosebumps all the way to my toes.

"Sunita could have *died*! Is she alive? Is she okay?" I sob.

"But *you* nearly died!" He counters, shaking, as though he is fighting back a rock in his gut that won't leave. Leaning back against the wall, he brings my body with his, continuing to gently rock me back and forth. "Do you know what it did to me when I saw you fall from your horse, underneath all of those frenzied hooves? And when I got to you ... all the blood!" Feeling his body tremble as he finishes, I wonder why it has affected this battle hardened warrior so much. The tales of his one-on-one victories are so much more gruesome than what I went through.

Looking up into his dark brown eyes, then at my surroundings, I recognize we are in my bedroom. Trying to sit up, and away from his body, I realize just how sore I really am. Fearing not only the gossip, but disqualification, I put my hands on his hard chiseled chest.

"Ohhhh, you shouldn't be in here! This is not appropriate! What will the girls think? Will I be disqualified? You definitely shouldn't be touching me this way." I bring my hands to my face in an act of embarrassment but find wrappings there covering my wounds. Remembering all of the blood, I fall back into rivers of tears and sobs against his chest. Shujae races across the bed and climbs the king's body to cuddle up under my chin. He knows something is wrong with me and is doing his best to comfort me too.

"What now little one?" Xerxes murmurs, shaking his head and scratching Shujae on the back lightly.

"Now I have to be disqualified. I guess I should be rejoicing, now I am free to go home and pursue a proper marriage according to my faith. But I had really come to enjoy your presence, your friendship, and I thought maybe I had a tiny chance. I know there are so many other girls here who are stunning, impressive and wonderful but I thought maybe. Just maybe ..." Covering sobs with my fingers, I notice his hold on me had tightened when I insisted I should rejoice at being disqualified.

"Why are you disqualified?"

"Surely with all of the blood, I have a disfigured face somehow. A queen cannot have a disfigured face. I can no longer be considered," answering while lowering my gaze, with tiny uncontrolled sobs still escaping.

"I am the one setting the rules and even if you were missing an eye, you would never be disqualified. Look, Hegai has been here the whole time, as well as a healer. They are here to testify nothing inappropriate happens and nothing that would jeopardize my choice for queen being fair. You are staying, and your name will most definitely be called. Stay strong." Then he turns my body for better viewing, and gestures to the other side of the room.

"Take a second, get your bearings, but then come with me," Hegai says gently. "It is the Blue Group's final day for hosting. You certainly should be there. Most of it was your idea and a result of your hard work after all."

Trying to reach for Hegai's hand is impossible when my shoulder jumps right up and all but yells at me. Maybe it is dislocated? Lowering it back to a happier position, I try to lean forward and scoot off of the bed. This time, my lower back sounds off in what might be very, very angry Anatolian. It is fluid, flowing up and down every rib and back muscle like music, albeit angry music. I realize I am holding my breath when I collapse back into Xerxes arms, unable to force my body forward and off the bed under my own steam. Every muscle and limb is determined to punish me. Or at the very least, give me a good tongue lashing.

With a sympathetic smile, King Xerxes scoops me up like a child, and places me in a standing position. It takes a couple minutes for me to gain enough strength to keep my balance without his hands on my waist. Taking Hegai's hand, I thank the King, and slowly ... very slowly ... follow Hegai to the dining room.

When the other ladies see me, they flock in my direction. The first to reach me is Sunita. We dissolve into each other's arms and cry happy tears at being reunited.

"I am so grateful for what you did, but you know I should kill you for the danger you put yourself in right?!" Sunita scolds and praises me all at the same time.

"It was all out of instinct I swear. I saw you were in real trouble and nothing in my head would let me stand back and wait for someone else to save you. I don't know, it was as if I didn't have any control, my spirit said, 'we're up' and away we went!" I say, laughing throughout. "I wanted Genet to get you, and I knew I had to be on the other side, to keep your horse from running away from Genet."

"Genet, you were so brave. Thank you for rescuing Sunita," I say, holding my hand out to her as well.

"Teamwork girl, teamwork," Genet says, reaching out and squeezing my hand.

"So! When are you going home?" Martha asks, smirking hatefully, "I mean, with a face like that, you certainly can't be queen. 'Ugly, is not an accepted trademark for a queen."

"Martha! Pack your bags. You are disqualified," a male voice says from the hallway.

Turning around, Hegai says, "Haman! It's good to see you've returned from your trip. How was business?"

"Ehh, it was business. I came by to have breakfast with this fine group of ladies only to find petty bullying and harshness. King Ahasuerus has no need for a viper as a wife. Pack this one up and send her home in shame," he says distastefully. "It is bad enough we have to put up with bullies when we are children, but I will not listen to it when I am an adult. I get no greater joy as King Ahasuerus' Vizier and Second in Command, than searching out those adults who think they can act like bullies in primary school and still get away with it. Makes me go from pleasant to lethal instantly. Leave without one word of protest Martha, or you will be branded unworthy as well."

"Yes sir, Haman. So close, and yet so far," Hegai replies, chuckling.

"You know, this sounded like such a great idea at the time, and now it feels like a terrible punishment having to deal with this many ladies all at once all the time. My business trip was a real holiday!" Haman mutters.

"There you are Haman! Accompany me to the throne room and fill me in on your trip," Xerxes says, slapping Haman on the back.

***

<Haman>

Today the King is dressed in his finest robe of red leather made in the regions of the Asian peninsulas. The formal name for this type of robe is a Kandy. It is luxurious, the hide was tanned and processed so expertly it almost feels like butter. They put the leather through an extensive dying process, producing a one-of-a-kind red color no one else in the world will ever own. The edges have the finest embellishments and embroidery patterns seen across the world. Sewn into the neck collar are rubies, diamonds and sapphires.

Since King Xerxes is nearly five cubits tall, his robes of royalty, especially this red one, make him seem all the more regal, imposing, and especially intimidating.

On his head sits a golden crown standing roughly two-thirds of a cubit in height. It is decorated throughout with red rubies, and oval cut diamonds.

It is a stunning piece one cannot help but admire repeatedly. His attire starts with his fighting shoes, and tunic. A golden silk shirt, also from the Asian region, adorns his torso, and the lacing at the top is left untied, barely showing off his heavily muscled chest.

He carries his black scepter topped with the largest ruby known in the world, encased with gold protective bars to secure it inside. If I ever decide to take this throne from him, I will burn them all and have robes and crowns far more grand made for myself. Zeresh has much better vision for such things than Xerxes does. She will make sure I look more grand and impressive than any other crowned king in existence.

Inside the throne room, many are milling about waiting their turn for Xerxes to offer the scepter in their direction. If the scepter is not offered, you may not approach His Highness upon penalty of death. No rank, file or relation, saves you from punishment if the scepter is not offered should you approach uninvited. Not even the Queen may approach unless the scepter is extended. If any female dare appear in my throne room, they would be the last left in the room before they were offered the scepter. The solutions would also probably not be something they would like. But a king is a king. A woman is a woman. They have but a few purposes, and if they need something from a King... especially if I were King ... they would pay for it my way.

"The Egyptians are amenable to trade a glass sculpture of your newly named queen in return for a team of our engineers to travel there and build them a yakhchal, allowing their engineers to copy the building plans for how to erect them in their country as well," I report. Getting those Egyptians to agree to anything is like pulling teeth. All I wanted to do was get back here and keep an eye out over Janeth to be sure I didn't lose her. But their negotiators were skilled, and not easily satisfied.

"Very well, this is acceptable. I want the sculpture to be placed in a very visible spot within the palace. It has to be transportable, and able to be protected. I need it set in a place of my choosing so the lighting and protection from the wind is perfect," Xerxes says deep in thought.

"I'm guessing you know exactly what this sculpture will look like already?" I ask, running all of the most beautiful contestants through my mind. It had better not be Janeth, with her beautiful eyes and body I cannot forget. He can't have her.

"Haman, wipe the look of lust off your face. This Queen is *mine*. She is interesting, beautiful, smart, brave and fearless. I've held her, and can tell you my last wife's body seems like one of a teenage boy compared to her. Should I see or hear any man lusting after her I will kill him with my bare hands. She is mine!" Xerxes proclaims slamming his fist down on the arm of his throne.

"When did you become obsessed, My King? I was only gone for a few days," I taunt him.

Xerxes shoots from his throne and grabs me by the throat before I knew what was happening. "I *am* obsessed with this woman. So much so, you should tread lightly when thinking you have the freedom to joke about her presence or status. Am I clear?" He growls in my face.

"Crystal," I reply, breathing heavily. He will pay for humiliating me in front of others here in the throne room. Just wait.

"Good," he says, releasing me and brushing off my shirt as though there was dust on it, "now, from the looks of this room, we have a long day's worth of arbitration ahead of us." Taking the scepter, he points it at the first person in the room he lays eyes on.

"Gabriel, I will hear your petition. Let's see what we can do," Xerxes says as Gabriel reaches forward, bows, and touches the scepter. It was the first of many important decisions to be made today and at the end we would both be exhausted. Deciding people's fates sometimes really did weigh heavy on him. Other times, when the arrogance, and pride of being king ravaged his blood and soul, he flippantly made judgments based on whomever he found more handsome or better educated to keep himself entertained. It was at those times he was more easily manipulated.

\<Xerxes\>

That evening, after the servants had brought us dinner in my quarters. Haman and I had discussed the quarrels or uprisings in the different provinces, I decided I wanted a bath and a girl from the harem. It had been three years since Vashti. She did many queenly duties well. Other duties she simply didn't do, or was terrible at them. There had never been one moment where I felt the urge to hold her in my arms to comfort her the way I had Esther this morning. Sure, I had brought Vashti to my bed but it was only out of duty to produce an heir.

With Esther, I could not stop thinking about how she would feel in my arms. I knew they were all virgins. Did I even remember how to be slow and gentle with a virgin? *Had I ever* been slow and gentle with anyone? No, I do not think I had ever taken the time to care about anyone's feelings except my own.

At first, I wondered if she had placed me under a spell. All witches who played with the dark arts carried tattoos, the symbol of the third eye. It was either placed on their hand or their forehead, and Esther's skin was clean. I had asked the servants performing the oil rituals to examine her body for any kind of witchcraft. They also reported she was clean. Knowing she had not placed a spell on me, how is it I am wholly consumed with thoughts of her daily? Surely this was not love? No, not me, King Ahasuerus would not be one to fall for love. I had witnessed other men of power be made weak by love. That would not be my fate.

Soaking my tired muscles in the warm bathtub, the nameless girl entered. With lowered eyes, she grabs a sponge from the side of the tub and sensually plunges it into the water to get it wet. Closing my eyes, I feel the cascade of warm water rushing down my head and onto my face, then down my chest. The feeling was calming and began to relax my tensed muscles. Next, she released a flow of water over my shoulders letting it slide down other parts of my body.

Placing the sponge on the side of the tub, she wordlessly reaches for a bottle of frankincense oil and pours some onto her hand. Her experienced fingers begin to gently work the muscles of my neck and shoulders. Responding with a deep moan, I lean forward a little so she can reach some of my muscles further down into my back.

Closing my eyes, enjoying the relaxing feeling of the massage and smell the oils bring to me, soon, my mind begins to wander. I see eyes the color of doeskin, and hair the color of the exotic delicacy known as chocolate. With my mind racing, I reach for what I want the most. When I open my eyes to see blonde hair and blue eyes, I deflate with disappointment.

"Please, return to your quarters," I murmur.

"Did ... did I do something wrong?" She fearfully inquires.

"No," I snicker, "just go. Have a good evening, miss."

'*Look at me, I might even be pathetic,*' I thought to myself. '*I'm being polite.*'

***

"Haman, do you ... *love* your wife?" I ask.

Pulling a greasy bone away from his mouth and slurping meat between his teeth, he examines me, "Which one?"

"Well, any of them I guess. *Do* you love them? *Did* you love them? What does it feel like?" I ask again.

Grinning broadly, Haman wipes his face on his shirt sleeve, spits out some leftover gristle, and slaps me on the back, "Why, are *you* in love?" Then he gets serious and says "I don't know. I don't really think I have loved any of them. I was excited to bed them - well ... one of them. With another, her father didn't have any sons and she was the only daughter. Marrying her meant I would inherit everything they had, and they were wealthy so, sure I loved her I guess. Is that love?"

"I don't think so. At least not what I mean. Have you ever thought about someone all the time? Wanted to do nice things for them? Took a girl from the harem, and then looked at her and decided, 'nahhh, go back to your quarters?' All because you couldn't stop thinking about *her*? Am I obsessed, or in love?" I push him.

"You sound crazy is what you sound," Haman said with wide eyes. He is the grossest male I know when he is eating and it makes me want to stop talking to him, but he is my Second, and a king does not really get to have ... friends, so this is what I've got to work with.

"Well alright, Zeresh is the closest to what you describe. If she died I would miss her friendship and her council. Everything she does is looking out for me and our family. We talk over morning breakfast together and drink tea outside looking at the stars at night." Pausing, he looks at me again. "But she is terrible in bed. The good thing is she hates it. After giving me sons she asked if she had to keep it up. Happily I said no. Now we are friends, and good ones. Concubines, and my second wife kept my manhood happy after that."

Laughing at his description I say, "Alright, fine. I'll give you that. Maybe I sound crazy. But I have never gathered more respect, interest, desire, and care for someone's well-being all wrapped up in one body as I have for this woman. And I've had a *lot* of women come through my life. She is so smart, I would possibly even run training scenarios by her on the off chance she would have an idea that might be beneficial to training the men."

"Alright now you have to tell me who this goddess is," Haman says, suspicious of who could have piqued my interest so deeply. "I mean, it sounds like you like her more than me."

It is time to end this conversation, now he is merely taunting me. "In due time Haman, in due time. Everyone will find out soon enough," I say leaving the table.

***

With each passing day, I become more and more consumed with Esther. Even with the new scar on her face. When the horse head-butted her, it tore her delicate skin wide open in two places. One, right at her hairline, leaving a scar that was not visible at all as her hair covered it up naturally. The other went right through her eyebrow. It left a line on the outer third of her eyebrow that looked like a warrior etching had been purposefully placed there acknowledging a dangerous accomplishment. It fit the occasion perfectly, and was the story I would tell when traveling and presenting her to dignitaries across the world. 'A Queen who risked her safety protecting her people.'

'I am a king. I am to rule the land and its people. I have been taught it is men first. Then women and children last. Women are inferior. How has this woman proven time and again to almost be my equal? How has this wonderful creature bewitched me? The more I watch her and her chosen inner circle, the more I see strength and wisdom in women. In some women. There is a large majority who have bought into the system of manipulation, to land a man with the most money possible so she can do the least possible in life and pretend to be important. But the ones like Esther shine like obvious jewels. None of them call to me like her. But many are like her. I see that now."

***

\<Esther\>

'As the days pass, I become more and more drawn to Xerxes. He is not of my faith, and I know it is less than ideal. I also know even in my faith, women are not allowed as many freedoms to choose their path as men are. There are many ways we are at the mercy of what the men around us decide. Many stories from my faith prove Yahweh allows hardships. Even hardships forcing us to hold onto our faith at all costs. I have heard the stories of how my distant kin walked through hundreds of years of slavery in Egypt. Until God sent Moses.

'Shadrach, Meshach, and Abednego were taken into slavery. When trying to uphold their faith in the one true God, they were thrown into the fiery furnace, where a form of Yahweh met them there, and endured the furnace with them. Three were thrown in, four were witnessed inside.

Daniel, captive as well, upholding Yahweh was thrown into a den of hungry lions. But Yahweh ... Again, Yahweh delivered him, holding closed the mouths of the hungry lions and Daniel emerged whole the next morning.

Samson and Delilah, Samson foolishly traded his faith for a woman who then betrayed him and Yahweh for her greedy desires. But Yahweh! Yahweh heard Samson's cries and honored his plea for redemption. Delilah fell at the righteous hand of Yahweh through his approved hand of Samson.

It was not my choice to come here. I don't know how my story will play out. I don't know if, as a woman, I am worthy for Yahweh to speak to me from a burning bush so I have clear directions on what moves to make next. I don't know if he will appear next to me in a fiery furnace, or in a lion's den. But I do know He saved and redeemed Rahab. Loved her, though she was forced to use her body daily in the physical act, simply to feed herself. He redeemed her for helping his army. Knowing He has done all of this, He will surely help me as well.

Papi always taught me to act on what I know to be true of Yahweh until I hear a new word. As a woman, I'm called to be true to Him, to love my husband and my people ~ both the Jewish people and my country. If I am called to be Queen of Persia, I will do it to the best of my ability. Trusting Him no matter what. Just like Daniel, Rahab, Shadrach, Meshach, Abednego, Sampson, and Moses, ~ Yahweh will make a way and show me. It might not happen until I'm already deep <u>in</u> the furnace, but deliverance will come.

I am already developing feelings for this King. I would have never thought it possible with the violence he has caused, and his arrogance. But he makes me feel safe. Accepting his life will be painful. But, as his wife, I will have the opportunity to teach Yahweh to our children and affect the next generation. 'Yahweh, if it be your will ... so be it. Amen.'

Chapter 11

ESTHER'S NIGHT WITH THE KING

<Esther>

Clapping his hands, Abagtha gathers the Blue Group together. "Ladies, Hegai has summoned all of the contestants to the dining hall for some announcements. We have ten minutes to make it there. Gather your things, we head out in five."

Many of the girls were curious but we would find out soon enough, so the murmuring was kept to a minimum. Upon arriving in the dining hall, pleasantries were exchanged, and friends waved across the room to one another. The eight or so months we had lived together had produced some really great long-lasting friendships which would likely remain into old age.

"Contestants, as I'm sure you have concluded, your purification and education months have been completed. King Xerxes will begin hosting you one at a time this very evening for private meetings regarding your worthiness for the title of *Queen of all Persia*." Pausing for the murmurs of excitement to die down again, Hegai waits with a pleasant smile on his face.

"Now there is the matter of the points contest between the groups. I am proud to announce, the group traveling to the Zagros Mountains for a one day pampering in the hot springs there, and clay facials performed by the women of the region issss..." his dramatic hesitation has several contestants twittering with excitement. I love how much he is enjoying this.

"The Purple Group! Congratulations Ladies! Your collective performance on the last test was what put you over. You will leave straight from here to the carriages waiting for you outside. Grab whatever you think you will need and meet the guards beside the carriages."

"Ahh, Congratulations Genet!" Mary and I yell over the excitement of the crowd.

"Thank you!" Blowing an excited kiss to us across the room, Genet rushes out to pack a light bag.

"Now for the rest of you, here are the protocols for your visits with King Xerxes. First, I must announce, the overall point winner for this group of contestants is Esther. You will be given a special piece of jewelry on your visit with the King as your reward." Hegai gives me a small bow.

Mary leans into me and bumps my shoulder, "Girllll, had anyone else won, they would have been given a golden vase from Rome or some dumb thing. You get a piece of jewelry given to you personally on your night of private time with the King. Should I just start calling you Queen Esther now?"

As she teases me, another contestant walks up and says, "Did you hear Hegai? Tonight's visit belongs to me!"

"Tomorrow's visit is mine," another girl squeals.

"And the next, mine!" Breathes yet another.

"I do not mean this in a hateful way Esther, but I really did feel like you were the favorite all this time, how are you not the first one?" Eve questions.

"Are you all daft? I do not care what order they present you all to the King in. The fact remains, every one of you given an appointment before Esther are all doomed. Hegai promised the King would be giving her the prize for having the highest points at her meeting. This means all of you before her are guaranteed not to be chosen queen," Mary chides.

Everyone's emotions did more flip-flops than if they were rolling down a hill in a barrel processing Mary's news. One thing was for certain, these next few weeks would separate the women from the girls.

Nightly, each contestant bounced off for their meeting with the King. As promised, they could request whatever they wished to bring with them. Several of them asked for fancy dresses from the market. 'Fancy' like the temple prostitute dresses and loud makeup. It surprised me, but the more I thought about it...everyone had to give it their all. Xerxes was known for being a ladies' man. It was reasonable to think maybe if they could impress him with their body, he would choose them for his queen. I would definitely not be chosen for those reasons. I barely had any more knowledge than a gourd and a carrot. Oh, I missed my Papi right now.

I cannot refuse him sex, it is, and always has been part of the rules. I had been given all I needed to know with the gourd and carrot evening after all. Snickering out loud, I continue to gather flowers for bouquets to set at tonight's tables during dinner. But seriously, even Papi knew it could happen. He tried to prepare me in the most awkward of ways, but yet he did prepare me.

"If only I had the power to make a maiden laugh as freely as those hyacinths do." A voice interrupts my musings.

"Xerxes, you frightened me," gasping aloud, "*King* Xerxes, oh heavens, please forgive me," I say, kneeling at his feet in apology. The burning of my ears and the tension in my cheeks tell me I have turned a bright shade of red once realizing my mistake.

"Think nothing of it. I very much like the sound of only my name rolling off your tongue." Smiling at me, he reaches down to pick me up by the arms. "I wanted to tell you something Esther. Do not fret I will find my Queen before your turn to visit comes. I very much look forward to having serious talks with you regarding your willingness and ability to consider the role. I have ripped these girls from their homes, and many of their families are very powerful. There is pressure to give everyone a fair chance."

"You do not need to explain anything to me, Your Majesty," I say looking around, "but thank you for doing so." The tension in my shoulders release, and I give him a relieved smile.

"I shall see you soon, Esther of Susa," King Xerxes says, backing away.

Losing myself in the fragrance of the bouquet and dreaming of what may be, I make my way to the dining hall. For the rest of the evening, our conversation plays through my mind.

***

After a week of waiting, tomorrow will be my visit with the King. I am a bundle of nerves. As I am sitting in my window petting little Shujae, I hear, "You no longer look like my little Nesicha, you look like a lovely woman now."

"Papi!" I breathe, barely making a sound because my throat is tight, and I am fighting tears. Shujae crawls up my chest, places both paws on my face and is trying to figure out the change in his favorite human's emotions. He looks at Papi with almost a perfectly executed frown of suspicion.

"I see you are still picking up strays everywhere you go?" Papi says, chuckling. "I also hear tomorrow evening is your visit with the King."

"Papi, you will not want to hear this, but I am so nervous. I already have feelings for him. He is *beautiful*. He makes my mouth water and when he stares at me, oh my goodness. He was so concerned for me when I was knocked unconscious on horseback. He held me so gently on my bed the next morning and cared for me so tenderly, stroking my face as I cried. What if he doesn't pick me?" I blurt out only a fraction of all the wayward thoughts that have been bouncing around in my head.

"What? Unconscious - horseback? What have they been doing to you here Esther? Hegai has not been keeping me informed well enough. I thought you were getting facials and learning makeup. And he was holding you in your bed? The King is not beautiful, he is scary and deadly." Papi was grimacing and trying to process through everything I had spouted without thinking.

"Um hmm, yes and so was Hegai and a healer, it wasn't just the King. All the other girls have been ordering dresses like the temple prostitutes wear for their meeting with the King. Is this what I should do? Help. Me. Papi." I wailed.

"Temple Prostitutes? No, absolutely not. Esther, You are a daughter of Yahweh. You live *in* this world. You do not become one *of* this world. If Yahweh wants you to walk this tribulation and embrace this life, he wants you to do it *and* honor him. Don't ever get so tied in a knot you forget who you are, daughter. It just so happens your old man brought you a gift. Approved by Hegai. Now, kiss me on the cheek. Approach your King as though he were your husband already. Be a blessing to him. How would you bless your husband? Do this for him tomorrow. You are already worthy." Papi sets his package down beside me.

"Papi," I sigh, "he's the King. I am but a simple Hebrew girl."

"You are worthy because *Yahweh says* you are worthy. No other outside circumstance tips the scale on that one way or the other. You are worthy. Period." Kissing me on the forehead, he says goodbye. As he walks away, he hands me a letter.

"Your step-mother wrote you a letter." His smile was as bright as the sun.

Gasping, I clutch the letter and whisper, "Rachael!"

**

Seeing my Papi and hearing from Rachael has centered me. Learning I was going to finally be a big sister delighted me in ways I could not explain. It was exactly what I needed to become focused again.

In his package, Papi had left me a beautiful silken dress in shades of red. Red matched the King's robe and crown, and I knew Papi was smart enough to be sending the King a subliminal message. The shoes he sent with it were flats almost matching the color of my eyes. The neckline plunges in a v-neck as low as it can possibly go, and still be able to hold myself in a ladylike posture. The sleeves end about three quarters of the way to my wrists, where Papi has left me a bracelet. It has been delicately hand tied between each pearl. He must have spent a fortune on this bracelet. I would cherish it forever.

I had sought Hegai's counsel to ask what he thought the contestants should be bringing with them. He advised me I should only bring to the King things that would tell him all about me. Things that were my favorites, or that symbolized a place I might really want to travel to, maybe something that held a great childhood memory, but most importantly, only bring things that truly showed the King my true self.

With his advice, I baked him a loaf of lemon blueberry bread as a treat since it was my favorite. I also brought a bouquet of flowers containing red poppies in the center, surrounded by white blossoms as accents. The poppy had always caught my attention. Tonight, it matched my dress, it was an unexpected, extra bonus. Then I brought one of the left-over decorations from the Asian peninsulas we had used during the daily change of decorations as a place I would love to visit. I had heard their beaches were something one *must* see. Some of the other contestants mocked me, but I was more confident in myself than ever. I am worthy.

Being led down the hall to his quarters, I really wasn't even nervous any-more. He surprised me and the guard when he met us in the foyer instead of the hallway to his room like he was supposed to. When the guard left, King Xerxes grinned and held his hand out in the direction of the room he wished to entertain me.

Walking in, there was a wide open balcony, with fine blue linens billowing in and out with the winds. There was incense burning, decorations, wine, and plates of food everywhere.

"It is like a dream, Your Majesty. So beautiful."

"Here, may I take this? What have you brought?" He asks, reaching for the bread.

"I wasn't sure what to bring so these are a few of my favorites," I reply, placing the vase of flowers on the reclining table.

"Your dress is stunning, red is amazing on you. Have a seat, I'll have them start bringing dinner." Gesturing to a seat, he claps as servants flood the room bringing drinks and dinner items of all kinds.

"Oh, King ..."

He holds up a hand cutting me off. "Please Esther, from this day forward, when we are alone, please ... only call me Xerxes."

Nodding my consent, I look at the table and say "It may take us a month to eat all of this food!"

"Mmmm, I am not against being locked up in this room, just you and I, for a solid month. What say you?" He is smirking at me, which makes me blush.

"Well, I say ... I have no experience in any of this. My faith doesn't allow any sort of dating or courting really until I am old enough to wed, which only happened right before the gathering. So I'm not even sure how to have these conversations properly ... although I know how I would tease you most of the time. I usually bite my smart tongue, for fear of not being a proper lady," I confess. *'Esther, stop word vomiting all over the King,'* I chide myself.

"Tonight's first rule. No holding back on anything then. I want to see the real Esther," the King grins.

"Pshhh well, then you are already down one, because that is the second rule. The first is, I am to call you Xerxes." Smirking, I strike one point for myself in the air.

'Just be yourself and minister to him as if he were already your husband.' The words of my Papi came back to mind. I hear Xerxes chuckling as he processes my teasing comment.

"Very well then, one point for the lady," he says, and I can smell his scent wafting on the breeze blowing through the room. I must think of something to keep my mind on before making a fool of myself. If left to my own devices, I would sniff the air and end up right in his lap with my nose pressed against his neck. How silly is that? *'Straighten up Esther, what is wrong with you?'*

"Would you like some of the almonds and cheese?" I offer.

Beginning to fill his plate as we make small talk about my experiences during the contest, I find my rhythm. Xerxes expresses he is impressed. I viewed the whole contest as though it were a battlefield experience. I could sense my enemies, my allies, and the ones who only used whomever they could use at any given moment. He explains this was one of the things they spent hours and sometimes even years trying to teach to their officers in the army.

"It's just something you either understand, or you don't. You do, Esther. So very unusual."

I felt proud I had caught onto something so easily he thought was only a man's talent. Moving to the couches, he held an arm out for me to snuggle into him and relax at his side. I was a little hesitant at first, but he remained calm and held his invitation steady.

"Xerxes, I... I don't know what to do. I saw all of the other girls leaving the quarters dressed as temple prostitutes and ...quite literally all I know about sex was explained to me with a gourd and a carrot. Well that and what I've seen the animals in the field do," I say blabbering nervously, unable to stop.

"Shhh ... you don't have to know what to do ... but what? What about a gourd and a carrot?" He asks, confused.

"Annnd the embarrassment continues," I groan, sharing how Papi tried to explain the mating process to me on that awful night.

Xerxes is now howling in laughter so much, tears begin to form in his eyes. He is wheezing and apologizing, and trying to stop but something comes to mind again and it starts all over. I adore the way his deep baritone laughter sounds, but each time I try to run away from the embarrassment of his laughter, he wraps me up in those massive arms of his and continues to laugh as he holds me.

Soon, my embarrassment gives way to my competitive nature, and I grab a pillow. Hitting him with it only makes him howl with laughter even harder. He is still holding me down to make sure I do not escape, and I surely would. This has been too humiliating, even though hearing his laughter is endearing.

"Oh you think so, do you Kitten?" He growls through his laughter. Grabbing my wrists, he wrenches the pillow away from my hands and bops me on the head with it softly once. Breathing heavily, and filled with adrenaline we both find exhilarating, we finally make eye contact. Slowly, he leans in, cupping my face with his free hand, and using the other hand to place my wrists around his neck. When he lets go, my hands stay there of my own free will and begin to play with his sleek black hair. The only reason my eyes break from his is to take a good look at his lips. I nervously run my tongue over my own lips and it must have dissolved his last bit of control.

Leaning forward he kisses me softly, sharing the kiss a virgin should experience. He is soft, and gentle, almost as if he is taking it slow to give me time to adjust. When he deepens the kiss, a soft moan escapes my mouth. I could never have imagined a kiss would have felt so good. He then grabs me by the shoulders and forces me away from him. Placing me beside him on the couch, and wrapping his arm around my shoulders, he snuggles me right up into him like he first offered.

"Did I ... did I do something wrong? I just do not know what to expect."
I say, studying my feet intently.

"Well, I never intended on just taking you straight to bed. You did everything so right, I had to stop you or we would have skipped everything else
and went straight to it," Xerxes replies.

"Oh. I thought ..."

"I know what you thought, and you're right. I have the right to do it. To
be honest it still might happen. I do want you more than anything or any
woman I've wanted in a very long time. But I want to share a meal, get to
know you, and ask you some questions. You see, I very much intend for
you to be my queen if you'll have me. Before we can do anything, there is
a whole lot we must discuss and negotiate. I will not do what I did the last
time. You see, last time I all but beat my chest and screamed 'I am King. I
am a god. I choose you. You do as I say. Be Grateful for me.' Then everyone
learned the painful way it was arrogant, stupid and doomed to failure for
all," he says, bowing his head in frustration.

"I won't let my country down that way again. So help me do it right this
time," he pleads.

"What should I do? What could you want to know besides the carrot and
the gourd?" I ask smiling.

"What scares you about being Queen?" He asks, trying not to go into fits
of laughter again.

"I don't want to come out wearing only my crown in front of a bunch of
men," I boldly state. It was a fearless thing for a woman to state right off
the bat to a man, but I wasn't going to pretend to be something I was not.

"With you? I like you as a friend, I want you as a lover. I crave your approval. I have never felt any of that before. I am already jealous over you. I think I would kill any man who accidentally saw so much as your knees, so I don't think it will be a problem," Xerxes replies sheepishly.

"You don't *think* it will be a problem?"

Smiling a very distracting, swoon-worthy smile, he lifts my chin, "It will not be a problem. I will not share you with anyone."

"Okay, I'm jealous over you too," I say, and he raises his eyebrows, "I'm serious. Your nights with the other girls were not fun for me. What will life be like as a Queen?"

Heaving a sigh, he runs his hand down his face. "As you know, a harem is an expected part of life for a King, but I can tell you this from a recent experience. When a harem girl came to me, and I opened my eyes to see blonde hair and blue eyes, I asked her to go home. I only wanted you. However, when Kings travel, to gift the traveling King women to satisfy his tastes is a normal expected activity. To turn it down is an insult. I can bring you with me on many of the trips. We can share sleeping quarters, even though it is unusual. But I cannot promise I will never partake in the harem forever. A harem is simply a major part of politics."

He told me later, a pang of guilt hit him for his answer, but the old Xerxes still lurked inside. He would not have a woman turn his life all upside down. Not all at once. Not even me.

"Will I have opportunities to improve the lives of women, under their husband's approval of course?" Hope laced this question from my heart.

"You have truly changed my mind regarding women. You and a few of your closest friends in this contest. Your intelligence and capabilities have truly shocked me. Small changes could possibly be made, but change has to be slow. Also, the men *must* remain head of household," he compromised.

"It's a start." I smile and hug him. "I'm sure there will be a lot more we will need to talk through as it comes up, but that's all I can think of now."

Hugging me back he says, "Children, right now."

"Yes, my dear," I say, leaning back from the hug and smiling into his eyes.

"In that case, it's time you receive the special piece of jewelry Hegai hinted at for your being the high point achiever in the contest." Kneeling in front of me, taking my left hand, he places a large oval shaped emerald on my left ring finger. "Esther, would you be my Queen?"

"I love emeralds," I gasp softly with tears clouding my vision.

"I might have known that, and had it specially made," he says smiling.

"How long have you known it would be me?" I ask, amazed.

"About the moment I heard Rajia's collar bone snap and you bend over to scream in her face like a true warrior," he grins proudly.

"Remind me to thank her if I ever see her again," I say smiling.

Chapter 12

THE WEDDING

<Esther>

Waking up to the smell of my man, I bring the sheets up to my eyes and reflect over the rest of the evening. Giving my body to him was nothing like the gourd and the carrot. Now, having experienced it though, I will let Papi off the hook. How could you accurately describe it to someone who has never partaken of its pleasures? You wouldn't want them to know honestly, until they were in love and married to the man or woman God made for them. I am yet not married, but I remind myself of the rare set of circumstances I'm in. Slowly, I raise my hand to examine the ring Xerxes had placed there while on his knees in front of me. Letting my hand sink back to my stomach, I am interrupted by his deep voice.

"I can see the entire evening playing across your face as you think Kitten," he murmurs.

"Be careful with 'Kitten' Xerxes, maybe you will turn around one day and see I am the fully grown Tigress," lifting my chin with a smirk.

"And that will be the day I send you in as a spy against the enemy forces. Behold my incredibly alluring Queen, who can also stab you in the throat unprovoked!" He proclaims.

"Then I shall expect the finest of daggers. Just tell me when, my love." Rising from the bed, I put on his silken shirt from the night before. "Let me get you a piece of the bread I made and brought last night."

Finding my favorite morning tea in the kitchen, I prepare two cups and several slices of the lemon blueberry bread, bringing them to the table on a tray. Hearing music in the streets, I cut my eyes over at Xerxes in surprise. His face is one of satisfied pride and joy. Holding out his hand, I take it and am pulled into his lap, and brought in for a kiss.

"That my dear, is the proclamation, letting all of Susa know they have a new Queen!" He is nearly bursting with pride.

When a look of fear crosses my face, he says, "Oh no you don't! You will not back out now Kitten, I need a little bit of the Tigress to come forth. We have to plan your staff, your attendants, decorate your quarters ..."

"My quarters? You mean we don't live together? I mean, of course we don't. I knew that. I just ... we in town ... poorer folks ..." heaving a big sigh, I look him in the eyes, "Xerxes I'm sorry. There will be many things different than I assume. I will do my best to accept them as you expect me to," I say with resigned struggle.

"I actually never thought of it. Waking up with you this morning was heavenly for me. For strategical, and political reasons, a lot of things a King does happens late at night. Scouting missions, negotiations, drinking with Kings and dignitaries, well as you can imagine, there are just a lot of things men enjoy in the evening. Coming in and waking you would wear on you after a while. Most queens honestly don't want it. If you do, I assure you, you will find me in your bed, or I will carry you to mine much more often than you expect," he says nuzzling his nose into my neck. "Now let's go see the parade!"

"Xerxes," I hesitate, pointing to myself only in his silken shirt, "the kingdom will see my knees, and thighs, as well as several other things if I go onto the balcony like this," I say smiling at him.

Frowning, he growls, "Hmm, that will never do!"

Disappearing around the corner, he comes back with a robe and ties it around my body. It absolutely drowns me, but he picks me up with one arm under my knees and one arm supporting my back and rushes to the balcony. When we appear, a small crowd of citizens below call out to us in celebratory congratulations and cheers. Setting me down in front of him, I have to stand on top of his feet to be able to see over the railing. I'm not short for a woman, but this man is a giant and so is everything made for him.

The music was festive, the people of the city were joyful, and decorations were being put up for a week of celebration. We waved at everyone before he scooped me up and whisked me away into our sanctuary once again.

***

\<Xerxes\>

The fact she wants me in her bed nightly branded her deep into my soul. Then when she reasoned with herself to accept my role without complaining as best she could, it nearly melted me altogether. Yes indeed, I picked the right one. The gods definitely blessed me this time.

"We will be wed within three days. I cannot wait any longer. I am granting you a staff of three, whomever you choose. They can have families, their children can be in the palace nursery and schools, but they are to help you in any and all endeavors, or I don't know … to be your companions daily. Give me their names as soon as you have them." I tick off item number one.

"Mary, Sunita, and Genet. Without a doubt."

"Decisive. But I knew that about you. I'll send a notice. Can they refuse?"

"Of course," she says while smiling and rolling her eyes.

"The wedding - what colors would you like us to celebrate with? Any specifics you want? The celebration usually lasts three days?"

"Red, gold, and … what do you think? You can do whatever you like except one thing. No concubines during our wedding week. Afterward, I know as the King and my being a woman, I cannot make demands on you," she says, looking down to hide a tear. Reaching over and raising her chin with a finger, I realize for the first time how much this topic cuts her heart, and it's not simply for control's sake.

"I haven't exactly given you all of the information about traveling dignitaries and concubines. It is equally customary when traveling to other kingdoms for men to be given to the Queen for the night the same as women from the harem are presented to the King.

Usually the men aren't publicly announced, they just show up in your chambers. The King gets women paraded to him publicly. But everyone knows the Queen gets her treats too. So, I ask you the same. Only me during our wedding. Please. I don't think you understand. I've never loved before. This is just as new to me," I finish quietly.

Stunned into silence, Esther grabs a slice of lemon blueberry bread and shoves it into my mouth watching me chew. Taking a bite for herself, she begins shaking her head back and forth still in shock. Knowing I had stunned her with such unexpected news, and then blown her mind with my admission of love ... I smiled really big and let bread crumbs tumble everywhere. She uses her hand to try and make me stop smiling, but pretty soon she was smiling too, and bread was falling everywhere from both of us as we laughed together.

"Well, I never ..." she chokes out. "Just try my bread please. I worked very hard on this for you and you spit it all over me."

"I'm sorry My Queen, I can clean you off if you prefer?" I offer, wiggling my eyebrows.

"Now, you are the predator," she says smiling. "Xerxes, were you trying to shock me or is that true?"

"Well Kitten, I knew it would shock you, but it is the truth," I say while running my hands through her chocolate hair.

"Then you need to keep me big and pregnant so the "sweets" they send to my room are truly sweets like desserts and not men," she says, shivering at the thought of it actually happening. She then leans over to kiss me fully, and heads for the baths to get ready for the day.

***

<Esther>

This is definitely not how a Hebrew courtship and wedding would have progressed. But all of my training and teaching of Yahweh has taught me hardships would come. They were part of life. Sometimes they came to grow your faith, sometimes to bring glory to God, sometimes to reach another, but you were always to be as faithful as you could.

Next, as a woman, you were always to stay under your father's covering. *'Two days ago, Papi had said, 'Act as if he were already your husband. Minister to him as if you are already his wife.'*

So I fixed his plate, we visited, we laughed, I massaged his neck, and we enjoyed being together. Then, we did what a husband and wife do. Now I am to be Queen. Is it right? I don't know exactly. But I do know I followed Yahweh, I stayed under my Papi's covering, I ministered to him exactly like I was told. Now I am Queen. One thing I know - I will teach my children of Yahweh. The next King will know who you are. Maybe the next reign will have the whole country honor you.'

***

Days pass in a frenzy of planning, preparation, and excitement. The rest of the contestants were sent home. Many of them were very excited for me. Others were not. I understood. They would return home. And they would be all-but sold off where the bride price was the greatest, regardless of the character of the man. I hope to improve life for women, but how?

Sunita, Genet, and Mary immediately accepted the request to be my personal staff. Such a relief. They are brave, intelligent, fierce, beautiful, and all have strengths in different ways so they compliment every facet a queen might need. If anything even bordered on dangerous, Genet would be at my side. If I needed organization, list making and prioritizing, Mary was all over it. Sunita was a perfect go-between for anything. She was brave enough to assist Genet, talented enough to assist Mary in public appearances, and all three were so beautiful they would be treated as honored dignitaries wherever we went.

Haman was teasing Xerxes relentlessly about already being made weak by love. I do not like that man, not even one little bit. Neither do my friends. My heart, spirit and soul scream in protest every minute he is around. But he is Second in Command, the Vizier, and if anyone could drive a wedge between my marriage it would be him. I must find ways to make him think I look up to him. Yahweh, give me strength because I would rather feed him rat feces.

***

"Can someone mute those blasted bells?" Genet is yelling at me from a finger's distance away so I can hear her over the incessant ringing of the palace bells. We have taken delicate cotton from decorations around the room and placed them within our ears to muffle the sound.

Suddenly, I feel calloused hands the size of plates cover my ears and I know it's Xerxes. Turning me around to face him, he mouths the words 'I'm sorry' grinning broadly.

Exaggerating my lips, I reply, "Will it stop?" and hope he will understand me. He busts out laughing. Mouthing "Yes" right back, he is still finding our distress comical. Punching him in the chest, I can't help but laugh a little at his antics. Noticing the bells are already losing some of their punch I am relieved. When the noise decreases where we can stand it, we remove the cotton and lay the little puffs on the table. Xerxes eyes go wide.

"We made ear plugs, your highness. We pulled them right out of the decorations in the room." Genet gestures to some of the decorations we had taken them from.

Looking back and forth between all of us, he finally shakes his head and mumbles, "Genius, who knew?"

Offering me his hand, we step out onto the royal balcony where the Zoroastrian Priest performs the ceremony binding us together as King and Queen. The balcony has been decorated in gold, red and white. Streamers and decorations are crisscrossing everywhere. I wasn't sure if this ceremony was binding in the eyes of Yahweh, but this was the closest I would get and I knew He would see my heart was pure. I didn't understand many of the words or even what I was agreeing to but when Xerxes gave me a slight nod, I knew I was supposed to nod. We had practiced the night before while sharing a plate of fruit in bed.

Many of the citizens of Susa were in attendance - even my Papi and Rachael. I could see the slight swell of her belly now. I couldn't wait to bless my little brother or sister. Papi still didn't want me to advertise that we were family. To keep my ancestry hidden was a really big decision for him. I wonder if he knows something I don't.

When the priest began to once again speak in the language we all understood, I paid attention. He was now admonishing Xerxes to love and protect Persia and his Queen with his life. To leave us with the gift of an heir should he die in battle. At the thought, Xerxes put an arm around me with his hand settling on my right hip, and drew me in closer as if already protecting me. I leaned into it and he squeezed my hip in response.

He turns to address the citizens, taking me with him. "Citizens, thank you for celebrating us today. This woman, your Queen, is different. She is strong. She is fearless, to the point I've already survived a few heart attacks. She has risked her very life to save one of her fellow contestants. That life was saved at the expense of her getting knocked unconscious." Gasps were heard throughout the crowd. "Hence, my first, almost-heart attack."

Chuckles ripple across the audience once again. Xerxes pauses, enjoying hearing the crowd ripple with excitement at the unexpected story.

"One evening, while walking through the palace, I happened upon the dining hall, where I overheard her addressing a group of servants who had intentionally failed to do their duties. She was fair, firm, and merciful. All but one responded to her correction with favor." As realization dawns on me which night he is referring to, my mouth drops open in shock. "You didn't know I was there that night did you?"

Feeling my hair fall over my eyes as I shake my head back and forth, I can also feel the heat and tingling sensation forecasting the new shade of red my face has obviously changed into.

"Well, the one who didn't like her correction rushed her as if to attack her. Being much bigger than she was, I almost intervened. Instead I motioned to a guard nearby, but she called him off," he said, clutching his chest and rolling his eyes as the crowd laughed again. "Instead she instructed Hegai he could still have one more chance. He could work and be paid his normal weekly salary, forfeiting the bonus for almost attacking her. Or not work and lose everything for the whole week. But then she said, 'Oh, write this down. *If* I am named Queen, you will be reassigned as a shepherd in the Mountains of Zagros. But I'm sure there's nothing to worry about. You, yourself just said, I am nothing. Right Seth?" The King pauses, waiting for the laughter of the crowd to die down.

"I got word today Seth has been eaten by the mosquitoes, trampled by one particular ram who sees him as competition for the ewes, and has no idea how to use his staff. But I'm sure things will get better," Xerxes finishes much to the crowd's delight.

"I know a King is not supposed to admit it, but this woman has already made me better. Because for the first time in my life, I am completely in love." Gasps and 'awe' sounds can be heard from men and women alike in the crowd at the admission of love from their King.

"Come, celebrate my good fortune. Rest easy, knowing Persia has a Queen who is finally worthy of the title. I am declaring a Holiday for all of Persia." The crowd erupts into cheers. A Holiday proclaimed by a King usually included time off work, freeing of slaves, and forgiveness of some debts along with gifts. He ends by picking me up bridal style and started walking to the celebration hall. The very one where Queen Vashti was supposed to show up wearing *only* her crown. I slowly began looking around. "Look at me Kitten, I felt you tense up. What is it? No matter what it is, I can fix it," he urges.

Smiling sadly, I say, "You cannot, my King. I was here the night Queen Vashti died. I was one of the very few people she last spoke to before she was beheaded. It just dawned on me this is the room she was supposed to show up in wearing only her crown." Seeing his face fall, I pick his chin up and say, "Just because I got tense doesn't mean I reject you. You already answered my questions about this. I still accept them. It surprised me to physically see it with my eyes, that's all. Now, let's celebrate our marriage." I lean in and give him a quick kiss to convince him I am telling the truth.

"Are you even real? Not even a tiny bit of manipulation. Yes, let's celebrate," he says while kissing me back. The kind of kiss that makes me blush ... again.

We are seated at a long table at the front of the room. There are eucalyptus leaves and poppies along with other plants and flowers decorating the table. Everything is draped in fine linens. The hall is the most beautiful I could ever have imagined and I stop a few of the servants to compliment them on it.

The wine is flowing, and many are getting animated with the drink. Xerxes had put away a few and was also feeling more than his normal self. Some actors were reenacting King Xerxes' fiercest battles of victory to declare his prowess for all in attendance.

"My goodness, My King, you most certainly fight like a god. Can you really kill twenty men hanging off of you at once?" I ask, smiling lovingly at him.

He places his goblet on the table loudly, runs his hand down his face, and leans in with only his lips on my ear, "Actually My Queen, this is embarrassing, they have exaggerated the stories so badly not even the gods themselves could have won these battles."

Before I can tease him again, we are interrupted by a very loud, wine-induced voice.

"The last time we were all gathered here I do believe King Xerxes made us a promise and didn't deliver. I feel like either he pays up this time in full, or he goes down in history as a liar," Governor Marcus Stathan states.

Xerxes immediately stands, seething, "Marcus, you had better get to the point quickly, and without any games."

Quickly, I reach over and pour a glass of water from the pitcher and cut a piece of bread to keep my hands busy and give the impression I'm about 'women's work'. Placing the bread and water in front of Xerxes, I smile dutifully, and contemplate all the many directions this could go.

"You promised us you would make your wife appear wearing only her crown because you alone had the best and you would prove it. She refused. You could not keep your promise. Now, I say you must keep that promise or be branded a liar. I mean, unless you do not think this girl is as beautiful as your first Queen? No insult meant M'Lady," Marcus finishes.

Reaching over and placing my hand on Xerxes' hand, I notice he is shaking in rage. "My husband, the man above *All* men. May I please speak to the fool?"

Addressing him as the man above All men must have reminded him of our conversation because he relaxes a little. Turning his head to me, he winks, but only I can see it.

"You see? The Queen of all Persia knows how to speak and address her King. She knows I am the man above all men. So gentlemen, let's gift her this moment as a wedding gift shall we?" Leaning in, he kisses me possessively on the mouth. I receive it willingly to show he is my husband and he is wanted.

"Thank you King Ahasuerus. Sir, no insult meant? Yet insults are all you speak. And you end with M'Lady, a known insult to a queen worldwide. You. Are. Something," I say, as I make my way around the table to stand in front of this monster. I feel my hair parting with every breath Xerxes takes, he is so close. He is a little bit large to be my shadow, nevertheless here we are. "I'll tell you what. Why don't we brand *you* a liar this instant?"

Scoffing, he crosses his arms, "What have I lied about?" Marcus indignantly bows up to me as if to strike me. He thinks twice about it when he notices Xerxes, reminding him who has my back.

"Everyone knows Queen Vashti was marched to her death wearing only her crown. Regardless of how it happened ... you got what you were promised. Am I correct?"

Stammering, he glares at me. "That is not the context he promised it in!"

"Did he promise context? Did he say, right here in this very room, you shall see Queen Vashti naked, wearing only her crown? Did he promise you those words? If not, then decreeing she be executed in her crown..."

vividly remembering the details of this evening as told all over the village, I am about to show these men how smart women can be. "Well, it proves my husband, and Persia's King is certainly a man of his word. Unlike some who are here this night."

He raised his hand again, this time, definitely intending to strike me, when Xerxes left arm cradles and moves me out of harm's way. At the same time his right hand latches around Marcus' throat.

"You have been proven a liar. You are free to leave for home now," I finish addressing Marcus. "Your Majesty, Haman is your trusted Second. I am assuming he could make sure Rome's Governor finds his way home?"

"We could do that My Queen, or we could let Haman challenge him in the ring? What say you?" My drunken, furious, husband offers me the choice, still holding Marcus and glaring at him intently. I must answer these questions correctly to uphold his power and reputation.

"No," Marcus answers hastily.

Sucking in my breath, almost making a whistling sound, I say, "Good choice Marcus, Haman is tough. However the King has left the choice up to me." Grinning at Xerxes I reply, "My husband has offered me a very impressive wedding gift."

Xerxes interrupts me, "One of only many, My Queen."

"Being new to this empire, I could make a decision based on emotion this evening. But while I'm still being taught all of the delicate matters, My King. I would not want to make a decision without all of the proper political knowledge and turn things upside down. Whatever you decide, may it take up the least amount of your time during our days of wedding celebrations," I say. Now it's my turn to flirt with him a little by suggestively winking at him.

The crowd is whistling and laughing when Xerxes lets go of Marcus and orders, "Send him home Haman."

Haman secures Marcus, bows in my direction and says, "My Queen," with his arm crossed over his chest in a warrior salute, and they all leave the building.

"I could have just killed him for you," Xerxes whispers in my ear from behind.

"Definitely not the memory I'm going for on my wedding night," I whisper back.

He picks me up and heads towards our quarters to boisterous cheers and clapping as we leave.

Chapter 13

SETTLING IN

<Esther>

The morning after our wedding, I awoke early to find Xerxes gone. Taking the time to meet with my staff, we eat breakfast together on the balcony. I couldn't define exactly what their duties would be because as of yet, I had not learned what was specifically expected of me daily. I spent the rest of the time sharing with them why I saw them valuable and how I saw their strengths working and benefitting our group.

Genet was born in Ethiopia. Taller than most women, she stands around four and a half cubits and is all muscle. Her physique does not make her look manly, however. She is beautiful and exotic. Her eyes are as dark as her skin but her teeth are as white as the mountain peaks covered in snow. With highly defined cheekbones, and a sense of humor that keeps me in a good mood on the most boring of days, she is a joy. She is confident and can daintily pour a cup of tea, or plunge a dagger into the eye of an attacker. I find comfort in knowing if for any reason, we ever find ourselves in danger and our guards have been compromised, Genet and I would be able to work side-by-side and give our group a decent chance at survival. I trust her implicitly.

Sunita's family originally came from the northern outer regions of the Anatolian islands, but moved to Susa as her father is an engineer who works on the qanats. Qanats are a tunnel system designed to carry water from the mountains to the plains. This helps feed the crops and livestock in the lower places when we don't get enough rainfall. Insufficient rainfall seems to be a problem every year. She has an exotic Asian look with long black shiny hair that resembles a waterfall down her back. A little smaller, she is not quite four cubits in height, but it never seems to slow her down. She doesn't draw as much attention to herself, but she seems to be good at everything. She doesn't mind speaking to a crowd but mostly prefers the background. She waits to find a place to be helpful and then steps in. She is athletic, proper, and a quiet wonder.

Mary is a ball of energy. Her blonde hair with red tints, and freckles splattered across her entire body like jewelry, make me feel as though she is springtime wrapped up in a body. When she is happy or excited, her green eyes bubble with energy. Born closer to the northern borders of Rome, her family made their way down here just about four years ago for her father to work on the yakhchals. She is an organizational dream and loves creating schedules and itineraries and making everyone stick to it. I am more whimsical and would definitely need those skills she has been gifted.

Once I expressed these traits about them I loved, and saw as assets for my staff, we discussed our plans for the day. I wanted to see my childhood best friend for a few hours.

Genet, Sunita, and Mary all wished to do the same thing. We did not realize how much this little outing would entail. Hegai quite literally lost his cool. He began mumbling, pacing back and forth, trying to plan how this could logistically work, and again, pulling at both sides of his hair.

We stayed seated on our cushions and stole confused glances between one another. Finally, when he turned to face us, he had pulled his hair so many times he once again resembled a tufted horned owl. It was the most ridiculous, comical scene ... and poor Hegai didn't have a clue. We froze, looked at one another, and turned our faces trying to fight down the pending laughter.

It's Mary... Mary is the one you cannot sit by when something is humorous but you know you are not supposed to laugh. First, we heard a *kkkk*.

Hegai spun on his sandal and narrowed his eyes on us. I duck my head quickly to try and keep my composure. The second he even acted like he was turning his back she let out a *kkkkkggnnkkk* and Sunita brought both of her shoulders forward so far they almost touched under her chin. Genet looks over at me with her lips puckered out in front of her, and her eyes are squinted with tears already in them. Sucking both of my lips into my mouth, I bit them as hard as I could. It was all Genet could take and started silently wheezing.

Hegai turned around and all four of us were caught red-handed. I look at him with very wide eyes, still biting my lips. I'm not sure if it was Mary or Sunita but next I heard a very, very high-pitched "Heeeeeeeeeeee," followed by knee-slapping.

Then the flood gates opened, I began laughing, but it immediately turns into the silent kind of laughter where you cannot control yourself. When mine turns silent I know one thing is coming. Eventually, when I inhale, I am going to make a very loud squawk, almost like a duck. I tried. I tried so hard to take a preventative breath early on, before the squawk could occur. But I couldn't. When the awful squawk rang out, Genet's eyes got so big they looked like plates. She fell right out onto the floor cackling, and holding her stomach.

I tried to apologize to Hegai, who once again ran his fingers through both sides of his hair and pulled in frustration to mutter 'women.' Of course, this only made his hair look *more* like an owl and it launched us on another uncontrollable round of squawking, heaving and hee-heeeeing.

"I'll try again in a few minutes," he grumbles and prances out the door.

"Maaa-ryyy! Oh My Stars, you cannot do that ever again! I'm supposed to keep my composure, and I'm over here howling like a hyena." I say, still wiping tears from my eyes. My stomach hurt so bad. Another round of that, and I felt like I might lose the breakfast we had consumed.

"Hyena? Then when did a duck run through here?" Sunita says, sending the other two off on another fit of oxygen-stealing chuckles.

Mary grabs a handful of reeds from a tall standing vase, and shapes them over her head. With the reeds sticking out from both sides of her ears, she clears her throat and says, "Yes, Ma'am, I shall never laugh at something amusing ever again in the presence of the Queen," in an overly mocking, aristocratic tone.

The look on her face when my pillow bounces off her nose almost makes me lose composure again. Rubbing her nose, she quickly picks up the reeds and shoves them back in the vase as I gesture to the hallway indicating I hear Hegai returning. When he appears, his hair is combed.

"I might have noticed my reflection in the shining metal mirror as I passed down the hallway. You are forgiven," he says, looking at me and patting both sides of his hair with a smirk.

This time when I hear a *kkk, I don't look over at my friends. I do, however, raise my hand and point a finger in the direction of their group while fighting back a smile.

"The reason you panicked me with your announcement, ladies, is you may not realize it, but from now on, you will never go *anywhere alone*. Ever. Not even the bathhouse. When you are going somewhere delicate, one of the eunuchs will accompany you. There will always be a guard within earshot. But the eunuchs will be there to bring you a towel or any other toiletry should you need something." He pauses to make sure we are listening.

"A trip into the village and protecting four different valuable individuals is for sure an impressive feat. But we can do it. We will be bringing a eunuch for each of you, plus a guard for each of Genet, Mary, and Sunita. Queen Esther, you will have myself, plus another eunuch, and two guards. I know you do not feel any different, but with your status changes, your lives have changed. You would not believe the people who might take their chance at harming or abducting one of you to receive some money in return. We cannot take those kinds of chances." He finishes very sternly with a narrowed gaze at all of us.

Please give us the addresses and whom you are going to visit. Miss Genet, you have a particular guard who is very interested in being your protector for this journey," Hegai says with a raised eyebrow and a smile, but she just glares right back at him.

"Tell Tereh I said hello." I encourage her, "Don't get all defensive. He's cute!"

"I will not repeat that to the King. You're welcome." Hegai admonishes, and hands our papers off to the guard at the door.

"Ugh, I'm encouraging her Hegai, not wishing my husband looked like someone else." I defend.

"Okay, I've given your names and addresses to your teams, let's split up and get going so you can be back when the King gets home this afternoon shall we?" Hegai asks.

***

In the carriage, Hegai eyes me closely.

"Why are we visiting your childhood best friend and not your family?" He inquires.

Reminding myself not to lie but not reveal anything unnecessary, I decide to tell him the truth but emphasize certain things and let him come to his own conclusions.

"I am an orphan, Hegai. My father died in a war before I was born. My mother died in childbirth. I was raised by a cousin, but what does a man know of raising a daughter?" I said, smiling softly. "We had many people in the city take us under their wing and teach me all of the things a daughter should know. First, he left me with a wet nurse most of the time, then an old widow took over, teaching me the ways of becoming a woman. When Rachael moved into the neighborhood, we became the best of friends. We played together all day. Her mom taught me how to cook and wash clothes and stuff like that. I came home at night to feed my cousin and sleep. He would probably be at work now anyway. So I chose to see my best friend." I smile hoping the explanation satisfies him.

He raises his chin, with a 'hmmm', and doesn't ask any further questions.

When Rachael spots me she squeals at the top of her lungs and rushes out the door to hug me. One of the guards tries to step in between us, but I swat him away. "Not with her... *ever*. She should always be allowed access." He nods affirmation quietly.

We lace our arms together and enter the house. Giving my guards the nod to stay outside, they begin pacing around the perimeter making sure all of the accesses into the house are covered and I am protected. It all feels weird.

"Rachael, look at your belly!" I exclaim with my hands on my face. "May I?" I ask, reaching forward with my palms outstretched.

"Of course Esther," she giggles. Then she reaches for my hands to place them on a certain spot. After a second or two I feel a little thump. There isn't a proper word, amazed, awed, shocked? I just can't find words to describe the feeling pouring through me when my little sibling thumps its hello. I can't help but take the opportunity to introduce myself. "Hello to you too little brother or sister. I already love you, you know? You have been blessed with the best Mama and Papi," I croon to him. For some reason I think it's a brother.

"Did I hear the word Papi?" Gasping, I jump up and give my Papi a hug as I recognize his voice.

"Papi, I thought you'd be at work," I said, so grateful to be able to see him.

"I didn't have any appointments until after lunch so I took the morning off to carry up the day's water for Rachael. The midwife says she's bigger than women normally are with just one baby and suspects there might be two in there. So I want to help as much as I can." Papi's chest swells with so much pride, his shirt might pop open.

"Rachael," I gasp in awe, "what does it feel like? Honestly, I cannot wait until I feel a child in my womb as well!"

"I cannot explain it other than to say it is wonderful Esther. You will understand when your baby is there." Rachael says smiling, her face completely content.

"Esther, how is it going? Really?" Papi asks me.

"Great so far. Xerxes is treating me better than you ever thought possible. He proclaims his love for me daily and is very kind to me."

Chuckling Papi says, "Yes him falling in love with you was something I hadn't counted on. But I saw it with my own two eyes at the wedding."

"Papi, why am I keeping you a secret? I don't want to lie," I plead with him.

"And I do not want you to lie. If push comes to shove my child, you may say it. But Haman is a vile man Esther. On top of that, he is a descendant of Agag, and we are descendants of King Saul. Mortal enemies at birth. The Agagites harassed and worked tirelessly to block our people from reaching the Promised Land when we left slavery in Egypt. He has never treated any Hebrew fairly unless the King is with him and questions why he would be so mean," Papi says, shaking his head. "It is like the harassment and war was reborn in his veins when he took his first breath."

"One, I just don't want you to reveal you are Hebrew to Haman unless necessary, so the fewer people who know the better. And two, there are Hebrews in this town who are readily starting to bow to him just so he doesn't get cross with them. He then uses them to get information on other Hebrew people he doesn't like."

"I will not bow to him, Esther. Bowing on your knees in the way he requires is a form of worship. I worship Yahweh, and Yahweh alone. That being said, I do not wish to bring trouble onto you if this issue becomes a showdown," Papi finishes. It's a lot to think about but I am glad to know the reason why.

"One last thing daughter, be wary of the King's Officers Bigthana and Teresh. They are becoming dangerous," he warns.

"I've met them Papi, what do you mean they are becoming dangerous?" I ask, leaning forward.

"The King has not chosen them for promotion and they feel insulted. They are furious about it. Their spirits are very mean and dangerous. I've seen it before. If I hear of them making plans to attack anyone within the palace, I will get word to you somehow," he promises.

"Thank you Papi. You know my staff ladies are Genet, Sunita, and Mary. They may be easy to call for transport of documents back and forth to the gate or something of that nature. Just keep it in mind," I encourage him.

"Will do Nesicha. I've got to go. Love you," he said, hugging me as he rose to leave.

"No! Papi, let me leave first, so Hegai and the guards do not see you. They are right outside." I stand, cautioning him. "Also, since I am now the Queen, Nesicha doesn't quite fit anymore does it?"

Placing a warm kiss on my forehead, Papi places his forehead on mine and says "Except you will always be my Nesicha no matter how important you become."

Leaning into him for another hug, reminding me of all the bedtime stories he would tell me and all of the ways he was such a good parent. I reveled in how grateful I was that my parents picked him as my Papi.

"Palace escorts now? I suppose we have to get used to this." He squeezes my hand with a smile. "Queen Esther, yes well, It's probably a good call. I'll see you next time."

Rachael walks me outside and hugs me goodbye. With one last good luck rub of her belly, I take Hegai's hand to climb up into the carriage.

***

Returning to the palace, I hear rushing footsteps behind us and know instantly it is my husband. His arms wrap around me from behind, and he plants a kiss on the top of my head.

"Did I surprise you?" He asks.

"Surprise me? You sounded like a rushing herd of camels so no I was fully prepared when you wrapped me up in your arms, but I stayed very still so you didn't miss." I smiled, winking at him.

"Ohh we have a jester in our presence today!" He grins, "Go freshen up, tonight is time for gifts. Everyone in the kingdom has been sent a gift from the palace. Every household in all of Persia has been given one of these." He hands a red velvet pouch to myself and each of my ladies. When I tip it up, out slides a large silver coin with a side view of my face on the front, and a picture of the palace on the back.

Amazed, I gasp, "My King, how? How did you make this many in such a short amount of time?"

"I might have started a *little* early. It would have been a real bummer if you had said no," he replies with a grin. "A few provinces will be late in receiving theirs but most will be on time."

"Oh, my stars," I say, shaking my head. "You are unbelievable."

"I'll take that as a compliment. Now I can't wait any longer and I am going to skip the part of letting you freshen up," he says excitedly.

Hearing Genet snort behind us, Xerxes says, "Don't get sassy back there. This gift is for you too Grumpy."

Leading us out into the training arena, he makes us wait there, covering our eyes.

"Now this goes against all of my sane instincts, so do not make me regret it." He paces back and forth in front of us like a royal windbag. I can hear a commotion somewhere in front of us. Horses are snorting and pawing the ground ... several of them. Unable to wait any longer, all of us remove our hands from our eyes. The guards are holding four horses, not just any horses ... but the ones Genet and I specifically rode on that fateful day. We looked at each other with great anticipation and smiles.

"I am giving you the one thing that made me almost drop dead of fear. However, the more I have thought about it, the more proud I am of all of you. For everyone but Sunita, I am gifting you ..." he gets cut off by yelling, and the sight of two horses running at breakneck speed right to us. The grey and black Caspian is racing toward me with no sign he remembers how to stop. Genet's gelding is also giving it all he has. Mine cuts in between Xerxes and myself to plant his head in my chest, giving a soft whinny as a hello.

"See, now you're already making me regret my gift!" Xerxes heaves, "The connection the two of you have is weird."

Watching us for a minute, he turns and sees the guards leading the other two horses up to the group.

"Sunita, this slightly blind, almost dead old nag is your new 'steed.' She only does slightly more than a walk and never, ever spooks. You should live many long days with her as your mount." Xerxes grins. "And Mary, we were able to find this horse for you, as we think it might be a better fit than the one you had on the day of the contest. Now, is everyone happy?"

"Yes! Thank you, Your Majesty," Mary and Sunita say together.

I jump at him and wrap my arms around his neck. "Very happy My King," I say with a kiss.

"Well I am not doing that, but I do thank you very much, King Xerxes," Genet offers with a precise curtsey.

Chapter 14

ATTEMPTED ABDUCTION

\<Esther\>

Walking briskly to The Marketplace, I try to increase my speed, seeing if I can lose 'the men' who are following us. Genet and I decided on a trip today to see the different items being sold there. I have plans to promote the women of Persia and the goods they make. When traveling with King Xerxes, I hope to bring items from women artisans here in our country as gifts and for possible trading events.

Mary and Sunita have been very helpful in creating a presentation for The Council and my husband. This will not only increase the fame of the country of Persia, but also set us apart as a country whose women are more than just baby producers, but they are also able to support themselves or contribute to the household in times of crisis.

The proposal asks for each woman to be allowed to keep twenty percent of the profit for their craft, knowledge, and time in creating quality goods. These goods would represent Persia, their husbands, and themselves with quality craftsmanship. We know it will never be approved, but we are asking big so we might be granted something. If The Council can tell us no, but "graciously" offer us even five or seven percent to appease "the women," it will be a victory. As of right now, women are not allowed to have any private or personal money unless they are widowed. If widowed, the bride price their husbands' have paid for them is supposed to be given to them from their fathers. However, too often it just simply isn't there anymore. There are always "reasons" why they broke law and tradition and used the money. But a lot of times the bride price rule is simply not honored. Being granted a sliver of the profits would be a beautiful place to start.

We plan to emphasize that by increasing the ability for women to produce goods, earn money and being able to keep a fraction for themselves they could feel real gratitude towards the country, King, and their husbands. Life would be better for all the residents of Persia. It might be too much too soon, but if Yahweh has his hand on me, hopefully I can make things better for them in the long run.

"My Queen, you know this is our job right? Walking as fast as you can and changing directions on your way to The Marketplace - you are not going to give us the slip you know that right?" Tereh teases me.

Waving at someone from my old neighborhood, I reply, "Not today Tereh, but stay on your toes. Genet and I can be slippery when you least expect it."

"I am third in command of The Royal Army of Persia. You are not going to give me the slip," he insists.

Putting her arm around my shoulders, Genet gives him a sly grin and says, "Challenge accepted."

I remember coming to The Marketplace with Papi, but I always viewed it through the lens of what I wanted and not really what could be promoted. Being Queen, my presence carries much more attention when I am here than before. As I walk the aisles taking in all of the locally produced products, I stop and compliment some of the finer goods made with more precision to detail. Selecting carefully, I purchase one or two items to be able to present as part of my proposal.

Genet has an eye for how things are made and asks questions to each woman about the process and how it could be streamlined. We are gaining quite a bit of curiosity with our questions and purchases. Hopefully our presence, and mentioning that I am looking for gifts to present to dignitaries as we travel, will encourage a fresh wind of creativity and production of goods. Loaded down with items, we head back to the palace.

I would love to see my Papi at work, even though he doesn't want us giving our relationship away. So I decide to take off toward The Palace Gates. The Marketplace is located very near The Palace Gates, except for the fact I won't be entering the palace through my private quarters, no one should suspect anything. I'm a little 'homesick' even though everyone's lives have changed and Papi's home is now considerably more crowded than when I was with him, I still miss it sometimes.

"My Queen? Are we entering right through the front door of the palace and not your private quarters?"

"Yes Tereh, keeping you guys on your toes is just my little contribution to helping you maintain your sharp skills," I tease him.

"When we get back, I need to visit with you and your staff about the actual need for protection outside the palace walls," he grumbles.

Making the clicking sound with her lips, Genet turns to him and says, "I am sure there is so much more to your job that we even know. But there is more to the Queen and I than you can begin to imagine. I suspect this discussion might educate both sides. Just tell us when and where."

Genet is aware of who my papi is and I trust her with my life to keep my secret. Seeing his station, I walk a little more in his direction. Papi looks up, and seeing me, his shoulders relax, his smile broadens, and he sets down what he was working on.

Nearing his station, I feel Tereh's presence on my shoulder and I stiffen. Papi's body language turns more formal, and rigid. Genet closes in on my right before the other guard can take position there.

"Good morning my Queen," Papi bows. "What a breath of fresh air to see you among the people of Persia. We welcome you." Tereh places his left arm between us in case Papi were to reach out to touch me, sending a strong message to those around that I am not to be approached.

"Thank you sir, blessings on your day," I answer, sharing a one-on-one personal smile with him as Tereh continues to escort me forward.

"Oh M'Lady, you dropped your fan," Papi shouts, waving a hand-held fan out to Genet. Giving me a glance first, she rushes back to retrieve it from him.

"Genet, get up here within the protection of our circle," Tereh hisses.

Rushing into our group again, she holds up her fan, "I apologize, I dropped my fan."

"Don't do it again, I'll get you another."

Tereh seems very uptight, like he has seen something I have not. Pulling back my independence and willingly ducking into his coverage makes him relax a little. He is giving commands to the three other guards with us, but they must be in code or something as I don't understand his speech at all. They have all assumed a rigid formation around us and now I know something is not right.

When the shouting begins, I am able to identify immediately where it is coming from. The guards shift formation around me and Genet, covering us as best they can. Bouncing off of each other, inside the circle I know the fighting has started. As the first assailant tries to cut Tereh down with a long dagger, I realize how much danger I put us in by changing the course without proper planning.

"Don't fail brothers, the King would pay a nice penny to get her back. Don't let her escape!"

Following the voice, I can see the leader of this band of criminals. He looks desperate and his eyes suggest maybe he is touched mentally. He does not look fully human. With skin beaten and weathered by the sand and sun of this region, he looks much older than his age I am sure. It is obvious the leader has had no formal training, but he is desperate and determined. Those two qualities bring a lot of strength to a man. He has seven men with him, making their group eight strong. The guards are much bigger and much better trained than this desperate band of low-lifes, but we are still outnumbered and that is serious.

There is much bloodshed but the guards keep taking out attackers one by one keeping Genet and myself within their circle of protection for the most part. With every swing of their sword, they are backing us toward the front doors of the palace. Trying to stay light on my feet and out of their way, I suddenly feel a hand on my arm. He is successfully pulling me out of the protection of the group. I don't scream for the guards, I scream for the soul sister Yahweh has given me on this journey.

"Genet!"

Turning in the blink of an eye, she grabs his arm with her left and yanks both of us toward her. I duck when I see her right arm is already across her body on the backswing with a dagger in her hand. Seeing it protrude from his eye a second later was surreal and yet ...interesting. But I didn't have time to study it as she put her arm around my waist and made a break for the palace doors just a couple strides away.

Reaching the steps of the palace did not provide instant safety as it should have. Bigthana and Teresh, the doorkeepers, hesitated before turning to open them, and when they did make a move to do so, they acted very slowly. People in the crowd were shouting at them to 'hurry' and yet they just continued like they really didn't care.

Looking down at me, Bigthana heaved a sigh indicating I was nothing more than a pest and without a word or even a movement like he might help to protect us, he just stepped aside. I didn't have the luxury to consider his movements at the time, but soon I would understand. Genet and I heaved the heavy door open ourselves and pulled it shut as fast as we could.

"Take them to the Queen's quarters. Put six guards in front of her hallway room entrance," King Xerxes shouted. The anger was rolling off of him in waves. His dark eyes were narrowed like a predator as he continued toward the front doors of the palace where we had just come from. Sword in hand, I could see the different cords and muscles in his arm clutching, moving and jerking in anticipation of the coming moments. My husband was on his way to spill the lifeblood of anyone who got in his way and it was entirely my fault. This blood guilt is mine to bear.

***

\<Xerxes\>

When the child raced into the courtyard where I was meeting with Roman dignitaries about trading agreements, I saw his frightened eyes and instantly knew my Esther was in trouble. My heart reached up and grabbed my throat squeezing off all air coming into and out of it. I don't even remember if I gave a reason for leaving the negotiation table abruptly. All I could think of was Esther. I frightened the child so badly it took him a second to be able to speak. Getting down on one knee before him, I assured him I was so glad he had come. Also, instructing the scribes to place his name in the book of the records of the chronicles helped. Watching his little chest expand, I knew he was feeling pride, but he was still more afraid. He began slowly, but once he got started, he talked faster and faster. By the end he was almost shouting and waving his hands in every direction. But he had let me know my love was in trouble and I rushed to her aid.

Grabbing for the comforting feeling of my sword in hand, I head to The Gates. My thumb runs over the top of the quillon, and my index finger starts to trace the groves in the grip. It was a ritual at this point, I had done this a million times rushing into battle. My sword was as much a part of my body as my arm and someone was about to be intimately acquainted with both.

Seeing Esther and Genet rushing through the foyer gave me relief and yet even more anger all at once. Knowing she was safe, allowed me to turn my beast of rage loose to run wide open at free will. Shouting to get the women to a safe place, I sprinted toward The Gates to see if I could get my hands on whomever dared touch *My Queen*.

Pulling the doors open, the gatekeepers were just standing there watching. I would have to deal with them later, the lazy fools. Looking around on the steps, I spot Tereh and two of his guards subduing the last of the rioters. Disappointed there wasn't a battle left for me to fight, I head to them anyway. Interrogations were almost as fun as battle, and I was highly .... persuasive.

"Your Majesty, this is the last of them. The leader is contained over there," Tereh indicates with his sword. Stalking this man, one slow footstep at a time, causes him to begin squirming. Narrowing my eyes, I slow my steps even further. He was my prey, and he knew it.

"Your Majesty, I didn't .. it was ... please! I beg for mercy! I'll never do anything like it again!"

"The stench of your urine and feces reach my nose already and I haven't even gotten to you yet. What caused you to try and kidnap My Queen?" I really wanted to put a hand over my nose because this wretch was disgusting. He only responds with more begging and pleading. May I never have so much fear I lose control of my body. I vow I will take it like a man if death is imminent.

Lifting him by the throat and bracing him against a tree, I take half a step back. "What made you think you could even tell *My Queen* good morning? What was your plan? Did you really think I would pay you money to get her back? I would simply have killed you ... and enjoyed every second of it."

Knowing no excuse would get him out of it, the attacker gives himself over to his insanity once again and spits at my feet. "I thought I would just see how she tasted."

Rage like I had never possessed before exploded out of me. My ears had tremendous pressure in them, feeling like they may burst. All of my skin tingled with venom. My fingers tightened around the grip as they had done thousands of times before taking a life, and I gave no thought before removing his head from his body.

"Put his head on display right in the middle of The Gates as a warning to all criminals what will happen to you if you do not give the utmost respect and care to The Queen of Persia when you should happen to be blessed with her presence."

Now, I had to see her. My arms felt weaker than I had ever felt before, and I knew the only thing to restore balance in my mind and my body was holding her.

***

<Esther>

"Whatever blood is spilled today is on my hands and my hands alone," confessing to my ladies, realizing what I truly have done. "I must go to offer a sacrifice immediately."

"Not without risking your heritage you will not," Genet reminds me.

Mary reaches over and places her hand on mine. "We shall find a way to bring one of your priests into the palace. Then you shall give orders to bless him with a sacrificial lamb when he leaves."

"Leaving out the word sacrificial of course," Sunita reminds us all.

Handing me the fan she had dropped in the courtyard, Genet said, "You should take a look at this Esther."

"Your fan? I have one just like it," waving her off.

"I guarantee you do not," she pushes.

Opening it, a folded paper falls onto my lap. Instantly, I know my Papi's handwriting. Reading it, and not being able to deal with everything all at once, I fold it and place it in my robes.

"How did Yahweh bring such wonderful, loyal friends to my side in the midst of this most unusual life?" Reaching out and holding hands with all three of them at once I shed tears of release, fear, gratitude, and remorse. Calling for a guard, I ask whether Xerxes had been made to leave the negotiations table to deal with this uprising I had caused.

"Well, this is again, not ideal and all my fault. Genet, please hand over all of the trinkets we purchased at The Market this morning. Guards, please have one of the staff present these in gift baskets along with a feast of flavorful bread, hot tea, wine, or water, and shower the Roman dignitaries with extra sweets for their pleasure." I could not let this hurt his reputation in negotiations.

"Yes My Queen," the guard bowed before me, and then left to carry out my instructions.

***

Hearing a scuffle in the hallway, I stand and prepare myself for whatever might come. Seeing my husband enter covered with blood, exceptionally wide eyes, and breathing heavily in the moment of the first real attempt on my safety, I prepare myself to be scolded or punished, or ... anything. He crosses the room in three steps and envelopes me in his crushing arms. Breathing in my scent, he just holds me. Placing his hand on my head, and the other arm around my back, pulling me in at the hip ... we stay there.

Having seen his condition before he embraced me, I knew he was covered in the life remains of some soul who had been a part of trying to abduct me. Blood covered his torso and face in splotches. There were pieces of what I could only suspect as parts of the victim's insides clinging to his shirt. I deserve this. No matter how sad and repulsive it is to be pressed up against the gore I will endure it. This is all my fault after all.

When his grip lessens and he pushes me back, holding me by the shoulders, I prepare myself.

"I'm so glad you are okay," he murmurs.

"Are you not going to punish me? I deserve it, this is all my fault," pleading with my head lowered.

"How is this all your fault Kitten?" The love in his gaze only convicts me further.

"Xerxes, I changed the direction we came home today. When getting done in The Marketplace, I decided out of curiosity to return home through The Palace Gates which would make us come through the front of the palace instead of the private entrances," my speech is rapid and pouring out of me mixed with two parts guilt, one part fear.

"Everything was going well, people were polite, going about their responsibilities, until one moment turned into another and then all our lives were in danger! Tereh had been frustrated with me all morning and I thought he was overreacting. I am not special. I am just Esther. I don't feel different just because I now have a crown. I still feel like me. I haven't heeded any of these warnings properly, because I really thought I am a nobody .. I'm just, well ... Esther." New tears are coming to my eyes and I am now on the verge of bawling.

"I made his job extremely difficult, put Genet's life in danger, and look at you! All of the blood you spilled is on my head. This is my fault. How could there be redemption for this?"

"Well good, now I don't have to give you the speech about being careful. Now you've experienced why," he croons.

"Why would they care - I'm just me," shrugging again, searching his gaze.

Finally showing a little frustration, he raises his voice, "You are not just Esther. You are the Queen of Persia. You are my wife. You are valuable just because of who you are to one who is looking for leverage. In this world you are valuable because you are mine. Life is not the same for you anymore Esther!"

His frustration actually makes me feel better, like I'm paying some kind of penance. But as he is finishing I hear the words of my Papi in my head.

"You are worthy because Yahweh says you are worthy. No other outside circumstance tips the scale on that one way or the other. You are worthy. Period."

Chapter 15

A Perilous Day

<Xerxes>

"Your Majesty, The Council is ready to hear from the Queen, they are waiting," Haman says.

Turning to him in rage, I ask for clarification, "Excuse me but ... what?"

Heaving a sigh, which irks me, Haman repeats, "The Council? The investigation into what happened in The Palace Gates? The Queen needs to give her testimony, and be reprimanded after all."

"Take a look around you. Really think about what's happening and say it again?" I dare him.

"The investigation into the incident in the Palace Gates is ready to begin. The guards say the Queen acted inappropriately. She's a woman. She must be punished," he finishes in a bored tone.

"Don't you ever, and I do mean ever, cross the threshold of Queen Esther's door without first asking permission. Do I make myself clear? The next time your feet cross that line, I will consider you guilty of rape and have you hung, understood?" He nods in affirmation, clearly irritated, but backing up to where he is out in the hallway.

Has Haman always been this way? Was he like this with Vashti and I just didn't care? Whatever is happening, he needs to understand this is *my* wife. Not his. Why does the way he treat her anger me so? Nevertheless he is right. The Council will be expecting her to arrive for an investigation.

"Please inform The Council, Queen Esther and I will be arriving at the hearing as soon as we have had a chance to clean up. Then she will arrive on my arm, *when I am ready.*"

Knowing he was dismissed, Haman turns on his heel and strides away.

"Xerxes, I am not trying to delay, but this is really important. When the Gate Advisor called Genet back for her fan, he had slipped a note inside to give me. His name is Mordecai, do you know him?"

"Yes, he is a hard worker, I only know good things about him. Let me see the note."

"Bigthana and Teresh are the same ones who guard the door. Today, when Genet was trying to get me to safety, they didn't want to open the doors for us. I feel like maybe his note of warning would be worth forming a secret investigation to look into the matter?" She encourages me.

Wrapping her in a big hug, I say, "I should just place you in charge of my 'secret investigation' unit of soldiers, shouldn't I? I will look into it Kitten. You have my word."

Wiggling away from me, and wrinkling her nose, she says, "Umm... thank you, can we bathe now?"

***

\<Esther\>

After Xerxes and I clean up, I follow him down the steps to the wing where most of the business is conducted in the palace. Sunita, Mary and Genet accompany us, but Genet will be the only one allowed inside, as she is to be interrogated as well.

"Remember, in these settings, I am the King. You are merely my wife. All informality should be strictly avoided," Xerxes states firmly.

His tone and attitude surprise me a little. If I were to be honest, I would have to admit it hurts my feelings as well. I had gotten entirely too used to the relationship we had within my quarters. Once again, I am reminded of a woman's place in this world. I am King Xerxes wife. Correction ... 'merely' his wife.

Taking his place on the miniature throne looking chair, Xerxes gestures to the two seats beside him for us to be seated. Clearing his throat, everyone gives him their attention.

"This council meeting is being held regarding the incident that happened today in The Palace Gates. One guard was injured superficially, no other injuries or deaths occurred for the palace residents. We will begin today's meeting with a statement from The Queen," Xerxes states and looks at his council.

"King Ahasuerus, this isn't how investigations go? You forgot to mention we will be looking into punishments for the Queen and her attendant Lady Genet, as well as deciding how their lives will change in the future regarding outings." Councilman Tarshish bitterly looks down the table toward myself and Genet.

"The guards have told us of her haughty attitude thinking she doesn't need to listen to them and can do whatever she wants." Councilman Shethar spits with disdain. With his remark, Genet sits up straighter in her chair and turns her burning gaze into Tereh. His countenance does not falter, but he also does not make eye contact with her.

"Let me interrupt you right there, as your King. I'll remind you, I am the one who sets the agenda as well as the punishments. I may take your advice into consideration, but you do not tell me what will be happening at any of my meetings. The purpose of a Council is to *advise* the King. Not to demand I do what you say. Remember your roles."

"But you left negotiation talks with dignitaries from Rome and they are still waiting. This makes it look as though you are not in control of the events of your Palace. Someone must pay for this," huffing in displeasure, Councilman Meres lays down his fan, and frowns.

From across the room, a servant raises his hand, "My King, if I may?" After getting a nod from Xerxes, the servant tells the room. "Queen Esther, while quarantined in her room for safety, inquired whether you were pulled away from negotiations. When she discovered you were, she sent gift baskets, food, wine, hot tea and water to the dignitaries. A musician was also dispatched for their entertainment. The delegation has retired to their wing, sending word that they look forward to resuming talks in the morning and thanking the Queen and King for taking such good care of them."

"Thank you for your report," then Xerxes looks at me and states, "We will now hear a statement from Queen Esther."

My legs were shaking and felt weak, however, I stood, "Councilmen, Haman, My King. Please let me thank the guards for doing their jobs outstandingly in the face of attack and being outnumbered. Also, I must acknowledge a very courageous member of my staff, Lady Genet. While the guards were battling and outnumbered, one of the assailants was able to grab me by the wrist and begin pulling me from the safety of their formation. Lady Genet stopped his progress, pulling me to safety, and stabbing the assailant in the eye within just a second. I fear without her bravery not only would my day have ended differently, but there would have been yet another attacker coming after the Royal Guards," looking around the room I could see not only did the Councilmen, not appreciate Genet's efforts, but they in fact, were doubting my version of events.

"After securing permission to walk to The Marketplace this morning, Lady Genet and I did walk briskly, and we did tease Guard Tereh we would give him the slip to test his skill in being guards for the Queen and her entourage. However, we did not run from him, nor did we hide from him. We were within his sight the entire time."

Several Councilmen were barely listening to me, Haman was frowning, Tereh had a straight face, but Xerxes cleared his throat and nodded at me. "Please, continue."

"After looking at the goods, and purchasing some of the finest items for traveling dignitaries, we headed back to the palace. When nearing The Palace Gates, I noticed it was very alive with traffic, people and noise. As Queen, I thought it would be good for me to have at least a superficial knowledge of all the workings of Susa and the Palace, so I changed course and headed in that direction," glancing at Genet, she nodded to encourage me to continue.

"One of the Gate's advisors bid me a good morning and we stopped as he honored me. Tereh blocked his ability to touch me and we proceeded forward toward the palace. It was then, the advisor yelled at Genet she had dropped her fan. She stepped back and retrieved it before rejoining our group. Just a few footsteps later Tereh noticed danger and directed his guards to move into a protective formation around us. Pretty soon a group of men attacked and several were trying to get their hands on me saying the King would pay handsomely to get me back."

Xerxes face was red, and he squeezed his water tin so hard it bent in an awkward shape. My eyes went wide at his strength but I continued, trying to finish in a hurry.

"Tereh and the guards fought valiantly but there was a gap in the circle, an attacker reached in and grabbed my wrist, pulling me towards him, when Genet saved me by stabbing him in the eye as I recounted earlier, and then because we were merely two steps from the palace doors she rushed me to safety. Or so we thought. The two doormen moved very slowly and didn't even open palace doors. Lady Genet and I had to do it ourselves. So we were exposed for quite some time. But Lady Genet and I took care of ourselves, and it turned out okay."

"My Queen, are you finished?" Xerxes asks. I simply nod my head. Several Councilmen were murmuring but none of them had questions for me.

"Alright, Lady Genet, Please stand and testify," Xerxes gestures to her.

Standing and looking around the room, Genet spoke slowly and clearly, "My Queen has spoken well and truthfully. I have nothing further to add," she said and slowly began to sit back down.

"Young lady, you were not given permission to sit," Councilman Tarshish all but throws his disapproval at her. "Did the Queen ask permission from the guards to see if she could change course and go through the Palace Gates?"

"Sir? I remember a conversation regarding the change of plans, but I don't remember if it occurred before we neared The Gates or not. I'm sorry."

"Did the Queen say to Guard Tereh 'I am the Queen and I'll go where I want!' when he questioned her change of plans?" Councilman Carshena was next.

Laughing out loud Genet spoke, "Certainly not, I encourage you to get to know your Queen. She never talks down to people the way that statement insinuates."

"Lady Genet, did you seek and obtain permission to carry a weapon?" Councilman Shethar smirks, pleased with himself.

"It is part of my job, Councilman..."

"Don't get smart with *me*, woman!" He fumes.

"My apologies sir, my intent was not to be smart. I was simply explaining my job description laid forth by the King and Queen. Her Ladies-in-Waiting are to be her last line of defense should there ever be a moment like today and she be left vulnerable. We are to use all means necessary to protect the Queen. A knife would be considered 'all means necessary.' Would it not?"

"It would indeed and thank you for a job well done. Persia still has her Queen," Xerxes nods to Genet gratefully, much to some of the Councilmen's displeasure. "Tereh, your quick action, fighting ability, and the fact you have the trust of your men all worked together to save the life of the Queen and her Lady, Genet today. I commend you and your team. Do you have anything to add to the testimonies heard here today? The Councilmen said you or one of your guards had told them the Queen was haughty and disrespectful to you as men. If this is true we need to hear about it."

Tereh stands, grabbing the leather bound bundle in front of him. "Lady Genet, your dagger. Your skills today were impressive. Any time you would like to train with the guards you would be welcome. You truly made the difference in the Queen's safety today," he said, holding her gaze and sliding her dagger across the table.

"The Queen and Lady accurately described today's events, Your Majesty," Tereh addressed the King.

"Councilman Shethar, I have heard no testimony as you stated of the Queen treating the guards in a haughty manner. Where is your proof? Or are we to assume you were lying?" Xerxes challenges with a dark gaze, clenching his jaws, and the muscles in his arms.

I can't help it, when his muscles in his chest and arms jump like that I am so attracted to him. Now that I am not a virgin any longer, it brings memories of intimate times to my mind and here I sit day dreaming of things I should definitely not be thinking about at a time like this. But my husband is certainly a beautiful man. I am startled out of my daydreams and jump, when Xerxes projects around the room, "I. Am. Waiting."

"What has happened to you, My King?" Councilman Shethar asks, appalled. "The Queen took an alternate route home. The planned route was to go back and enter the palace through the private royal entrance. She took it upon herself to change those plans. If that isn't haughty I do not know what is. Women …"

"Are not slaves."

"Excuse me?" Shethar asks, startled.

"Women are not slaves. Just because men are the head of the household and they must defer to us does not mean they should be hated. It does not mean they are not worthy of love. It does not mean you get to believe they are all dumb, worthy of punishment in every scenario, and incapable of adding value to any circumstance," Xerxes is processing out loud as though he cannot stop.

"Furthermore, as my wife, in a lot of situations, she is more valuable than you, Councilman Shethar. She is mine, she carries my worth. You do not. I have seen her capacity for loving all other people, and even animals for that matter. I've also seen her intelligence, and even though many of you will refuse to believe it, she could outsmart several of the men I know. For today, the guard who was with her says she did no wrong. She does have the right to change her path home if she so chooses because she is not a slave. I rule today was an attack by a worthless band of men. Our guards, and Lady Genet acted exemplary, and no punishments or future restrictions will be placed on any of them. As for my council, you will be tasked with removing the hate in your attitudes towards women. You can still be head of household and hate women I guess. But you cannot be a *Councilman* and hate women any longer. Meeting adjourned."

With those words, my ears began to feel smaller and tighter. The floor started to widen, and tilt. One minute I was fine, but the next minute I was reaching out to steady myself with a hand on the table. Missing it, I went straight to the floor. As all of my vision went black, I thought to myself, *'Oh I hate it when this happens. It is so annoying.'*

***

\<Genet\>

"Esther!" In less than a second the King is on the floor beside Esther feeling her forehead, shaking her shoulder, rolling her onto her back. The tenderness he uses placing his head onto her chest to check her heart was still beating is … well for a King … it is precious.

I know what is wrong with her, but I've been sworn to secrecy. She is white as a lamb right now. There is no color in her face at all. I send someone into the hall for Mary and Sunita as fast as I can and within seconds they are on their knees beside her clucking and fussing like the chickens running around the city.

"Do not touch her!" Xerxes bellows at everyone gathering around trying to get a look at the Queen.

"Stop panicking King," Sunita scolds him. "Women been passing out since the Garden of Eden."

"The What? What is that?" He asks, completely lost.

Frowning, she spits, "Are you a heathen?"

Mary reaches forward and claps her on the back of the head. Pursing her lips while her big eyes and bobbing head are trying to remind Sunita, Esther's condition is a secret. Sunita either doesn't care or is not catching on.

"Ow, Stop hitting me Mary. She needs the healer, you know this. We've been here before," Sunita says.

"You have, why? How many times? How often has Esther passed out and why has no one told me?" Now we are getting the third degree. And it's heated. Thanks Sunita.

"Because you are not supposed to know. Sooo … can you let us do our jobs now?" she gives him the shoo signal.

"What Am I Not Supposed To Know Ladies?" Xerxes is yelling so loud all of Susa can probably hear him now.

"Ahhh, you caveman. Do you want your child to be deaf before it is ever born? Sheesh just because you are King does not mean you can just …"

Now King Xerxes has Sunita by the shoulders and is shaking her like a rag doll saying, "Baby? What baby? Is Esther with child? Are we having an heir?"

With all of the ruckus happening around everyone, I reach down to hold Esther's hand concerned she still hasn't woken up yet. It is then I notice the spot of blood forming on her dress. No, oh no, not now little one. Your Mama was so happy you were here.

"Guys," I try to interrupt, but no one is listening to me. "King Xerxes,… everyone… You Guys!"

When they all turn my way, I look down at the blood stain that is now even a little bigger than when I first noticed it. The King went from looking elated to devastated, and now he looks terrified. Scooping Esther up in his arms, he runs out of the room.

"Which healer does she prefer? Which one has she been seeing?"

"Miriam, in the village, has come to the palace to check on her a couple of times. I know where she lives, you get her in bed. I'll go get Miriam!" I say now, coming alive and jumping into action.

"Take Tereh with you!" Xerxes demands with concern.

Rushing to the stables to grab Kasha, my gelding, the King gifted us during his wedding week, I run into Tereh along the way. Thank God, what is his name again? Esther has been telling me about her God. Yahweh, that's it. If he is her God, he is the one I need to be praying to right now so he can take care of her right? *'Okay Yahweh, this is your girl, and she needs you. Show up big for her, can you? I am begging you.'*

"Tereh, grab a horse and help me please, I don't have time to explain!"

Grabbing a mount and riding bareback, Tereh doesn't ask any questions. As much as I swore I would never give myself in marriage, this man is worming himself into every crack of resistance I have. He trusts me. He respects me. And he is wearing down every single argument I have for not trusting men.

Jerk.

"We have to get to Miriam in the village. The one who has been coming to see Esther. She collapsed after the meeting today. She is with child, but she passed out and did not wake up. Then she began to pass blood. We need Miriam to get there fast."

"I got you Genet. Lead On, I won't let anything happen to you," he reassures me.

See! I tell myself, he's unbearable.

***

<Tereh>

We got the midwife back to the palace. I take the horses back to their stalls, brush them down and feed them so Genet can be with Queen Esther. She really loves the Queen as a sister. I really love *her*. I wish she didn't have so many walls up. I will spend a lifetime breaking them down to have her.

And by the looks of things, it will take me a lifetime to get them all removed there are so many of them.

Walking myself to the royal quarters, I find Lady Genet standing outside in the hallway with Lady Mary and Lady Sunita. When she turns and finds me, her eyes alone tell me the news is not good. As she continues to look into my eyes, tears well up in hers. Not knowing what to do, I just open my arms. Fear flickers for just a moment, but then she rushes to me. I don't say anything. No expectations, no pressure, just comfort. But I have to admit the feeling of her in my arms finally is much better than I even imagined it would be all of those many nights I laid in my bunk thinking about her.

Now if I can just do this right and not mess it up! As strong as she is, she tucks her arms inside my embrace and grabs my shirt with her fists. Using her fists to shield her face, she stays there and cries for several minutes until she leans back and tells me the baby is gone.

The Queen was finally awake but very weak as she had hemorrhaged. Luckily the midwife was able to stop it before Esther had bled to death. She said the King was in shock, sad of course, but very grateful Esther would make a full recovery. Xerxes had said the trip for negotiations on trade to Egypt was cancelled. Esther insisted it was still on and needed another trip to The Marketplace to purchase gifts for the dignitaries. The stubborn woman. One thing is for sure, Persia has a very strong queen. Sighing, I wondered which one of them would win this silent stand-off.

Chapter 16

BROKEN LULLABIES

\<Esther\>

"Yah - weh delivers ..." singing Hebrew lullabies is one of the things that brings me comfort. It has been six months since I lost our first child and heir to Persia. I miss him or her terribly. It wasn't as real for Xerxes as he only knew of the pregnancy for about twenty minutes before it was over. He just wants to make sure we actively try for another one. At least he says he does, but then Haman comes in and steals his attention.

Haman has somehow wormed his way into my marriage and I'm not liking it at all. He pulls Xerxes away and has women from the harem waiting while he gets Xerxes drunk with wine. The more often he does this, the more my husband's feelings for me wane. If there were only a way for Haman to find himself accidentally in a pit of boiling tar, or maybe, oops - stuck in a tiger's den.... I would not sing lullabies missing him.

The note my Papi left about Bigthana and Teresh turned out to be true. Xerxes had Haman conduct a classified investigation and it proved them to be plotting to kill the King at the next festival where he would address the people from the steps of the front doors of the Palace. They planned on handing him a goblet of poisoned water after his speech. He would not have been able to taste it, and it would not kick in for a few hours. It would be difficult for anyone to point a finger at them for blame. In their arrogant impatience, they had begun to brag to a couple of the other gate workers who then ... also couldn't keep their mouths shut.

Once Haman captured the gate workers and interrogated them for a testimony, he arrested Bigthana and Teresh for intent to commit murder of the King. Xerxes had them hung in the gallows for plotting to murder their King. Their bodies were put on display for all to see what treason will get you. Mordecai was immortalized by the story being recorded and giving him credit for saving the King in the book of the annals, in the presence of the King. Xerxes also issued a decree elevating Haman above all other officials and stating he should be bowed to in honor and reverence. I am so glad this is not required of me. I would have a very hard time doing so.

We are leaving in two days for Rome. We will be visiting dignitaries there as the guests of Consul Vopiscus Julius Iullus. We shall attend gladiator fights, the men will negotiate over land, and slaves, and whether we will be allies or enemies. I have purchased two carts full of the best trinkets Persian women have to offer. I am also bringing a couple extra women to set up tables in approved market places and earn money by selling the goods we have brought.

Some will be used for gifts, and some will be used for profits on a women's group I've started. We haven't gained the freedom I was hoping for with The Council for women yet, but we did gain permission for a women's group. Whatever goods we can sell from the group, can be split from amongst the women. It's a start.

I want to take a walk through the Palace Gates today to see my Papi and hear about my twin little brothers who are almost one year old by now. They are chubby and full of life. Their giggles light up my soul. Tereh and Genet are inseparable now and I won't be surprised if they are wed within the year. Tragedy has a way of cutting off all the unnecessary ridiculousness from your heart and leaving you with the raw reality of life. When I lost my baby, and almost my life, Genet had all of her superficial silly reasons for keeping Tereh at arm's length cut away from her heart and now, she is head over heels silly in love with him. Good for her.

Setting out with four guards including Tereh, Lady Genet and myself, we stop by Mordecai's table.

"Good Morning sir," I greet him.

"Good morning, My Queen," he responds.

Reaching out my hand, I offer it to him to kiss. He takes it politely and places a proper kiss on it like a gentleman would. Because we have practiced this several times, no one sees the note I have pressed into his hand at the same time.

"I pray you have a blessed day My Queen," he offers with a bow.

"To you as well."

Reaching The Marketplace, we grab one or two more bags of items we had ordered for the trip, and then we begin to return home. However, nearing The Palace Gates, we hear a lot of commotion. There is screaming and I can tell it is Haman.

"You filthy Hebrew, I told you to bow to me whenever I walk by. Do you know what I could do to you?" Haman spits on someone, but I cannot see who it is. "The King himself has ordered all of the Gate officials to honor me by bowing down to me, yet you refuse."

"I only bow to Yahweh," Mordecai answers as politely as he could, considering all of the emotions surfacing and swirling front and center between the two of them.

"Yahweh," spitting again at Mordecai's feet, "we shall see about that."
Haman proceeds past Mordecai, shoulder checking him as hard as possible
when he gets close.

***

This outing was incident free and what a relief. Tereh ushered us on, but I
had heard enough to know it was my Papi Haman was tormenting. I would
get to the bottom of this as soon as I could. Returning home, I stop by
to see Hegai while Tereh and the rest of the guards disperse. We are safe
within the palace walls and have much more freedom than when outside.

"Hegai, that special guest who wanders by occasionally? He will be around
tonight. Will you make him comfortable?"

"Yes, Your Majesty. I always look forward to our visits while waiting for you
to arrive," he nods his head patiently.

"You know how much this means to me right Hegai?"

"Yes, Your Majesty, your secret goes to my grave. I swear on my life," he says,
and bows.

Tapping my heart, I stand on my tip-toes and kiss him on the cheek. "7pm
- I'll see you then."

***

Once again, Xerxes did not come to eat the evening meal with me. Nor did
he even send word. Tereh had seen Genet so she let me know he was eating
with Haman. We discussed a lot of these situations in our talks on the night

before he announced me as queen, but I sure didn't imagine Haman being the cause of these disappointments happening.

"Heyyyy wife. Hows wuz your day?"

"Xerxes, you have had too much to drink ... again," I sigh.

"It jusst makes me a betterrr lover."

"Trust me. It does not." Turning out of his awkward reach for my body, I move a step away from him.

"Whoaaa, where did you go?"

"About a hand width to the right," I answer.

Chuckling he says, "So the little woman is playing hard to get."

"No, your wife is playing impossible to get."

"What do you mean Esther," he is still slurring every single word in each sentence. "We need to get started on the next heir. I love you. You are all recovered."

"I am. But we will worry about it when you are a little closer to sober. And maybe when you are not wasting your seed daily on the harem girls."

"We talked about that. You don't get the right to be angry," he trips over the reclining table and falls to the floor. "I am the King."

"Mmmm, and so very impressive. Actually what you said was I would have to put up with concubines on dignitary trips. You really did not say anything about spending all your evenings with Haman and wasting your seed into harem girls daily. I cannot believe you have made me so miserable, I am looking forward to this trip and the possibility they might actually send me a harem man as well." Oooh that was a low blow. I didn't really hope for any such thing, but I wanted to hurt him at least a little bit as much as I was hurting. Great, now I would have to repent and offer a sacrifice somehow.

"Oh no you will not," now his eyes are shooting fire. It might be a little scary if I thought he could get up and walk to me.

"Xerxes you would actually have to pay attention to me to know what I am or am not doing at any given moment. And besides, judging by your pattern of actions here lately, you will be avoiding spending time with me. You will be drunk, unable to walk, talk, or make love before the sun goes down. You will pass out early, and you will be wholly unaware of anything I do the rest of the visit. It will be just like another day here in the palace."

"What does that mean? Huhh? Do you have harem men in the palace? Are they some of my guards?"

"Wow. Xerxes, just go to sleep. Or go find Haman. I really don't care anymore. We are not in a good place right now. Goodnight."

***

"Hegai, hello my friend. Just a word of warning. The King is very drunk. He is unable to walk without falling. Unable to talk without slurring. Very stubborn and just wants to fight about anything right now thanks to Haman. If you happen to see him coming, please come knock on the door so I can send my guest away through the window. I will go to the barn, and brush down Stormy."

I am feeling exhausted after my encounter with Xerxes. Brushing down my gray gelding would be very therapeutic right now. There is nothing more calming than putting my nose in his neck and breathing in. When Hegai nods and winks, I head for my old bedroom and close the door. Papi is already there. Wrapping me in a bear hug, I can't help but hang on a second longer. He raises an eyebrow asking me what's wrong, and I spill everything to him.

"That Haman really is a snake. It seems he knows how to cause real trouble everywhere he goes," sighing with the weight of the world on his shoulders, he hugs me again a little tighter.

"Now, was it you Haman was tormenting in the Gates this afternoon?"

"Yes, he was. He is obnoxious. He is forcing all of the Hebrew people to bow down to him. I won't do it. The way he wants people to execute the bowing is too much like worshipping. I won't do it. Can you imagine a Hebrew bowing to an Agagite? Unheard of," crossing his arms he is frowning and looking just as stubborn as Xerxes was a few minutes ago.

"Papi, try to stay out of his way, okay? He will look for you. Just to make a scene, he will go out of his way to find you so he can humiliate you. Please be watchful and stay out of his sight while we are gone. Promise me."

"I will do what I can, daughter, but I have a job to do. I can't just stand up in the middle of an appointment and run. That is not who I am. But I will do what I can."

"Okay Papi, we are leaving the day after tomorrow for Rome. Figuring travel time, and the visit I am going to say we will probably be away for eight weeks give or take. Haman will be left in charge most likely, so please be careful. Now, how are my brothers?"

Before he could answer, I hear three soft knocks at the door. Knowing it is our signal, Papi quickly hugs me and dashes out the window after checking the coast is clear. Hearing Xerxes interrogating Hegai as to my whereabouts, I make my exit out the window as well. Running for the stalls, I slip inside to be with my gelding. He bobs his head up and down, throwing his black mane wildly when he sees me. I love that he is excited to see me each time I visit.

Pretending I haven't brought anything with me, I hold my hands up in the air as if I don't know why he is pawing the ground with his hoof. Soon he starts nudging my hips, first the right and then the left. His search intensifies and becomes not-so-gentle anymore. Giggling, I reach inside my shift dress and pull out small pieces of carrot I snuck out with me just in case I got to see him. Smoky is happy munching on the carrot pieces I brought him and life is all too simple for him. Burying my nose into his neck, I wrap my arms around him and let my stress melt. The smell of a horse is comforting, calming, and cannot be duplicated by any other animal. Not even close.

"You used to make that face when you nuzzled me in the crook of the neck," came the voice of my husband.

"Yes, well it ceases to become inviting when all I smell there are other women and alcohol. At least Smoky is consistent. His smell is always his and he never waivers in his desire to see me."

"Esther," Xerxes voice cracks "I ..."

"Don't bother husband. You have told me repeatedly. It is your right as a man. As the King. Did I leave out anything?"

"Yell at me, ... something," he pleads.

"I gave you my word I would handle it as best I could. Although it is not nearly like it was presented to me, I am doing the best I can. If you ever find any of those desires you once had for my friendship, or love, seek me out. I will try again. But tonight Xerxes, leave me with the one who loves me the most." The tears running down my cheeks silences the moment.

After watching me brush down Smoky for a few minutes, his hand falls to his side, his chin lowers to his chest, and he slowly retreats to the palace. But not before I hear him place a guard outside the stalls to watch over me.

***

<Xerxes>

I would have gotten a better reception in Sheol. She isn't wrong. I have been selfish, I deserved that. Vashti never once was with child. When Esther lost our baby, it devastated me. First, because I saw how easily she could be taken from me. She turned so white, so weak, and nothing would wake her. To see the blood coming from her body and staining her dress sent panic through me like no battlefield had ever before. But learning the blood represented my son, or a tiny daughter who would fill the palace with giggles and think her daddy was the strongest man in all the world, left me with a grief so deep it dug into every muscle and organ I had.

After losing the baby, when Haman invited me out to drink, it was such a relief. To let strong drink carry away those feelings of fear and sorrow. In the beginning, I sent away every girl he had waiting from the harem. But as the weeks passed, the more I drank, eventually I gave in. I couldn't face Esther. I couldn't talk about the baby. Or my fear of losing her. Yet I also knew by not doing so, I was a coward. I knew she needed me to hold her, to let her cry. I knew no one else would be able to heal those wounds within her but me. And I chose night after night to stay away. I do not deserve her. I have failed our love.

Standing there tonight watching her brush down Stormy I could almost reach out and touch the hurt she carried. I could see night after night of rejection and abandonment at my hands. I could imagine her lying in bed missing our baby and knowing I was holding another. How will I ever forgive myself? I will never expect her to forgive me. I have failed as a man. I am supposed to be a god. But I cannot even be a husband.

When I left, I stationed a guard to protect her because that's what Kings do. But I am not just her King, I am her husband and it is time I start acting like it. Turning around, I go back to the guard and talk to him in low, whispered tones so she will not hear. Dismissing him, I do what I should have done from the beginning. I take care of my wife. I will stand guard over her. No one will protect her as well as I will, because no one loves her as I do. I need to start doing all of the little things to remind myself of how much I do still love her.

It is a good thing I am a highly trained warrior. If I were not, I would have missed her sneaking out of the stalls, trying to avoid the guard ... a.k.a. me, who had been stationed to watch over her.

Catching up to her entering the palace, I gently say into her left ear, "Why must you be so difficult with protection detail Esther?"

"Twice Xerxes, this is only the second time I've tried to avoid a guard. And maybe it is because I'm suffocating. I cannot go anywhere without people a hand width from me, judging me, breathing down my neck, and having a million opinions about whether I should be doing the thing I am doing. It is infuriating."

"You are precious Esther, you are the Queen. We are only trying to keep you safe. By the gods will you ever listen?"

"Most likely not. Things that are precious are usually given attention, not guards Xerxes."

I accompanied her back to her quarters without pushing myself on her. I could still smell the alcohol on myself so I knew I must reek of it. My tongue stuck to the roof of my mouth and my cheeks clung to my teeth like the whole thing was filled with cotton. The pressure at my temples and the base of my skull was building and I knew I must look as awful as I smelled. She wasn't wrong in any of the things or feelings she expressed tonight. I had been a terrible King and had displayed no redeeming qualities as a husband over the last several months.

When we reached the door to her quarters, she turned at the threshold, crossed her arms, and her look dared me to even try and come in. I had at least caught onto that much this evening. King of Persia or not, if I tried to force myself on her this evening, I would be leaving her room less than what I entered with. I'm not sure of what she would take, but I would pay. Of that I was sure.

"Goodnight Esther, I will not disturb you any further this evening. To-morrow, you will find the man who much more resembles the one you married. When you are sure he has returned, please give him a chance to apologize, and redeem himself."

Her arms never uncrossed, her face never softened. What have I done?

Chapter 17

WHAT HAPPENS IN ROME ...

\<Xerxes\>

The caravan is ready, the goods for trade are all packed appropriately, and maps for land negotiations are loaded. The Romans are shifty and I would not put it past them to use falsified maps to cheat me out of land. I have tried to think of everything so I am fully prepared for negotiations.

Esther and her staff have arrived and mounted their horses. They all expressed their preferences to ride horseback or camels, at least for a while. We have a small cart able to carry six people following the caravan and if they should prefer to rest, they can switch over to it.

The weather is good, a little windy but not horrible. Esther and all of her ladies are in lightweight dresses that Esther has modified into pants with really flowing legs so they can ride astride, but you can't tell they are not dresses. When I try to compliment her on them, she thanks me with the same fervor she would a stranger.

They have covered their heads and faces from the harshness of the blowing sand and heat of the sun. The only thing I can see of her are her eyes. Eyes which used to look at me with love, but now look through me as though we have never formally met. The old me is irritated with her. The one who loves her knows better. I've been a jerk and I've wounded her. I can't expect her to just snap out of it.

Stopping about mid-day, I reach over to take Stormy and water him for her. She pulls his reins back and says she can do it.

"I'm just trying to lessen your load Esther, let me make things easier for you," holding my hand out.

"It is fine, I have grown quite used to doing everything by myself," she bites back with a twang of insult.

Something in me snaps. I know I shouldn't. I am pulling at myself the whole time to stop, but something in me says she is going to at least meet me on equal ground right now or we will begin a battle the likes of which no one has ever seen before. Dust swirls up as I stomp over to her, grabbing her by the forearms bending them down to her waist. I then pick her up and throw her over my shoulder, giving her a good smack on the backside.

"Listen to me, My Queen," I shout. "You are not the only one who lost a child. I did too. I handled it in the worst possible way, but I have finally pulled my head out of my aaaa... rear end, and you are going to listen to me!" Stomping forty paces away from everyone else, as they stare at us with their mouths wide open, I pull her off of my shoulders to find she is *spitting* mad.

"No, quiet. You are going to hear me out. When we got married I told you I had never loved anyone before. When you passed out, I found out I had a child and the craziest thing happened. I loved them. I *really loved* them. Twenty minutes later they were gone. But worse than that, before they were gone, I looked down, and saw all this blood coming from you. You were pale, and weak, and would not wake up. I could have lost you. I barely find out I am a Dad and I lose them too. I would rather die a thousand times over in battle than to feel what I felt that day. I do not know how to help a woman heal from a broken heart. I know how to train a warrior. The thought of holding you while you cried terrified me. So like a coward, I took off with Haman every night. And every night I felt guilty. I have never been a coward in any way before. So every night I drank more.

At first, I yelled at him and told him to send the girls away. But the more I drank, the more I stopped thinking. The harder he teased me for not being a man anymore and how you must be holding my ... *ahem my ... man parts in your dresser in your room, I decided to prove him wrong and I took them to bed. None of them were fulfilling. All of them made me drink more because I knew I should be in our rooms holding you. Helping you heal. You can be angry at me. But you will stop acting like I didn't love you and I never thought about you. I am as sorry as a man can be. I know forgiveness will take a while, but I am willing to work for every inch of ... *oof"

The sand created a puff I wasn't ready for when she knocked me over. It got in my mouth and I started coughing, but I held onto her for dear life. She shouldn't have been able to knock me over with her tiny miraculous body, but she did.

"Shut up you big oaf, just hold me," she sobs. And I did. For as long as she wanted. I did not care we were losing valuable travel time. The Romans could wait. I pulled off her head covering and buried my nose in her hair. Gods how had I survived for six months without the intoxicating smell of her hair. The pulling of my chest muscles burned slightly, and I wasn't the least bit ashamed my tears mixed with hers at our reunion. For the first time in a long time I finally felt like a man again.

"Alright, much more needs to be discussed. I am relieved to know all of the things you said. But we have an entire caravan waiting on us. We will have serious talks later. I will ask you for them. Please make time to listen when I do. But we have responsibilities," wiping her face and kissing me briefly, she commands, "Let's go."

With that, she wiped off her dress and left me sitting there, staring at her in more confusion than I started with. But, she was talking to me, and she kissed me. It was a good enough start for me. So I followed her and got the caravan back on the road.

***

\<Tereh\>

With the King and Queen being at odds with one another these last several months, Genet cooled our relationship as well. She didn't want to flaunt happiness in the Queen's face when she was so miserable. Plus, watching King Xerxes bring so much misery upon her friend, she began to view me with a suspicious eye as well. As if all men would be guilty of the same offenses. The more upset she got at him, the more I suffered. I was very relieved when they had a moment of understanding, even if the King slapped her on the backside like a child and carried her off into the bushes. I was sure it was going to cause a war as fierce as any of the ages to break out, and somehow Genet would hold me as accountable as Xerxes. But it must have been a big enough shock that everyone's walls crumbled. At least enough to call a truce and start over.

Since then Genet and I have been drawing closer and closer each day as well. We have stopped for the evening, and the camp is almost set up. Even though I am nervous, I plan to approach King Xerxes and seek his blessing to ask Genet to marry me.

Before approaching his tent, I stop to wash my face as best I could in our conditions, and call out, "My King, may I have a moment?"

"Tereh?" The King answers.

"Yes Your Majesty."

"Then enter."

The rough canvas flap brings some reality to my anxious mind and hands as I lifted it to enter. My breathing is a little heavier than normal just out of anxiousness. This is the biggest moment of my life in a very long time. I am glad to see Queen Esther is here as well. I can take care of everything with just one conversation.

"Your Majesties, everything is in order for the camp. A few last minute things getting finished, and the cooks should have the evening meal ready within a few minutes," I blurt nervously.

Grinning, King Xerxes says, "Thank you for your report Tereh, but I doubt that's what has you sweating, and breathing like you are in battle. Is there something else you would like to say?"

I try to swallow, but there is not one drop of moisture in my mouth, or my throat. I wonder if I will even be able to make a noise. The Queen smiles, and approaches me with an outstretched hand offering water, "Ignore him, he enjoys his teasing far too much."

"Yes My Queen, I come today Sir to inquire about asking for Lady Genet's hand in marriage," choking and stumbling over my words. It would have been nice if I could have sounded like a man and not a teenager asking for money.

"Well, Well I ...."

"He has no say in the matter actually, so I will put you out of your misery Tereh," Queen Esther says, placing her hand on Xerxe's arm. "Do you love her? You do not have my blessing if you cannot honestly say you are head over heels, crazy in love with her."

The relief in my body causes my muscles to relax, and a smile to jump across the entirety of my face, "Yes, I can honestly say I am in love with her. Before King Xerxes announced you as Queen, I was a tangled bundle of nerves, scared her name would be called for her private evening with him, and I would lose her forever."

Snorting his disbelief, Xerxes interjects, "Genet? No, she doesn't like me. Plus, she scares me a little."

"Ya, that's one of the things I find really attractive about her. I mean, if I decided to just wrestle her one night, it does not automatically mean I would win. That excites me. Her strength and determination to win," my admission makes me turn as red as a little girl.

"Okay then what kind of bride price are you bringing," King Xerxes turns the topic serious.

Blowing out a big puff of air, I say, "Well I have saved as much as I can from my guard salary ..."

"And you will use it to start your life as a married couple. Women are not possessions. They cannot be bought and sold like oxen. Your bride price is to love her and serve her. For if you do, she will reciprocate. Women are responders. If you love her properly, she will love and serve you as well," The Queen says, taking me by the shoulders. "If you do not, just remember she has a really powerful best friend, and you may ... no you will definitely regret life if you don't live up to your promises to me today."

"Yes Queen Esther, I understand. But you do not have to worry. She is my love and my heart. Thank you so much. Don't spoil the surprise. I am waiting for the perfect time okay?"

"Do not take forever, I am terrible at keeping secrets from my best friends," Queen Esther warns.

"Tereh," The King calls after me.

Spinning to give him my full attention, he gestures to a chest full of gold, "All my money is on Genet in said wrestling match."

My ears travel almost to the crown of my head when I break out into the biggest smile I've had in weeks. I might just have to try it one day. Nodding to him, I rush out to plan our moment.

***

<Xerxes>

The rest of the trip to Rome has been exactly what we needed. In fact the last two nights before we arrive, Esther agrees to come and sleep in my tent instead of staying with her ladies. To have her in my arms again and hear the little noises she makes as she sleeps is heartbreaking and healing all at the same time. On the second night, she reaches for me and we make love.

Haman's voice in my head was saying 'It is about time. Don't let a wretched woman use emotions over a baby as a way to control you Xerxes. Do not let her get away with this.'

But the man who loves her and knows it is an honor to love a woman properly says, 'Love her better Xerxes, it is the biggest crown of glory a man can achieve, to love his woman well.' This time I will listen to the voice within.

As we are pulling through the front gates of the Roman Empire, Consul Vopiscus Julius Iullus and his wife Priscilla are waiting at the gates to greet us. "Welcome King Xerxes and Queen Esther of Persia! My Honored Wife Priscilla and I are honored you have traveled all this way to be our guests. Please come, William here will show your men where to store your carts and animals, and John will show you where to freshen up. We will meet you in the Great Hall in one hour?" Julius gives the formal greetings and instructions.

"Thank you for the warm welcome Julius, that sounds perfect. See you in an hour," I inform him, and give a nod to my company to follow his orders.

As we near the sleeping quarters, they show me where mine are located first. I pull Esther to me and give her a deep kiss before allowing her to be ushered to the ladies quarters to freshen up. I should have pulled her into my room, but I know what the Romans expect and I should probably play along for dignitary sake. I don't know, maybe I will just move her in here later.

***

"Great, you are all here. It is almost time for the main event being held in your honor. We are fighting our top Gladiators in the ring tonight! The house is packed, and we have arranged a personal one-on-one meet and greet with them before the event. If you will follow me, we should get going," Julius takes off and I fall in beside him. Esther and Priscilla are right behind us introducing themselves and getting to know one another.

When we get to the balcony overlooking the fighting ring, there is table after table filled with some of the most exotic and delicious food I have ever seen. As soon as I walk in, I am handed a plate by a beautiful woman, with barely anything on. She takes her hands and places them on my shoulders. Then when she asks me what I would like to drink, she rubs them down my chest and stomach. This is not unusual for political trips with the intent to negotiate and secure allies. Not once did I give any thought to these activities with Vashti, but love changes a lot of things. Taking her hands I politely remove them and tell her I would like to just start with water for now. It was a long and dusty trip.

Julius introduces me to a man almost as tall as myself, and a bit more muscular. His name is Simon and he is one of the gladiators who will be competing this evening. He hails from the Northern regions above Rome and is fair skinned with brown eyes. He looks strong, but I can tell he is a new fighter by the lack of scars on his body.

The next to be introduced is Lucius. Built as solid as the pillars on the colosseum, Lucius appears to thrive on the thrill of the event. Plenty of scars show he's been here a time or two. Julius boasts that Lucius has been offered his freedom once already, but when he was handed the rudis, he threw it back and claimed being a gladiator was an honor. With brown skin, perfect teeth, and the lightest green eyes one doesn't normally see, this gladiator was also a favorite with the ladies. Julius slapped me on the back and chuckled saying Lucius had even stolen a woman or two right out of his own bed. But he didn't mind because Lucius always made him fistfuls of money.

The last to appear was Titus. He was from the Sudan desert in northeast Africa. He was sold to a Roman officer by the Sudanese soldier who owned him. He was black as night with yellow eyes. More like hazel. Sufficient scarring to make me think he had survived a round or two. He was pleasant but not as talkative as Lucius. Tonight's events should be interesting.

"Will they be fighting one another?" I ask.

Julius' eyes light up and he says, "Oh, noooo, we will be releasing several dangerous beasts from different regions of the world who will all stalk them as prey. They can work together or alone. But we wanted to give them the chance to survive so they could pleasure Queen Esther throughout the night. You know, keeping her busy so you can have your fun with the finest delicacies Rome can offer you," he is pointing out the maiden servants he plans to send to my quarters. With raised eyebrows, he points at Esther, "Looks like she will be more than willing."

Turning my head in the direction he gestured, I see all three gladiators gathered 'round Esther. I can see she is flushed. Her arms, her chest, and neck, leading to a perfectly pink face. I've seen her flushed like that and I know what causes it. I am not liking this at all. She is so naive to the ways of the world and the things other countries will throw upon her to get the upper hand. She is in way over her head.

"Julius, you are such a low life," I grumble, heading over to save my wife, while hearing his laughter behind me.

"Do you know your hair is the same color as this rare delicacy called chocolate? Here try it," Lucius says as he is reaching to place the chocolate inside her mouth. This is way too intimate of a moment for my liking.

"Yes, My Love, try some I want to see what you think," I encourage her, but my eye contact is a challenge to Lucius, who merely smiles before turning back to my wife and continuing to feed her.

Taking the bite, Esther heads my way savoring this new delicacy. Still flushed, she links her arm through mine. "Lucius, it is *delicious*," she groans, licking her lips. She is unknowingly making this whole thing worse. She doesn't understand how alluring she is. Lucius licks his own lips with a gaze I definitely recognize.

"When I survive this event tonight, I shall bring some to you so you can enjoy them all night long," giving her a smile, he bows and turns to exit.

"All of the gladiators are yours for the evening to ... um ..." Priscilla hesitates looking at me "meet any need you may have."

"Although it is a very generous offer, Queen Esther will not have any needs this evening as she will be with me, in my quarters. Having her needs met. All night long. Do I need to be any clearer?" I question the crowd on the balcony. Esther buries her face in my chest out of embarrassment, while I cover her in a hug with both of my massive arms.

"King Xerxes, do you mean to tell me you will be snubbing your nose at all of the gifts we have so carefully chosen and prepared for you and your bride on this trip?" Julius narrows his eyes at me.

Shrugging my shoulders, I look at him and say, "Well Julius, it isn't meant as an insult. You see, when we wed, we just happened to fall into the once in a lifetime marriage which also includes true friendship. Several months ago, we lost a baby, Persia's first heir. The healer just informed us My Queen is finally healed, and my best friend is able to try again. Not only that, but the timing is perfect right now. So, I want to be the one to hold her, talk to her, and to try again. No insult intended," I offer smiling.

"Well that certainly does clear things up! My apologies for losing your baby, Priscilla and I have gone through the same loss twice. Thank the gods we have little Correandus. I will send my finest vat of wine and a tray of chocolate to commemorate your healing Queen Esther," Julius offers.

"Ya, but they are really good at ... meeting your needs ... especially if your husband is not concerned about being your friend. If you know what I mean," Priscilla leans over and whispers in Esther's ear. Esther takes her hand, looking into Priscilla's eyes and they both break out in laughter.

***

\<Esther\>

Well, *that* was uncomfortable all the way around. I have to admit, I can kind of see how temptation could rise up and pull at a person, even when they are married and in love with their spouse. Because my gosh, those gladiators were certainly physical masterpieces of creation when it comes to manliness. Temptation is something I had never been faced with before. I am glad Xerxes stepped in and put a stop to everything. May God forgive me, I would like to believe I would have said no, but ... Lucius was very bold and persistent, and I might have been tempted.

The gladiator matches were fascinating. The blood didn't bother me. When the trumpets sounded, the three gladiators were in the ring. Several doors opened and the first beasts to be released were hyenas. They circled the men and hunted them as prey, and yet the gladiators took most of them out with ease.

On the next trumpet, the doors opened and many different bears came out. The white one I am told was a polar bear, and he was out to kill. Then a great big brown bear, called a grizzly, was the next fiercest. Simon suffered a deep injury to his arm, but Lucius saved his life. In doing so, he looked up to me and blew a kiss. Once again I blushed deep red. Xerxes laughs and kisses me on the forehead. I am glad we have made up. This certainly could have been something that would have ended our marriage altogether had the 'Gladiator Factor' come into play while we were still at odds. Thank God we cleared things on the way up to Rome.

The winners of the night were Lucius and Titus. Simon eventually was taken out by a lion - may God rest his soul. Lucius survived by gutting a smaller black bear quickly and using its hide to disguise himself and sneak up on the polar bear for a kill shot. Then while Lucius distracted the lion, Titus leaped across the arena with amazing skill and slit the lion's throat, killing the last standing predator. I felt bad for the animals losing their lives, but I understood its popularity. To see the physique of the male body on display, fighting for their lives, using strength, skill and wisdom all at once was exhilarating.

Chapter 18

THE WEARY HOMECOMING

\<Sunita\>

Finally, after the loss of the baby, things are beginning to ease back into some sense of normalcy. The King had been a Royal insensitive jerk for months and I thought we might lose *our* Esther forever. The day he hauled her over his shoulder and smacked her on her backside before carrying her away from the caravan I thought we may end up turning around and staying at the palace while the King and his guards continued on to Rome alone. But when they returned, Esther seemed to have thawed out a few layers and the more we traveled, the more he checked on her and paid attention to her. She responded with kindness finally, and one day ... They rode side-by-side to have actual honest conversations.

To be honest, if Haman just stayed out of the way ... the King and Queen have the kind of friendship that was unheard of in royal marriages and they would have worked it out just fine. Friendship can be rare in common-wealth marriages as well. For the most part, it didn't matter your status, women were sold off every time for money. Most of the time we didn't even get to meet our husbands before he showed up, expected a grand reception complete with a feast, and then carted us off to his home. So ya, friendships were rare.

Queen Esther, in effect, owns us by making us her Ladies-in-Waiting. Of course she rolls her eyes at the description and adamantly denies any such thing. She says we are able to marry whomever we want to marry. At first the news delighted me. But now I have to admit, I have no idea how to go about a life and courtship in this manner. A woman cannot just walk up to a single man and say *'I like you, I choose you as a husband, now go talk to Queen Esther about a wedding date.'* The men would first laugh, and then say no way do they want a wife who is so bold. I have to admit, my freedom has left me at a loss. After getting the freedom I wanted, I realized it might not fit very well within the world I'm forced to live.

***

<Esther>

Returning home in the caravan seems to be taking longer than our trip there. I know it is just because I want my bed and my comforts again but this trip is a killer. Today, I have asked my staff to ride in the canopy covered cart with me so we can reconnect and catch up. Sunita seems down, for some reason, and Mary has been working so hard we haven't had any times where we are together just for the fun of being together again.

"So tell me what you all thought of Rome?" Mary instantly pulls out her books and wants to read off documented information. I reach over and put my hand on hers. "No Mary, I want to talk to you. Not my head of organization. What did Mary, my friend, think? It has been too long since we were all just Mary, Genet, Sunita, and Esther. Maybe I should stop the cart and dig out purple, white, and blue dresses for us to wear?"

The thought of assigned dresses lightens the mood a little bit, making everyone smile. Mary looks up at me and says, "My gosh Esther, it all seems like it was years and years ago. Doesn't it?"

Genet breaks in, "It really does, but it also seems like yesterday. Rome was interesting and exciting all at the same time. The Gladiator exhibition was fascinating. I wonder how many times a man can fight before he falls. They have to get really creative at killing strategies just to stay alive in the ring."

"I was not watching the beasts or the strategies or anything else, Genet did you even see the men? I have never seen as fine of men as those gladiators in all my life!" Fanning herself Mary is now blushing and nervously giggling. All of her freckles are standing out under the tapestry of red, flushed skin underneath and she is hiding behind her fan. Her hair is flying out around her face, because her wrist is slinging the fan back and forth furiously. "The one with green eyes. Mmmmm I've never seen eyes that color before and gracious sakes. His brown skin, those green eyes and perfect white teeth. Rrrrawwrrr."

"What just happened here? Our little blonde haired, shy virgin just turned into a harem girl in one moment before our very eyes. Look at the flush on her body, young lady you need to pray, or be dropped off at a temple or something," Genet is pursing her lips in mock horror, which causes Mary to flush an even deeper shade of red I did not think was possible. Laughter is floating around, but Mary is serious.

"Are you jealous Genet? Does Tereh give you these feelings?" Mary tries to get even and embarrass her too.

Genet's cheeks fall and her eyes widen in surprise, but all Genet will say is "Hush child, don't be asking such personal questions."

"Speaking of you Genet, congratulations are in order! The sunset, the Roman Colosseum, and Tereh asking you to marry him. It was beautiful!" Sunita offers.

"That man can make any moment all mushy," she cuts her eyes at us even though she can't hide the smile playing on her lips. "I am happy. He is very good to me and doesn't expect me to be all frilly. It is nice to be loved for who I am."

"I would settle for being loved," Sunita trails off. "I mean being loved at all in our world is pretty rare."

"You've seemed a little off lately Sunita, is this weighing you down?"

"Esther, I don't know. I mean yes and no. Since I was a little girl, I wanted to be able to have a say in who I marry. Now I have that say, and it makes me so different, I fear men are hesitant to approach me. It's either that or I have a giant wart on my nose I am unable to see or something."

Snorting a slight chuckle I put my hand on her lap, "I won't spoil the surprise, but I just gave permission for two men to begin courting you. Old habits die hard. I did inform them though. I have no say so in who wins, you alone are the keeper of your heart and bride prices are not a factor here. You are not to be bought with a price. Mary, had someone get our blessing for her hand as well."

Gasping out loud, Mary's hands flew to her chest. "I've been dying to tell you!"

"It seems you had a little bit of a courtship you hid from all of us while we were in Rome?"

The squeal that peeled out of such a tiny woman's body could have been heard for miles. The guard who had been riding past our cart got bucked off his horse, and Xerxes raced over demanding to know what was wrong.

"Nothing is wrong husband, we are just sharing some exciting news with one another." I said smiling.

He is not impressed, and looks back and forth at us for a minute. When he shakes his head and rides away, Genet and Sunita resume staring at Mary and I. Mary is trying to stretch out the anticipation, and I'm smiling because I'm the only one who knows the secret.

"Who is going to spill it? What's going on?" Genet demands.

"So, after the gladiator event, the ... um ... gladiators were supposed to 'service' Queen Esther all night long by order of Julius. King Xerxes, of course, didn't like the idea at all and moved her into his bed chambers. When I was heading back to my room that night after helping her move, they were waiting in the hallway. They were instructed to be nearby to fulfill the order of Julius in case there was a change of mind," wringing her hands, Mary looks up at our group trying to explain.

"And.....," Sunita demands with a raised eyebrow, imagining all the different ways this could be going.

"Well, Lucius stopped me and struck up a conversation. We talked the entire night. And we met up several other times during our stay. I just thought it was a sweet encounter and it would die off when we left. But that man .... I cannot stop thinking about him. He gave me this ring as a reminder he loves me... in front of a priest ... when we secretly wed."

"As soon as he wins his freedom, his plans are to relocate here in Persia." I assure everyone. "Now we should all pray for his successful wins in each fight. He needs two more," sighing, I reach over and squeeze Mary's hand. "He will be with us in no time."

"Girl you move so fast!" Sunita cuts her eyes over at Mary. "How do you know he don't refuse to wash his armpits every day or something gross?"

"I am not worried about his armpits," Mary's response turns her face so red again, I'm afraid we could use her as a light in the darkness if we needed to. My heart swoons, watching my friends find love.

"Hold up. They were supposed to service you? What exactly does that mean?" Genet inquires with some sass.

"Exactly what it sounds like, and Xerxes saved me from that awkward situation. Yahweh expects better of me. Besides – it is Mary's husband, or was going to be … umm these people and their pagan gods. I feel bad for Lucius still having to do as they order!" I say

"We weren't married then, but it would have been incredibly awkward now if it would have happened. I am crazy about him though. I cannot wait until he makes it to Susa!" Mary smiles brightly.

Sunita finally stops teasing and hugs Mary, "Okay then, I'm happy for you."

"Let's do the boring stuff now and go over the sales from the market and what the dignitaries thought of the goods from the women of Persia," I say.

***

\<Haman\>

The King's entourage should be back any day now. I do not relish the thought of giving up this power. I should be King of All Persia. I have spent many days making Janeth pleasure me. Xerxes choosing Esther when he did almost caused me to lose her. She was still a virgin and had not completed her night with him yet. Technically she was supposed to be returned home to her family. Fortunately, thanks to quick thinking on my part, I came up with a title for her to have bestowed upon her, requiring her to live within the palace. Kavan was not happy his daughter was not being returned, but knew the consequences of going against the crown. At the pleading of Janeth assuring him she would be okay, he gave in and went home. Little did she know, her 'title' was my favored consort from within my own personal harem. She was a slow learner for the pleasures of my taste but she would learn. She bruises too easily though, I must control myself so no one begins to ask questions.

Mordecai has begun to reside in every corner of my mind. My revenge and rage for him grows larger within me each passing day. I cannot pass his stall without fantasizing about plucking his beard out one scraggly little hair at a time. Or maybe by the handfuls because he would shed more blood that way. When he has the audacity to look me directly in the eye, I have the fiercest urge to stab him there and see the juices squirt from each eyeball. One of these days, I will kill him. And then I will be honored for it. Just wait and see ...

***

\<Xerxes\>

We will be home within the day. I am weary, thirsty, and mentally exhausted from not only the trip, but planning my attack on Rome. After being there, I know my army can take them. We could add Rome to our lands and move our ruling palace closer to the middle of all the lands.

Their sewer systems are their weakness. They are efficient, and state of the art, but they are not monitored. Tereh and a few guards took a couple shifts scouting the lengths of the tunnels and they aren't closed off anywhere from the distance of the bath houses to the outlets. It will be where we send the first attack through.

When we have conquered, and are rebuilding a new palace, I will build a statue in Esther's and my honor as the ruling couple. I am so relieved we have worked things out. Sometimes, discussing things with her is more beneficial than with Haman. No one would suspect she is my confidant. If Haman doesn't know anything, and isn't bragging about upcoming battles then I will be able to hold my plans until it is time to prepare the army and move out. He will be furious, but too many times he has ruined things with his big mouth.

As suspected, when we return to the palace, he has some urgent drama he claims must be dealt with immediately. It is always something with him. He claims there is a race of people within our lands whose customs are different from those of all other people and who do not obey my laws.

"It is not in your best interest to tolerate these people any longer King Xerxes, with every year they grow bolder and more audacious," Haman stokes the fire with his words. I am too weary to really want to listen, but I would not be a good leader if I didn't give this some sort of consideration.

"What laws do they have disagreement with Haman? What are they protesting?" I ask.

"My King, what does it matter? Whether they are not deferring to your chariots in the street, or not paying their taxes, if they are breaking one law they are breaking them all. It is their hearts that are wicked. The reason this is so problematic is it's an entire race of people," Haman urges. "If it pleases you my King, let a decree be issued to destroy them, and I will put ten thousand talents of silver into the royal treasury for the men who carry out this business. I have spent many a day gathering evidence against this race of people."

"How many are there in this certain race of people we are talking about Haman? Can we not require they all travel to the palace for me to address them, negotiate, and issue a final warning? I do not like the thought of wiping out an entire race at once."

"Is this the same King Xerxes who is ruthless in defending his power? His rule, and authority? Are you asking me if we could just talk to an entire race of people, and ask them to pretty please, honor the laws of the land when they blatantly disregard them now? I cannot believe my ears. You are losing your bite Xerxes." He sneers at me.

Not even rising from my seat, I grab his cloak and pull down hard enough his nose meets the table with sufficient force to break. "You think too highly of yourself. You think every idea you propose must be enacted or I am a fool. Haman, there are a lot of times *you* are the fool. This is my country after all. I can ask every question possible under the sun before I am comfortable making a decision and your opinion of that does not matter. We have been having problems with this since before Vashti was beheaded. Watch yourself before you step into her shoes. I do not have the patience to give you very many more chances," I push him up to look at me while still holding onto his cloak and see blood pouring down to the floor between his feet. "Tell me you understand Haman."

"I understand," he chokes out spitting blood from within his mouth as well.

"Good, now while I do agree with you I cannot have an entire race of people refusing to obey the laws of Persia. I have too many other things going on right now to deal with it. Keep your money. Take my ring, issue a decree dealing with this and then bring it back to me. Do it right Haman, or it's your head, understand?"

"I understand," he says, grabbing my signet ring. His eyes light up like I just gave him a birthday present and he leaves my office. There may have to be something done to replace him with Tereh in the very near future. For now, I am heading to bed to rest my weary body and hold my beautiful wife.

***

<Esther>

We are finally home. I am so looking forward to sleeping in my bed tonight. Laying down and snuggling with Shujae I am surprised when he darts down to my belly and puts his nose there. He looks up at me and then nose down again. Casually sauntering back up to my chest, he places a paw on my cheek and licks me, then cuddles into my neck.

Immediately, tears spring to my eyes, as I already know. This is just perfect confirmation. The only other time he ever did this was when I was expecting the baby I miscarried. The first time Xerxes returned to my bed was about eight weeks ago heading to Rome. We had not been apart from each other every night after that. When we started our journey home, I had a few moments of queasiness but convinced myself it was just the traveling and reactions to new foods.

By the time the traveling trip back home was almost over, my breasts were tender and I was sore in my lower stomach during different times of the day. *'Oh Yahweh, please give this little one the strength your first gift did not have for some reason. Let this little one stay here on earth and bless us with its presence. Thank you for another try. Amen.'*

"Were you praying I would hurry up and get here Kitten? Look 'et there, I am an answered prayer!"

"Oh husband, you make me laugh. That's not what I was praying for but it is a really great side effect. I feel like I got a present just for being obedient to pray," using my fingers to motion him over to the bed, he undresses as he comes.

The whole bed shakes and I bounce a little off the mattress as Xerxes jumps and lands on all fours straddling my body. Laughing until I cannot catch my breath, the duck squawk makes an appearance and Xerxes has tears rolling out the corners of his eyes.

"I love times like this with you woman," he says perched up on his side, cradling his head in his hand.

"Me too, ... Xerxes. I have a confession," I say hesitantly.

"Ooh, girl talk," he mimics and spins upright sitting crisscross applesauce.

Rolling my eyes, I try to find the right words, or how to tell him so it won't freak him out, ... now he is scowling at me and I can tell he is getting worried.

"Stop that, no getting worried. We are going to be nice, normal, rational people. I … I think I am with child."

"What have I done? How could you let me do that Esther?" He grabs me by the shoulders, eyes are wide, and his voice is rising in panicky volume with every syllable.

"Well, I quite enjoyed it Xerxes, what do you mean, how could I let you do that?"

Smirking just a little, he squeezes my shoulders again and says, "Not *that*, but thank you, I quite enjoy that too. I just jumped on you and mauled you like a tiger? What if I hurt this child like the last one? What if…" I can see reality settling all over his face by the second. All of the fears, and all of the what-ifs are running through his mind un-checked.

"Where does this mid-wife live, I'll go get her right now to be sure you are okay," he stands to begin getting dressed again.

Patting the bed, I plead, "Please, come back to bed honey, put your arms around me. Everything's fine. We will have her secretly come over in the morning. I do not want to tell anyone until we are past the time where the pregnancy is most vulnerable."

"What makes you suspect you are pregnant?" He asks gently.

"Among other things, Shujae just went down to my stomach, smelled it, then looked at me. He did it twice. Then he came up to my face and put a paw on my cheek and licked me," I replied wistfully.

Xerxes lips were pursed together, first he puckered them out and then he bit them while looking at me. "You've gone daft."

"No," I said laughing. "He has only ever done it one other time. I swear! Plus the whole traveling time home, I felt a little nauseous at times, my breasts were swollen ..."

"I know, they looked great!"

"Ahh!" I gasped in protest.

"What, you even admitted it! I'm trying to compliment you and point out I *did* notice!" He smiled like he had just won an argument.

"Why are you so cute?"

"Ahh!" He gasped in protest this time, "Handsome, chiseled, a man above *all* men - remember? Not cute - that's for babies and children. Ahhh babies. Maybe you will have two!"

"Xerxes, I cannot possibly have two little versions of you running around, I would never survive."

Chuckling, he gave in, "Okay one at a time. Come, let us sleep. But until this baby is safe. Either myself or Tereh will be with you twenty-four hours a day."

A cold shiver raced down my body as I thought to myself ... *'At least he didn't say Haman.'*

Chapter 19

HAMAN'S MOVE

Decree of King Ahasuerus,

The King of Persia

127 provinces from India to Cush:

On this day, the thirteenth day of the month of Nisan,

the first month of the year:

The following decree is issued into law:

On the Thirteenth day of the Twelfth month of the month of Adar, all of the Jews - young and old, women and little children - are to be destroyed, killed and annihilated. On a single day, the thirteenth day of the twelfth month, the month of Adar, every man of Persia may participate in the removal, killing, and annihilating of the Jews and they may plunder the goods of the Jews as their spoils.

Issued by the authority of Haman, Second in Command to King Ahasuerus, and sealed with the King's signet ring,

So let it be written,

So let it be done.

***

\<Mary\>

"Good Morning Esther, we have to talk. Now!" Skidding into her room, I am already out of breath and ... ohhh my gosh the King is still in bed with her.

"Excuse me, King Xerxes, Queen Esther, I certainly didn't mean to interrupt," I say, while wringing my hands, and dancing from one foot to the other. "It's just, well, the Queen has things to attend to, *right away* this morning."

No one knows where the decree came from, or why. There doesn't seem to be any reason why an entire decree would be calling for the complete annihilation of all the Jewish people. I am certain if King Xerxes knew he had just sentenced his wife to death he would have not allowed Haman to issue such a decree. All the same, I need to get her up and out of bed to meet Mordecai as quickly as possible. He has torn his clothes and is wailing bitterly in the streets. We sent word to him early this morning. We expressed Esther would be distraught, and would not want him to be this dismayed.

We even sent him a change of clothes with Hathach who went out to him in the open square inquiring what was causing his distress. Mordecai tore down a copy of the edict and gave it to Hathach to bring to Esther. Holding it in my hands is scary, what has this world come to? The whole country is in a panic and I don't mean just the Jewish people. Nobody understands this.

"Mary," the King growls. "Do you always bust into your Queen's room demanding things so early in the morning?"

"No, Your Majesty, it's just, well … she is needed this morning," I reply, making faces in her direction so she will understand the urgency of today.

"Today, whoever needs her will be disappointed. She is not going anywhere. She will be with me the entire day. If not with me then with Tereh. There will be no arguing. Please go send Tereh to me so I may send him on an errand. Do not delay." Xerxes rolls over and pulls her closer.

I wave a copy of the decree in the air and slide it into her table drawer at the entrance of her room. Smiling and nodding her head in my direction. I know she will find it soon and figure out how to handle this. An entire race of people is to be hunted and killed in a single day. Evil has an appointment. And it occurs on the Thirteenth day of Adar.

\<Esther\>

"My love…"

"Don't you, my love, me," Xerxes growls. "I couldn't sleep at all last night worrying about you. We are getting you checked out before we move a muscle today, do you understand?"

"Okay, but honestly life goes on, we have to take each day by faith and just trust everything is going to be okay. I need to be able to live my life. I need to walk, work, and laugh with my friends. To ride Smoky …"

"Have you lost your mind? You are not riding that beast," he all but growls at me.

"What we are not doing is arguing, I am going to bathe while you send for the midwife. After she sees us we will discuss life afterward, but I will not be a prisoner in my own home Xerxes. Big, big emphasis on the 'will not' part."

"What if you slip ..."

"Stay right there!" Pointing at him, I dare him to move one step closer. This is over the line.

***

When I emerge from my bath, Xerxes, Tereh and the midwife Miriam are all waiting in my room. Crossing my arms and frowning, they all look at me with concern.

"Esther, what is wrong? I am just protecting you and the baby," he says, crossing the room, gently rubbing my forearms.

"Xerxes, what happened with the last baby... it is not something you can protect me from. Pregnancies end in miscarriage, it happens all of the time. They just do. You cannot control what is happening inside my body. Maybe the baby had something wrong with it that made her not strong enough to survive. There could be so many reasons."

"It is true my Queen, especially with you passing out repeatedly during that pregnancy. But I cannot express strongly enough how dangerous it is for the mother to be under stress during these early months as well," Miriam cuts into the conversation trying to diffuse our building argument.

"How often were you passing out before?" His brows are furrowed at this news.

"It had happened maybe five or six times, but every time I checked her, all of her vitals were normal, and her skin tone was normal, there was no swelling. There were no other factors than her just tipping over for a quick nap occasionally," Miriam smiles at me.

"Five or six times, and you didn't tell me?" I could tell he was hurt, but I didn't know what to say other than the truth.

"I didn't feel right Xerxes. The whole pregnancy I felt weak and dizzy. I don't think anything could have been done to save that baby. This time I haven't passed out once. I have felt nauseous several times, but I have not thrown up, and I feel much stronger than I did before," I assure him. "I didn't want to cause you undue worry until I could figure out if everything was okay and if that baby was going to make it past the first several months. This time I told you right away because I feel stronger."

Seeing his shoulders sag in relief made me want to comfort him. He really must have suffered so much more than his words could explain to me.

"Not to mention on the day you lost the baby there was incredible stress with being attacked, fighting for your life, and then the whole inquiry by The Council who were adamant about punishing you no matter what was proven," Tereh spoke up from the corner of the room.

At the mention of The Council, Xerxes grows dark. His fists clench and muscles jump from his fists to his jaws. Stepping forward, I take his cheek in my right hand and pull him down to look at me.

"Don't waste anger on things of the past you cannot change. Look forward to better things that will come."

"Shall we get her laid down and get her checked?" Miriam offers.

***

Judging by the dates of my last cycle, and the size of my womb, Miriam figures I probably conceived on the very first night in the tent on the way to Rome when Xerxes and I finally made up. What a beautiful symbol of reconciliation.

Xerxes agreed to leave me in the protection of Tereh's abilities, but warned him to keep me free from stress and not let anyone but the ladies-in-waiting approach me. Tereh feels the weight of this responsibility, it is written all over his face. As soon as Xerxes leaves, I go to the table at the entryway and pull out the piece of paper Mary had left for me.

Reading the decree made me dizzy, I certainly cannot pass out today. Xerxes would probably go so far as to lock me up in a cage until I delivered if it were to happen. Feeling sweat beads appear on my forehead, I grasp the table to try and steady myself. The noise alerted Tereh from where he was resting, and in a second he was by my side. Knowing Xerxes was only about fifteen paces away from my room, Tereh was going to yell for him to come back. I could tell when he leaned over to peek his head out into the hallway. As he takes in a very deep breath, I place a hand on his mouth and very weakly ask, "Tereh, where do your loyalties lie?"

"What?" He is shocked, and distracted from calling Xerxes back into the room thank goodness.

"You are assigned to me as my head guard. My closest protector. If I were to tell you something, do your loyalties lie with me, or would you tell my secret to my husband?"

I know I am putting him on the spot and I feel terrible for it, but there is only one way I am allowing him to help me here and that is if he pledges his loyalties to me. This situation cannot be handled with a knee-jerk reaction. He cannot run to Xerxes and simply tell him what has happened, or it puts me in danger.

Xerxes would fight with Haman, reverse the decree, and then Haman's rage would grow. By then I would be exposed. His revenge would extend to me, and I now have a child to protect. I will never let that man have any opportunity to harm my child, not even if I have to draw the dagger across his throat myself.

"I have pledged to protect your life with my own. I will die for my King and my country as well. As long as you are my charge you come first, by decree from the King," he says while giving me the warrior's salute.

I hand him the decree. After reading it, he looks up at me in confusion. He tells me he's never seen it before and none of it makes sense. There has been no uprisings from the Jews, no organized skirmishes or wars against the crown. Why would Haman have issued this decree and why would he have had the King's signet ring?

"All really good questions Tereh, before I call in my staff there is something you should know. I am charging you with secrecy and have made the decision to tell you so Genet will not have to keep secrets from you. But the fate of the entire Jewish race may lie in your hands if you do not follow my lead and play this right," I explain.

"My Queen?"

"My Papi is Mordecai." It's all I offer and sit back, watching his face as all of the pieces fall together.

"By the gods," he stammers.

"God, there is but one God Tereh and I would love to tell you about him someday if you agree," I offer. "But now you understand. Haman has just issued a decree for my death, as well as the next heir of Persia who is in my womb. Today I need to talk to my Papi, my staff, and plans need to be made."

"But Queen Esther, you are to avoid stress," he says with round innocent eyes. "We should tell the King."

"If you do, I will surely die. Xerxes has given Haman a very wide road to roam. At every turn, Haman is merely reprimanded but left to scatter his chaos again. I must find a way to tell Xerxes and not allow Haman to have an escape, nor an excuse that can work. Please follow my lead on this. I am seeking Yahweh first, then I will move," pleading with him, he sees now all of the pieces to the puzzle.

"Could you, carrying your son or daughter, just sit back and hope no one ever finds out your heritage and watch while Haman slaughters your little brothers, your Papi, your Papi's wife, who is also your childhood best friend. Could you Tereh?"

"No, but, oh I am already tarred and feathered six different ways here aren't I?" Smacking himself in the forehead, he spins in a circle.

"I promise to lay down in my bed so no harm will come to me, please go get my ladies so we can discuss this and find a way for me to talk to my Papi," I tell him as I am already crawling back under my blankets.

***

\<Genet\>

It is unusual for Tereh to gather us in Esther's room, but I am assuming we will find out soon enough about what all is going on. Mary is as jumpy as the ants in the chicken yard. She knows something we don't and I don't like it. I can already tell it is bad news. Sunita has barely been up long enough to have her coffee drink and a bite of eggs so I am pretty sure she does not know anything. Tereh is avoiding my gaze so he is not sitting in my good graces right now. I wonder if there will ever be a time of peace and relaxation around this palace where we can just enjoy being alive. This constant tension is too much. Entering her room, Esther is still in bed? Is she sick or something?

"See? Still in bed just like I promised," she smiles up at Tereh.

See everything is unusual, but if there is anyone on this earth I trust with my man it is Esther. Telling myself to give it time, I find myself a comfortable cushion and wait for whatever she wants to share with us.

"I have a lot of big news to share with you this morning," Esther says. At the same time, Mary drops her chin, looking at the ground like someone just ate her last piece of dessert. "This morning, Miriam confirmed for me I am with child again! Another baby is on its way!"

Mary came alive. Squealing and clapping her hands, while tears stream down her face, she rushes to Esther's bed and bounds up onto it hugging her like the heir was already sleeping in a bassinet beside her bed with a crown on. Mary comes with so many emotions, I don't know how she contains them all.

"Congratulations my friend, there is no happier news," I say smiling at her.

Raising her coffee cup, Sunita simply says "Congratulations!"

"Now for the other news," Esther says, and Mary goes quiet. "First you should know, before allowing Tereh in the room for this conversation, I asked him where his loyalties lie."

Cutting my eyes in his direction, I am hoping to God he answered correctly. I do not think I could go through with marrying him if he were to ever say he is not loyal to Esther. I didn't realize my face was giving so much away when Esther cuts through my thoughts.

"Easy there killer, his answer was the correct one Genet," she says laughing. "Although it warms my heart to see the depth of loyalty all over your face just now."

She hands me a piece of parchment paper with a decree written on it. With every word I read the more angry I get. On the last word, I look up and realize I am huffing through my nose like a runaway horse and saliva has pooled at the corners of my mouth.

"When do we kill Haman?" I simply ask.

"There is so much more to this than killing him. I wish it were that easy. We have months and months to figure this out, but step one is communicating with my Papi. Xerxes is so freaked out about this baby, he has declared for every minute of the day and night I have to be accompanied by either himself or Tereh. This makes everything tricky. Xerxes will want it to be him at night. But during the day, I can't send Tereh to the Gates to get Papi because if Xerxes comes in here and he is gone, Tereh will be punished.

"Then I will go," I say easily.

"I figured you would volunteer, but Tereh, how dangerous is it really?" Esther asks. The smile she gives me is one of those connecting moments where your souls briefly connect and the depth of your friendship sparks between the two of you. No words are needed. She knows I would give up my life for her, and I know how very much she loves and appreciates me. We are closer than sisters.

"Sometimes it is safe enough for children, sometimes you could die. It cannot be predicted. I can send one of my trusted guards who is also a close friend with her though. It will have to be secretive, and Genet, please don't take any unnecessary chances," he replies. Everyone can see the worry stitched all over his face. It is as if 'I love you' is stitched into one eyebrow, and 'Be careful' is stitched into the other. I prefer not to have public mushy moments so this is equally annoying as it is endearing, I am not Hebrew after all, I will be safe.

"Genet, pass the information the same way I do every time," Esther says, and I nod.

"What? You have been passing information on our walks through the Gates?" Tereh asks, a little surprised.

"You really should employ us as spies. We are just that good Tereh," she laughs. I turn my gaze to him smirking. He blows air out in a half chuckle and shakes his head as he drops his chin to his chest. It makes me proud we were getting things past such a respected, well-trained guard as my man.

***

\<Esther\>

Xerxes met me and we ate lunch together for an hour or so. He was working all morning on physical training and keeping the guards' fighting skills up. He had picked up a thing or two from the Gladiator Event in Rome and used the maneuvers on the guards to make them sharpen their skills for attacks from a different direction. It made them think through their responses from an alternate angle and was very beneficial.

I reminded him of the combination moves the gladiators used together when there were only two left. How they clasped hands and pulled each other in mid-air switching spots. It left the beasts bewildered and off task for a split second. But that was long enough for them to get in a devastating blow, bringing them the upper hand. His eyes lit up like the sun and then he sank again because Tereh was the only other guard with us on the trip he thought could perform the skills with him in a mock battle. This was perfect. If I could get him to use Tereh, I could easily get in a visit with my Papi unnoticed.

"I am the worst father and husband on earth. It hasn't even been one full day and I am already considering removing your protection for a short time," he said, beating himself up.

"Or maybe you've had time to think about it and you realize it is just a little bit over the top," I say leaning in to kiss him on the lips. "The ladies and I were planning on going to visit Hegai, and spread our things out in the old dining hall to plan for the next visiting dignitaries and what events we could plan for entertainment and meals to impress them. If we promise to stay within sight of Hegai, would you just take Tereh already and go beat up all the guards? Pretty please?"

Leaning in to kiss me deeper, he says, "Can I make them bleed?"

"A little."

"Yay!" He mimics a child before bouncing up and yelling for Tereh. "Tereh! The Queen says we can go make the guards bleed for a couple hours together!"

The predatory grin that comes over men's faces when they are getting ready for something like bloody battles is downright comical, but they absolutely love it.

"Get out of here, both of you," I say, shooing them to the door.

Within just a few seconds, Tereh comes running back in while yelling "I forgot my dagger, I'll catch up!" But then he looks at me and says, "Queen Esther, you got dizzy this morning remember? Should I be leaving you, really?"

"Well, that decree was quite a shock you have to admit. I promise to go slow all day. Now get, so I can discuss this with my Papi!"

Saluting, and smiling from ear to ear, he runs out the door to make some guards bleed ... men.

Chapter 20

...For Such a Time as This

<Esther>

Our cover is set. Mary has everything spread out in the old dining room, she and Genet are pouring over plans and ideas for entertainment. Sunita is discussing meal options with the cooks and bakers. As soon as we enter the corridor, Hegai walks up beside me and grabs me by the elbow, escorting me to the hallway outside my old bedroom.

"You have no idea where this decree came from, My Queen?" He is so concerned. He has known who my Papi is since early on into the purification and competition process. He and my Papi had apparently become acquaintances many years ago and somewhere along the way had become friends. Actually, they had become close work-type friends, and had helped one another out on numerous occasions when things had gotten dangerous, or when one of them might need a friend in certain places of importance within the Gates or inside the palace. They had gained mutual respect and trust before I had ever come to the picture. Early into the contest, Papi had told him to watch over me. I only found out months after being married.

Kissing me on the forehead, he whispers "He is waiting. Good luck my dear."

Rushing into the room, Papi embraces me instantly. He looks horrid with ashes all over his head, mustache and beard. The sackcloth does not cover his legs and his skinny knees are poking out for all the world to see. He looks like a beggar on the side of the road. I understand the meaning. But it is still heartbreaking to see.

"Esther, you must do something!" He is more excited than I am used to seeing him. Usually when dealing with something of a crisis nature he is more calm and thoughtful.

"Papi, this cannot be dealt with quickly. If I were simply to go to Xerxes and tell him what Haman has done, there is at least a small chance he would reverse the decree, argue with Haman, reveal my identity as a Jew, and nothing more. Haman's rage and hatred of our people would only grow and now I would be the number one target for his hatred. He has successfully driven a wedge between myself and Xerxes once before. I cannot give him all of the tools to do it again. Papi, this must be thought out like moves in petteia. When playing, you must think two or three moves ahead. Knowing what will happen after you make your current play," I explain.

"The only way to win against Haman is to know what he will be doing after you make your first move," I ponder, thinking out loud pacing the room.

"We also do not have all the time in the world," he sighs, frustratedly.

"Papi, I will not go into this lightly," I warn him.

"Do not think that because you are in the King's house you alone of all the Jews will escape," he says quietly.

"I know Papi, I am just trying to plan with wisdom," I say, taking in the comfort of my surroundings. This room holds wonderful memories for me. It helps me plan my actions easier.

"For if you remain silent at this time Esther, relief and deliverance for the Jews will arise from another place, but you and your father's family will perish," he says. Grabbing me by the shoulders, he forces me to look into his face. "And who knows Esther, maybe you have been made Queen for such a time as this?"

At that moment it didn't feel like my Papi speaking, it felt as if I were in a void. Like that phrase was coming at me in all the different forms, voices, and ways. '...for such a time as this...'~ 'who knows...' ~ 'maybe you were made Queen...' ~ 'for such a time as this...' ~ 'a time as this' ~ 'the Jews will arise ...' ~ 'you and your family will perish ...'

"Whoa, Esther, are you going to pass out? Should I call Hegai?" Papi is speaking frantically and rushing for the door.

'No Papi, I ... I just ... I am with child," I finally confess. "But honestly I don't think that is what was wrong. I think Yahweh might have been speaking to me. I kept hearing fragments of everything you said, in a much more commanding voice, rushing at me from every angle just repeating over and over. I feel fine, do not call Hegai."

"Oh Nesicha, I am going to be a Grandfather? How wonderful ... What horrible timing!" He sinks back into lamenting.

"Shhh, we have not told anyone because I miscarried about six months ago. It was somewhat traumatic. Xerxes is an anxious mess and threatens to have guards follow me everywhere, even the bath houses when I relieve myself," I complain. "Between then and now, Haman had my husband completely under his control. They stayed out drinking every night. Xerxes refused at first, but eventually he began taking up with the harem girls again, we were not speaking and the only time we did speak, we were fighting."

"Esther, this is not something that can be put on hold," Papi pleads.

"I agree. Go, gather together all the Jews who are in Susa, and fast for me. Do not eat or drink for three days, night or day. I and my staff will fast as you do. Save for the fact I must adjust for the baby. When this is done, I will go to the King, even though it is against the law. If Haman or The Council interferes and I perish … then I perish."

"You are with child," Papi whispers. "Fasting is not healthy."

"I am Papi," I say, rubbing my still-flat belly and smiling. "I will be smart. I will not harm the blessing Yahweh has given. But I will show Him I am honoring His Word. The child is in no more danger if I stay silent, or if I act. I will do as I have promised."

"This is why you are convinced the King had no part in the decree?"

"One of the reasons Papi, our marriage is a good one again, we are friends. Some things are still the obvious man vs. woman dynamic of our time, but he is not cruel, like he appeared to be with Vashti, Papi. I truly believe him when he says he loves me. It is true he does not know I am a Jewish woman, but I do not believe he even has knowledge of this decree."

"Then I shall put away the sackcloth and ashes, and go to the temple. I will continually make sacrifices morning and night each day, and work my job. My prayers will not cease for you and my grandchild. Even for the King to have his heart and eyes opened. I love you child. I will spread the word. The fasting will begin this evening."

"I love you Papi."

***

\<Esther\>

Out of love for me, their Queen, my staff left their gods and agreed to pray to my God, hoping he really was real and could save my people, and of course me from Haman's plot..

As God began to show me things I prayed for exact specifics. I had an answer and a plan I could not get away from, it kept coming to me stronger each time I prayed. I approached my staff and we discussed it. The other ladies were surprised and questioned how it could be that we all had the same answer right down to the tiniest details.

"That is how powerful Yahweh is, friends," I beam at my God-given sisters.

There was to be a banquet. Well ... two banquets. The trickiest part would be approaching the King in the throne room. Going in without an invitation could technically mean death for me. If any of The Councilmen or Haman threw a fit, they could try to force the King to order my death for approaching without an invitation. My friends are worried, they are not willing to risk my life, but we can't come up with any other way.

"There are no 'what-ifs'. This is where faith comes in. I am more than confident this plan is the will of Yahweh because it came to me and then it was confirmed for me three times by being given to each of you. He confirmed it three times. The same number of days we have been fasting and praying. Yahweh does not operate in coincidences. That was on purpose. Now it is time to act on His word in unwavering faith. Help me prepare my body and clothing Genet. Mary and Sunita please prepare the banquet, do not leave out even the tiniest detail from the vision God gave us all."

***

Dressed in my finest royal robe, the red one matching Xerxes', I also wear the most royal shoes I own. They have a tall heel and I know he loves to see them on me. Having bathed and anointed myself in the proper ceremonial oils, Genet places the appropriate makeup for royal appearances to my face.

"Stunning, Your Majesty," she says, stepping back to view her handiwork. "Esther, should I bring weapons and be in the hallway to give you an escape in case …"

"Genet I love you. There is no need. The Lord is my protector and provider."

In a second, her eyes become very clear, then almost the same as watching a bath fill up with water, her eyes fill with tears. My lungs expel a quick rush of air with a smile when I see her lips purse. It was the smallest of sobs and I know if I give the depth of her loyalty one more thought, I will be bawling. Steeling my face and nodding, she gives a quick nod of her head, and says, "Very well, I shall escort you to the throne room, then break off to the kitchen to help with the banquet. Your private dining room will be waiting and perfect when the three of you arrive."

We both ignore the tears falling from her eyes, and clasp hands. Almost as if we share the same mind and body, our shoulders square, chins lift, and we march ourselves to the throne room, side by side.

From the first step I take into the throne room, there is no other noise but the marble floor and my heels greeting one another in rhythm, making all eyes turn toward me. My lungs refuse to open and take in oxygen. I feel the sneers of each Councilman as their heads turn, watching me approach the throne. The sensations of crawling ants up my shoulders and into my ears magnify their whispers. They could be deciding to end my life, and those of the Hebrew race right now and there is nothing I could do to stop it. Nothing, except pray. It is the most powerful thing on earth. *'God, I am being obedient. I need your help. My life is in your hands.'* Squaring my shoulders, I take a few steps closer to where Xerxes is seated on his throne.

For a minute, no one moves ... or breathes, or blinks. Xerxes is staring at me, but I do not feel any malice from his stare. It is when I see his eyes take in my heels, I know I will be okay with him. If he were angry, he wouldn't let me see his attention wander from the moment where my very life could be decided. Now I am praying I will not create a fight for him with his Council, or Haman.

I have lowered my head respectfully, but still allow myself enough room to see what is happening. Haman is half grinning at the situation, but it feels predatory to me in some way. The Council has been shocked into silence until the moment when Councilman Shethar leans over to whisper in Councilman Meres' ear. At the very same moment, Xerxes, without giving them a sideways glance, extends the golden scepter to me.

Taking four more steps to be close enough to touch the scepter, all eyes are watching. Feeling every muscle from my hips, to the back of my thighs, knees, and calves contracting and pulling my body into the correct bowed position, I stay focused. At the same time my hand reaches for the scepter, I feel the motion of my ankles bending, my thighs squeezing, and my toes digging in for balance. Reminding myself to breathe so I do not faint facing the tallest giant of my life, I hold my position. This is the moment The Council and Haman could pronounce me rebellious and worthy of death. Then a fight would ensue.

"What is it, Queen Esther? What is your request? Even up to half the kingdom, it will be given to you."

"If it pleases the King. Being so grateful to be the Queen of the man above *all* men, I have thought of ways I could show you my gratitude. Today, let the King, together with Haman, come to a banquet I have prepared for him."

When I included the private joke, 'man above *all* men' Xerxes' lips battled to keep from smiling. From the corner of my eye, I can see Haman's chest swell when I include him in the invitation. The Councilmen continue to whisper back and forth, but now that Haman is proud to be invited, I think I have outplayed their objections. For now ...

"Rise my Queen, Haman, our Queen has prepared a banquet for us. We leave at once so we may do as she asks."

Stepping from the throne platform, Xerxes extends his arm to me and I place my hand in the crook of his elbow as we have practiced hundreds of times. Following his lead earns me a wink. Like I told my Papi, I am positive this decree has nothing to do with Xerxes. How it happened I haven't yet discovered, but I will.

When the three of us enter the room set aside for the banquet, my staff and Tereh collectively showed their relief. Some of them exhale audible sighs, Tereh's shoulders let down so far it's noticeable. Raising my eyebrows at them to keep going, they all scurry back to work.

One of the banquet details all four of us received in prayer, turns out to be a specific dish Haman's Grandmother used to make as a child. Sunita was the only one to ever have had it, she was able to get the recipe from her Mama, and he loved it. He loosened up to the point he began to visit normally with us as if we were old friends. '*Thank you, Yahweh.*'

As they were drinking wine, Xerxes again asks me, "Now what is your request? Even up to half the kingdom, it will be granted."

"My petition, and my request is this; if the King regards me with favor and if it pleases the King to grant my petition and fulfill my request, let the

King and Haman come tomorrow to the banquet I will prepare for them. Then I will answer the King's question."

"Granted," he said, leaning over to kiss me on the forehead. "I look forward to tomorrow's feast as well. Haman, I'm afraid we must go to the training grounds to work this off," standing and rubbing circles over his belly, as though he could ever gain an ounce on his heavily muscled build. Reaching for his weapons, he then attaches them to his body.

"Esther, thank you Kitten. No one has ever noticed my hard work and honored me this way. Sincerely, thank you," the eye contact sent a ripple down my spine. I know for absolute sure he knows nothing of this edict.

"Oh, Queen Esther, the food was delicious. But his news dismays me! The King is likely to beat me to a bloody pulp!" Haman chuckles. "I do sincerely appreciate your repeated banquet invitation, I am certainly looking forward to tomorrow!"

"My pleasure Haman," I choked those words out pretty well if I do say so myself. "I apologize for my husband being such a brute. I will ask the cooks to make your family dish again tomorrow to make amends for this afternoon. Also, my dear husband? Maybe just for today, go a little easy on your Second in Command? He has an important banquet tomorrow and doesn't need to attend with a swollen lip!"

Everyone laughed, and the two men headed for the training grounds.

"Ooh, if Xerxes just," *mmmph "accidentally," *hurmph "punched him in the throat too hard training, maybe he could do our work for us?" Sunita says, acting out throwing viscous punches.

Staring at her with wide eyes, Mary says in shock, "Goodness Sunita, remind me not to ever steal your dessert. You are vicious."

"*Pow! *umpf" Sunita mockingly throws two imaginary punches at Mary. She takes two quick steps back, and Genet begins to tease her for being so afraid. In response to the teasing, Mary points at Sunita, and turns her large frightened eyes to Genet as if there are no explanations needed.

***

\<Haman\>

What a crazy day. First, Queen Esther marches herself into the throne room, all dressed in her royal robes. Not only does she get away with it, but she is only there to invite him to a banquet lunch. Then to make things better, she invites me along! When I am seated, one of the dishes served is Zareshk Polo. I have not seen anyone make that dish since my grandmother passed away. She and my mother fought terribly, so my mom refused to make it after Grandmother died. The old wench was always so jealous of my Grandmother's attention she couldn't even give her son the meal he loved the most. But low and behold it was there today. How did the Queen know? I have to get the recipe from Lady Sunita so Zeresh can start making it. She loves to cook.

Was she trying to get my attention? Does she have affections for me? I do have that effect on women a lot, it wouldn't surprise me. I cannot let her act on it while Xerxes is alive, but if I decide to take the throne from him soon, I could make her another wife. Janeth will have to stay a concubine. She has not loved me as much as I was sure she would. She loved the extra attention at first. But she bruises every time we are together. I would love nothing more than to take her in public, but she is just too fragile. Could you imagine if I were King and I descended the throne with Queen Esther on my left and Queen Zeresh on my right? I would be a legend.

I will keep my eye on Queen Esther for sure. If it is not her, then maybe it is one of her Ladies-in-Waiting. All beautiful, and all such different colors of the rainbow. Xerxes didn't even work us too hard in training. My skills have come back to the level that landed me the position of Second in Command to begin with. I had gotten lazy and let them slip. It almost cost me. Xerxes was not about to let me continue in such poor shape, so I had to step it up.

It's time to head home for the day and I'm actually looking forward to it. Taking a shortcut through the Palace Gates, my entire good mood is ruined when I spot that filthy Jew Mordecai. I had heard when my decree came out he had torn his clothes, and covered himself in sackcloth and ashes. He was supposed to be wailing bitterly outside the gates. Just the thought made me happy. Now he is here, dressed as normal, looking at me as if nothing ever happened.

Of course the vermin isn't bowing. When will these Jews understand they are unworthy. They must bow to an Agagite, as we are far superior to their unclean blood. Yet he looks at me as though we are equals.

"Hello Mordecai, you know there is an edict stating you must bow to me?"

"I bow to none but Yahweh," Mordecai says to me with a straight face.

I can feel my face getting red, my heart pumping my blood faster and faster through my body, there is no one in this whole world I hate more than this man. When I take him down, I will not only take him and his family, I will take everyone with Jewish blood in their veins down with him. He will not be so smug then. Maybe he will even beg.

"Okay, I can wait until the thirteenth day of Adar. Can you?" I say, sauntering past him to join a game of streetball with the young boys. I love jumping in a street game. The kids usually beg for me to be on their side and grumble if I choose against them. It is a good teaching lesson to encourage them how to strategize to your own strengths and look for your opponent's weaknesses. It is a great stress-reliever for me.

Kids are affected by every decision adults make and still laugh, run, and have these great outlooks on life. At least part of the day anyway. I remember. I was bullied by kids and adults alike. But when I got with my group of friends, my childhood was all laughter, hunting bugs, and playing games. I turned the tables as fast as I could.

Growing stronger, I became the bully to the bullies. Even now, when I find a bully who is an adult, I make them pay. I do not care about consequences. Those who deserve it, pay in the most frightful of ways. Like the Hebrews. Their day is coming. They should never have been released from slavery in Egypt. History is full of stories of how my people tried to stop them, but they kept fanning out like the plague of locusts. I controlled my feelings in front of Mordecai, but I will get my revenge. I daydream about that moment all the way home.

"Oooh Husband, you are as dark as a storm cloud. What is wrong?" Zeresh meets me at the gate.

Seeing several neighbors and friends in the streets coming home from work, I call them over too. "Friends, wife, behold my lands," I gesture from my front gate to my house, and beyond it into the hills behind. "I have earned and been given vast wealth. Livestock, jewels, honorable wives, strong sons and beautiful daughters. Being named Second in Command was a great acknowledgment of the hard work I have paid to my country. Even today, the Queen herself risked her life and entered the throne room."

While my captive audience gasped, wondering why Queen Esther would ever risk entering the throne room, I wait for them to imagine the scene. They know the risk of being executed if not offered the golden scepter. Having their attention, I continue.

"Her only request? She wanted to honor the King and myself, with a lunch banquet to reward us for how hard we have been working for Persia!" Looking around I make sure everyone knew the Queen had specifically invited me. "Me. She risked her life not just for the King, but for me as well. And yet, there is this Jew who sits in the Palace Gates, and since the day King Xerxes issued the edict that all Palace Gate advisors should bow to me in honor, Mordecai refuses to bow to me. Even this very day. The thirteenth day of Adar is coming, but it is too far away. What should I do?"

"Send your soldiers this night to build a gallows seventy-five feet high. In the morning, ask the King to have Mordecai hanged from it. Then go to your second lunch banquet happy," Zeresh suggests, and all of my friends agreed. This suggestion delighted me, so I sent the orders to my guards and had the gallows built overnight.

I promise myself while heading into the house. 'I shall see you in the morning filthy Mordecai. You will bow ... minutes before you die.'

Chapter 21

BUT YAHWEH ...

<Xerxes>

Lying here watching her sleep, I cannot help but relive all the moments since I met her. I wish my mother lived and could have met her. I know she would have loved Esther. Since Esther's mother died in childbirth, I believe they would have hit it off and loved each other immediately. My grandmother was alive when we got married but passed away shortly after. It is just the two of us here for our baby. That makes it all the more important that we are careful with our lives.

Knowing my baby is growing in her belly makes me want to go through each day with my arms wrapped protectively around her for every step she makes, but I fear that she may try to assassinate me. The thought makes me smile, she is not tiny for a female, but she is small compared to me. I know that I am just being eaten alive by fear after losing the first baby, but it is hard to battle.

Twice, I have seen Esther's body losing blood. As tough of a man as I am and as much blood as I have poured into the ground from other people's bodies, I cannot bear the sight of her blood. It is truly my worst fear.

I am not going to be able to sleep. Quietly I remove myself from our bed and walk down the hallway toward my quarters. Summoning the book of the chronicles, the record of my reign, to be brought in and read to me, it was found recorded there that Mordecai had exposed Bigthana and Teresh in the murder plot to kill me. He had put the note into Lady Genet's fan the day of the attack. They were two of my officers who guarded the doorway, and had conspired to feed me poisoned water on an upcoming day where I would be giving a speech to the people of Susa.

Stopping them as they read, I ask, "What honor has been given to Mordecai for this? He has always been an honorable man who worked hard for the crown. He has been faithful, and the people have always been pleased with his rulings or mediations. Now that he has performed this highest act of loyalty for his King, something surely was done for him right?"

"Nothing has been done for him, Your Majesty," my attendants answered.

Knowing it was almost morning, I begin to get ready for the day. Mulling over the options for how to honor Mordecai, I hear noises outside my chambers. "Who is out there?" I ask the attendants.

"Haman is standing in the outer court, Your Highness," the attendant replied.

"Bring him in."

"Haman, I am glad you are here. I couldn't sleep last night so I had the book of the chronicles brought out and read to me. I discovered an event where a man did a great thing for me and he has yet to be honored. What should be done for the man the King desires to honor?"

I have done many things for the King lately and have not received honor for them. Who could he be referring to but me? I am Second in Command after all. No one does more for the King than myself. There is not one other person he could delight in honoring except me!' Haman thought to himself.

"For the man the King delights to honor, have them bring a royal robe the King has worn and a horse the King has ridden, one with a royal crest placed on its head. Then let the robe and horse be entrusted to one of the King's most noble princes. Let them robe the man the King delights to honor, and lead him on the horse through the city streets, proclaiming before him, 'This is what is done for the man the King delights to honor!" Haman proudly proclaims.

"Go at once," I command Haman. "Get the robe and the horse and do just as you have suggested for Mordecai the Jew, who sits at the King's gate. Do not neglect anything you have recommended," I proclaim. I am happy this was caught. I have only ever heard good things about Mordecai and am so glad his good deed did not go by without reward.

***

\<Haman\>

'How? How could I be made to suffer this humiliation? This repulsive dog has refused to bow to me for months and now I have to parade him through the streets of Susa praising him? May the gods strike me dead now! I have been faithful! If I am not dead before I reach Mordecai, I will know there is no such thing as gods. I will be my own god. I will serve no one but myself forever more. I cannot bear this humiliation.'

I did exactly what I was commanded to do. Every time I had to open my mouth to shout, "This is what is done for the man the King delights to honor!" I just about threw up. My humiliation is too great. Mordecai dies today. I will not wait for the month of Adar. The whole time he sat upon that horse in the King's robe, other Jews would come into the streets smiling greatly at him. He would smile back and shrug his shoulders, then look down at me where I would have to shout his honor again. I hated it. But if I refused, I would be punished, and would not be allowed to carry out my plan for this Hebrew. I had sucked it up and endured. I know all of the Jews are laughing at me. Well we would see who had the last laugh.

When it was all over, the wretched dog went back to his place in the Palace Gates, but I covered my head in grief and raced home. Zeresh, and several of my friends were there. They were concerned about what had caused me so much grief. I had almost lied to them as it was humiliating to have to repeat the events all over again. As we were discussing what I should do next, one of the King's guards rode up on his horse in a hurry.

"Excuse me for interrupting Sir, but the King has ordered you back to the palace. It seems you are late for the Queen's banquet and the King said you have three breaths to get there."

"That is what he says as his last warning before you are punished," I say.

Zeresh grabs my collar and says, "Pull yourself together before you get there husband. "Your face is a mess. Remember, the Queen invited you and none other. Now hurry."

My horse was foaming at his mouth and about to his breaking point by the time I reached the palace. Entering the King and Queen's private dining hall, I was breathing like I had run the distance myself.

***

\<Esther\>

When Haman rushes into the dining hall, I breathe a silent prayer, '*There he is Yahweh, my hungry lion, the consuming fire in my furnace. Protect me spiritually, emotionally, and physically. Give me discernment, wisdom, and favor. ~Amen*'

"Oh, Haman, let me pour you a glass of water," I stall, trying to gather my courage.

While pouring his glass, Xerxes asks, "How did honoring Mordecai go?"

At the mention of my Papi's name I dropped the pitcher of water and Haman's glass all over the floor. Mary rushes to my aid and begins cleaning everything while Sunita pours him another.

"Are you alright?" Xerxes was out of his chair almost before the glass hit the floor.

"Yes, I apologize, I bumped it onto the table as I turned it around and dropped them both. Forgive me. Go back to your talk. We will bring the food," I distract them from my nerves.

Genet is eyeing me. She straightens herself and makes fists with both hands out in front of her firmly encouraging me to buck up and pull it together. I respond with a nod. The kitchen staff are serving the first and second courses since Haman was delayed and I do not want them running behind because of the banquet. '*Lord, Please calm my nerves and give me the words.*'

"Queen Esther, what is your petition? It will be given to you. What is your request? Even up to half my kingdom will be granted," Xerxes now suspects something else is afoot and is pushing to get to the bottom of the matter.

"If I have found favor with you my King, and if it pleases Your Majesty,"
I begin with a formal curtsey, "grant me my life – this is my petition," I
pause to let it sink in." And spare my people – this is my request. For I and
my people have been sold for destruction, slaughter, and annihilation. If
we had merely been sold as female and male slaves I would have kept quiet,
because no such distress would justify disturbing the King." Lowering my
head, I give Xerxes a minute to see if any recognition dawns on him. I can
tell he has no idea.

First, his eyes narrow on me and he looks angry toward me. Maybe he is a
little, for not just bringing it up to him earlier in private. Then I see his eyes
go to my belly, and anger does not even begin to cover the look that comes
over my husband then. His eyes grow so cold I would not think there could
be any softness capable within that body. The cords in his neck strain, and
the muscles in his jaw begin to jump.

You can audibly hear him clench his fists, the room is so quiet, and his
strength so powerful. Taking a chance to look at Haman, I can tell that he
is at a loss, unable to connect the dots. At first anyway. When he raises his
gaze to meet my eyes is when it begins to make sense to him. I see his nostrils
flare, and his ears turn red. He looks like a cornered animal. It hasn't played
out yet, but that is exactly what he is.

Deathly silent, Xerxes walks to me. Gripping me by the shoulders, he raises
me up a little and shakes me. "Where is he?"

His grip is getting tighter and tighter. His thumbs are pressing in on my
collarbones and his other fingers are spanning across my shoulders in my
back. Tears spring to my eyes and he softens his expression just a little,
but not his grip. Hearing the first tiny crack, the shocked look in his face
accompanies shivers through his body. He immediately lets go, then pulls
me to his chest for an embrace. I did not fight him, I knew his anger was

directed solely on whomever it was threatening his wife and secret unborn child. Fear and what ifs played out through his fingertips on my shoulders. When the cracking sound occurred, I knew my left collarbone had suffered a fracture, but was not broken all the way through. Gritting my teeth, I did my best to bear the torture of his transferred fear without whimpering.

Whispering into my ear declarations of love and apologies, he gently pulls me back to arm's length again. From the corner of my eye I see ever-faithful Genet reaching for her dagger. Raising my right hand in her direction and shaking my head she slides it back into the holder, but leaves her hand on the grip.

"I am so sorry," Xerxes says aloud. "Who is he? Where is the man who has dared to do such a thing?"

"The adversary, and enemy is this vile man," I point at him. "Haman. With your signet ring and a swipe of a pen, he wrote an edict to declare open hunting season on all of my people the thirteenth day of Adar. Any man is allowed to hunt down Jewish men, women, children and kill them by any means desired, and plunder all of their belongings. My people are not allowed to fight back by punishment of law, and we will be wiped out.

It all started because he is an Agagite and we are Jewish. Then he put his plan into action because my Papi, Mordecai, will not bow down and worship him. Hebrew people bow down and worship no one but Yahweh." Collapsing onto the couch holding my collarbone, I have now broken out into a sweat from pain and nerves. I have played all of my cards. Now I will either die with my people, or we will all live. Genet is by my side in an instant with Sunita and Mary right beside her. Tereh takes position in front of us all.

In a flash, Xerxes turns cold, and dangerous again. Spinning to look at Haman, he takes one step in his direction, then walks right out the door into the garden. Staying close enough to hear what is going on in the dining room, Xerxes is trying to get control of his rage.

In a split second, Haman charges me. Genet and Sunita step in front of me, charging him. "Haman, I *will* kill you old man. Just lay one finger on her!" Genet shouts.

"Just do it!" Sunita yells at Genet. "It solves our problem!"

Mary jumps on Haman's back, which shocks everyone. He throws her off easily, but she charges right back. Tereh tries to step in, however, my ladies are causing so much chaos, Haman slips his grasp. Ignoring Mary's return, Haman reaches for me but only gets my dress, and in all of the chaos it rips.

"Queen Esther, I'm begging you, forgive me?" Haman is pleading.

Xerxes had raced for the door the minute Genet threatened to kill Haman. When he made it into the room from the patio, he hears my dress tearing. "So even now, you will try and molest my wife Haman? With a room full of people and me standing right outside the door? It was not enough to plot her death with all of her people. You want to molest her under my nose too?"

Grabbing Haman, Xerxes throws him across the room into the wall as easily as if he were throwing a ball. Harbana, one of the eunuchs that assists the King in the palace, came rushing into the room.

"Your Highness, Haman had a gallows built outside his house that is seventy-five feet tall and planned to hang Mordecai from it this very day."

"Then take him, hang Haman from the very gallows he prepared for Mordecai," Xerxes said. Making his way to me he calls out, "Someone please call the healer Miriam."

Harbana hesitantly responds, "Sir, Miriam is a midwife, shall I call ..."

"Miriam is who we like Harbana."

"Yes, Your Majesty. I shall fetch her immediately."

Gently lifting me, Xerxes heads straight for our room. Seeing the bruises on my collarbone, his face almost turns an actual green color. Placing his forehead on mine while he is walking, he breathes in and out. In and out while taking deliberate steps to our room.

"Esther..."

"Stop, Xerxes. I understand. I love you even more. You do not owe me an apology." I place my hand on his cheek.

"So, Mordecai. Why? Why did you not tell me he was your Papi?" He sounds crushed.

"It was Papi's plea. It was his most urgent request when the contest started. Tensions between him and Haman had been high for a long time. He felt like if Haman had known I was his daughter, Haman would have found ways to torture me. He wanted me to keep it secret as long as I could."

"He was probably right," Xerxes agreed. "To my shame I kept Haman close because he was always happy to torture enemies for information or other nasty jobs I sometimes didn't want to do. I kept him around for the vileness inside him, to do the dirty work because he loved it. And look, it almost cost me the only woman I have ever loved."

When Mordecai was brought into the room, Xerxes took off his signet ring and presented it to Mordecai. "Mordecai, my humble apologies. The sacrifice you made keeping your identity as her father a secret was huge. But it was one of great wisdom. For the part I unwillingly played in that, I am so sorry. We have a lot of clean-up to do, if you will accept the position

Mordecai, I am in need of a Vizier. Your role will only encompass things of the Palace. Tereh will be my Second for matters of security, leading the army and matters of war. Do you accept?"

"It would be an honor My King," my Papi bows.

Falling to my knees, I beg weeping at the magnitude of everything coming to pass, "May it please the King, Xerxes, please put an end to the evil plan of Haman the Agagite. Please, My Love, write an order overruling the dispatches that Haman devised and wrote to destroy the Jews in all the King's provinces. How can I bear to see disaster fall on all my people?"

Reaching to pick me up off the floor, he hugs me. Running his hands through my hair and kissing my forehead, he orders me to quit falling to my knees, or begging him, or curtseying until my body is fully healed and well.

"My Queen, stay, see Miriam and rest. I will be back to check on you shortly and then will not be leaving your side for days. Mordecai, on me."

As the men left the room, Miriam entered with her supplies and began a check-up of my body, and the baby. It will hurt to lift my arms or use them for a while because my collarbones were injured from Xerxes grip, but I will be fine. One was just bruised, while the other did have a fracture. Our little peanut is growing right on track, safe within my womb.

How the evil one meant to destroy us and our people was scary ... But Yahweh!

Yahweh is good, All the Time.

And All the Time, Yahweh is Good!

~Epilogue~

\<Esther\>

"Push Esther, I see the baby, it is coming," Mary is doing her best to encourage me, but I can not tell if she is excited or about to vomit.

"I think one more good push will deliver the head. When I say breathe, I want you to stop pushing while I clean off the baby's face and nose. Then I will tell you to push again and we will deliver the body. You are doing great. Are you ready?" Miriam asks me.

Nodding my head, I can feel a contraction building. When it feels like it is nearing the top of the pain level, I begin to push. As I begin to run out of air, I feel like something splits wide open and pain like I have never experienced before, tears through me from head to toe. My scream splits through the air with frightening strength and consistency, even to me.

"That is it, Tereh is never getting a child." I hear Genet proclaim from my right side.

"Oh my gods, I'm not going to give birth to this baby. It has to stay in. I cannot do this. I cannot!" Mary is stepping away from my bed.

Throwing my hand out to the side, I grasp for her. "You don't have a choice anymore. Baby is already here! Have you gotten word back from Lucius?"

"What?" She answers looking bewildered. "Oh gods, I just said that out loud didn't I?"

"You did," I smile at her right before another contraction rips through me without warning. Squeezing her hand with all my might, Mary and I are both screaming as though a bear from those gladiator fights is ripping our arms off.

"Get out of my way!" Xerxes shouts and I see two bodies be thrown against the wall mere moments before he barrels into the room. At the sight of my blood and the head of our child protruding from my body, the largest, strongest man I have ever known goes weak and sinks to his knees right in front of my birthing bed. Fighting to regain his feet, Xerxes gets to me right as the next contraction hits me and Miriam tells him to grab me by the shoulders to help me sit up a little.

"Oh, that helps Xerxes, a little more," I say, and grab the back of my knees to help me push. With that contraction, the rest of the body delivers. I do not hear a cry right away and struggle to sit up on my own.

"Xerxes? What is wrong? Why don't I hear my baby?" I ask, frantically clawing at Xerxes arm.

"Because he has perfectly good manners. I so hate to ruin it, but I'm going to have to. He needs that first good deep breath." Miriam says. Turning him around, I see the most beautiful little boy I have ever laid my eyes on. He is just blinking and looking at me, when Miriam tilts him forward and gives him a good smack on the bottom. His eyes go wide, then his bottom lip drops way out and he takes that first deep breath in protest. Finally, the most beautiful sound I have ever heard breaks through the morning.

After a bit of squalling his displeasure at the move, Xerxes reaches for his son and says, "Here son, you are with your Daddy. I am giving you a pass today, but young Darius II you will learn to grow and be strong."

As my beautiful husband walks Darius to the window, the baby quiets. "You must learn to rule Persia fairly, putting all of the people first. To find your queen and love her with all your heart, no matter what The Council says. And above all, follow this Yahweh your Mama is teaching me about. When I met her I thought I was a god. She didn't think so."

Genet, Mary, Sunita, and I all quietly laugh at Xerxes' narrative to his son. "She did think I was a man above *all* men, so I forgave her. But I think she is right about this Yahweh, so you should listen to her."

Holding Darius up so they are looking eye-to-eye with one another, Xerxes continues, "Always protect her Darius. If there ever comes a day I cannot be here, protect her with everything you are. She is blessed, strong, courageous, loyal, beautiful, and so very smart. Not every woman is like her Darius. She is more precious than all the jewels, remember that."

After his soliloquy, my husband laid my son in my arms. He kissed me passionately, and then left to prepare a present for me, which I said was ridiculous. He was determined to do so though.

A few days later when Darius was nursing, Xerxes came in and gave me a ring of the precious stone blue sapphire. It is Darius II's birthstone, it is set in a white gold we have been mining in the northern regions.

Xerxes told me he had wiped out all of Haman's family, and Haman and his ten sons' bodies had been put on display as a warning to the people about trying to be treacherous and deceiving. All of their spoils had been given to my Papi and Rachael and they were moving closer to the Palace.

He had finally gotten word back from Lucius. This time when being handed the rudis, he kissed it and claimed his freedom. He should be here before his child is born and cannot wait to hold his wife again

The years passed, and eventually all of my favorite ladies from the contest were married with children and all of our families played together on holidays and fun events. Especially on Purim, the holiday established for the Hebrew people to celebrate escaping the mass slaughter Haman had planned for us.

But *for such a time as this*, God had appointed my time to fit the exact moment we would need a way out of the fiery furnace. I was humbled and grateful Yahweh chose me to carry out His purpose. If it be your will Yahweh, so be it.

When Lucius did arrive, he became invaluable to Tereh and Xerxes. They planned for years how to overthrow Rome. Xerxes planned and planned. He was convinced he could conquer Rome and be the King of all Persia plus all of Rome. When they launched the campaign to acquire Rome, Darius and I kissed him on the balcony and wished him well. It was the last time I saw my love ever again.

He died a happy man though. Darius II was the light of his life and he had doted on every first he had been there for. He loved us both well. He cherished my mind and my body as a husband should. If he ever did use the women from the harem again, I never heard about it. He absolutely just became, "my man."

King Ahasuerus, Xerxes, the fiercest warrior King of Persia, fell in Rome with stars in his eyes, having seen the miracles of Yahweh and honoring him more than once. I believe he is in heaven right now with Him.

I believe that when he closed his eyes, he was seeing Darius run to him. He is almost old enough to wrestle his dad to the ground now, they had such a great love for one another. I believe he saw me. With my arms open wide waiting for my favorite embrace. My favorite passionate kiss. And as _the man above all men_ walked into heaven, he turned and winked at me, then blew me a kiss.

Until heaven my love.

Until heaven.

CITATIONS

Holy Bible | YouVersion Bible App

Book of Esther Chapters 1-10

Translations: NIV, NKJV CSB

Life.Church | https://www.youversion.com/the-bible-app/

Chapter 5

Jewish Virtual Library. I Jewish Bedtime Prayers I Hashkivenu I

https://www.jewishvirtuallibrary.org/jewish-bedtime-prayers

Traditional Rosary I Protection Prayer I

https://traditionalrosary.org/deliverance-prayers/protection-prayer/

Chapter 9

Traditional Rosary I Protection Prayer I

https://traditionalrosary.org/deliverance-prayers/protection-prayer/

Acknowledgements

There are always so many people to thank when writing a book. In my case, at the top of every list, every time has to be my husband Corey. You don't like the spotlight, but you know what you have done and continue to do. I cannot ever be as valuable and supportive to you as you are to me. Forever grateful you moved to Sully Buttes Schools.

As always, to those who purchased in the presale campaigns - you are my Rock Stars! We need shirts or something right?

To my sister Sarena Nuttall, for every late night beta reading session, every 1AM line editing session while we are both chasing children and puppies, your friendship means the world to me.

My friend, editor, and favorite horror author Stephen W. Scott. Thank you for all of it.

Read. Write. Critique. I can't wait to cheer the publication of your novels! Thank you!

Tallgrass Literary Collective. Ana Maddox, Aubrey Green, Linda Berry, & Cheyenne Pauls. Thank you for standing elbow to elbow together as we formed this literary group in Tulsa. Inspirational women one and all.

Zealot Branding, Everything you have done for this series, has been high quality with the utmost professionalism, and it has been one of the best experiences I've had when publishing.

To every friend I have called while pulling all the skin several inches down my face and wailing "I'm a terrible writer!" You reminded me to ignore the 'imposter syndrome.' Thank you, especially for taking me to lunch, and then telling me to 'hush, and keep writing.'

For the prayer warrior God gave me to. You must be exhausted. I forever love you Barbara Billingsly.

CHOSEN AND COURAGEOUS

Chosen and Courageous is a powerful book series by award-winning author Heather Nuttall Westover, highlighting five women of the Old Testament who changed history. They didn't just break the mold - they crushed it. In a time when women were expected to stay small, out of leadership, and above all stay quiet, these ladies stepped up, spoke up, and said 'yes' to God's calling. Even when it meant risking everything.

With courage, faith and just a pinch of holy stubbornness, they used the gifts they were born with to change the world around them. Through vivid storytelling and a wink of humor, Heather reminds us that God doesn't just call the qualified - He qualifies the called, even if they're a little feisty.

Book one introduced us to Esther, she doesn't settle, won't make herself less than to make someone else feel better, and knows Yahweh well enough to know he will move mountains for His children.

Keep your eyes open for the upcoming stories of Miriam, sister to not only Moses, but Aaron as well. How would you like to have to keep those two little brothers in line? Following her will be Ruth, ever loyal. Deborah, the first actual female *superhero*. And rounded out with Rebekah, the answer to Abraham's prayers, no pressure or anything.

AUTHOR BIO

Heather Nuttall Westover is the award-winning author of *Growing Old: One Lucille Ball Moment at a Time, Being Married: One Lucille Ball Moment at a Time*, and *A Walk Through December*.

A wheat farmer's daughter from South Dakota turned proud Oklahoman, Heather has been married to her high school sweetheart for over 36 years. Together, they've raised five daughters, gained several wonderful sons-in-law, and now proudly answer to Granny and Papa from five adorable grandchildren.

When she's not writing, Heather is coaching other authors, consulting and speaking at writing conventions, churches, and local writers' groups - basically anywhere she's allowed to talk about books, Jesus, and how to survive marriage or children with a little grace and a lot of humor.

Heather loves dogs of all kinds, though her current attempt at bonding with a high-octane boxer has left her questioning her life choices - and her stamina. "Walks" have turned into sprints and "playtime" is now a full-body workout. She's fueled by coffee, faith, friendship, and a solid sense of humor. She loves singing, traveling and finding joy in the smallest of moments. Want to connect, laugh, or book her to speak at your next event?

Visit her at: www.heathernuttallwestover.com - She'd love to hear from you.

www.ingramcontent.com/pod-product-compliance
Lightning Source LLC
Chambersburg PA
CBHW050032120726
47903CB00006B/2013